P9-EEN-209

FRIDAY
NIGHT
LOVE

*Dedicated to*
*Carter, my pleasant surprise.*

*You were in my belly with the first word and*
*in my arms as I typed the last word.*
*I'm glad you're here to add a new chapter and story to our lives!*

# FRIDAY NIGHT LOVE

TIA McCOLLORS

WHITAKER HOUSE

*Publisher's Note:*
This novel is a work of fiction. References to real events, organizations, or places are used in a fictional context. Any resemblances to actual persons, living or dead, are entirely coincidental.

Scripture quotations represent several versions: The King James Version of the Holy Bible. The *Holy Bible, New International Version*®, NIV®, © 1973, 1978, 1984, 2011 by Biblica, Inc.® Used by permission. All rights reserved worldwide. The *Holy Bible, New International Version*®, NIV®, © 1973, 1978, 1984 by the International Bible Society. Used by permission of Zondervan. All rights reserved. The *New King James Version*, © 1979, 1980, 1982, 1984 by Thomas Nelson, Inc. Used by permission. All rights reserved.

**Friday Night Love**
**Days of Grace ~ Book 1**

Tia McCollors
www.tiamccollors.com
tia@tiamccollors.com

The author is represented by MacGregor Literary, Inc., of Hillsboro, Oregon.

ISBN: 978-1-62911-010-3
eBook ISBN: 978-1-62911-034-9
Printed in the United States of America


Whitaker House
1030 Hunt Valley Circle
New Kensington, PA 15068
www.whitakerhouse.com

**Library of Congress Cataloging-in-Publication Data**

McCollors, Tia.
Friday night love / by Tia McCollors.
pages ; cm. -- (Days of grace ; book 1)
ISBN 978-1-62911-010-3 (alk. paper) -- ISBN 978-1-62911-034-9 (ebk.)
1. Marriage--Fiction. 2. Christian fiction. I. Title.
PS3613.C365F75 2014
813'.6--dc23
2014006333



1 2 3 4 5 6 7 8 9 10 11 𝔴 21 20 19 18 17 16 15 14

# Prologue

"You got what you wanted, but you lost what you had," I told my husband as I tossed the packing tape dispenser on top of three unassembled cardboard boxes stacked in a corner of the garage.

Roman had come home three hours earlier than usual, catching me off guard. He stared in disbelief at the boxes of his belongings that I'd already assembled, packed, and labeled. Anger clenched his jaw, and the tension between us hardened his normally laid-back expression. As far as I was concerned, I'd done him a favor. I'd given him thirty days to move out, and this was the twenty-eighth day. Now he could be ahead of the game.

"So, this is how you get your point across?" Roman sliced his car key across the clear tape sealing the box marked "T-SHIRTS & UNDERWEAR."

I took my time answering as I finished off the last of the bitter coffee I'd bought from the gas station around the corner. Caffeine wasn't my thing, but I'd needed the extra boost of energy that morning. After the final sip, I said, "You have two days till you're supposed to be out, but you haven't touched any of your things. What did you expect me to do—let you casually move out at your own leisure? I'm not going to subject my children to watching you leave us sock by sock." I shook my head and turned my back to Roman's annoyed look. He didn't have a right to question any of my decisions. After all, this was his fault.

I popped the trunk of my car and tossed in two garbage bags full of summer clothes my children had outgrown in the past year. Things had changed in our family over the last twelve months, and it wasn't just that Kyle's height left his jeans two inches too short, or that Zariya's bustline pulled her shirts too snug. Evidently Roman and I had outgrown our marriage, too. No woman stands at the altar with plans to throw out her husband during her annual spring cleaning ritual.

Roman yanked his bow tie loose, leaving it dangle around his neck. "You're putting me out. I'm not leaving you, remember?"

Yes, I remembered. And I remembered the reason why half our bedroom walk-in closet was virtually empty now. I wanted to re-knot that bow tie, pulling it tighter and tighter around his neck, until... *Jesus, help my mind.*

Roman paced back and forth like he always did when he was in deep thought. He was an even-tempered man and slow to anger, but I'd pushed his buttons. He pressed his lips together as if trying to hold back words that would pierce like daggers and clearly make matters worse.

"You're unbelievable," Roman finally said.

"Me?" I snorted. "Well, there are plenty of things about you that I never would've believed. Where should I start?" I parked my hands on my hips in preparation for a verbal battle, but this time, *Roman* turned his back on *me*.

He slashed open another box, this one containing his jeans and polo shirts, and rifled through it, disheveling the neat stacks I'd made. I checked my watch. I had another two hours before I'd need to pick up Zariya and Kyle. It was the first week of spring break, and Roman had left early that morning for work so that he would have time to drop them off at a music and arts camp at the local community center. Since eight o'clock, I'd been working like a determined woman—make that a scorned woman—to pack his clothes, toiletries, and some basic household items that he would need for wherever he found to lay his head. I'd started in the kitchen, giving Roman two place settings. It was meant to be an intangible slap in the face, to let him know I didn't care if he used them when he invited over the woman he'd put before our marriage vows. I still choked on the word *affair*.

Maybe I hadn't been the best wife, but I surely hadn't been the worst. Marriages had peaks and valleys. That was life. But never, not even once, had I considered cheating on *him*. Roman would never realize the pain I felt from his betrayal.

I wanted to forget everything about *that* Sunday—the day I'd discovered his infidelity. Even the dress I'd been wearing was stuffed in the bottom of the donations bag. For two months, I'd cried every moment I was alone, until the sorrow had left me physically ill. Migraine headaches and stomach problems had plagued my nights. Days of silence would mount between me and Roman until things would finally erupt, and then the cycle would start over again. The atmosphere in our home had been tense with unresolved issues, words thrown at one another out of frustration and rage, and the residue of deceit.

Zariya and Kyle were emotionally fragile, and I crawled into a social cocoon. My longtime friend Caprice Mowry was my only confidante; I was too ashamed and embarrassed to tell even my mother. Roman had to leave. There was no other option. It was only a matter of when. A month ago, I had been searching the trunk of Roman's car for the instruction packet for Kyle's social studies project when I'd discovered instead the Greensboro apartment guides that he'd collected. That's when I told him he had to leave. I would never let it be said that *he* walked out on *me*.

It irritated me that Roman kept opening the boxes that I'd spent my morning arranging. He folded back the flaps of a smaller container filled with miscellaneous items from his nightstand. Inside was a dusty book about the history of music in the South, a men's study Bible, and a handful of business cards. He thumbed the pages of his Bible.

"If you're looking for a reason why our marriage failed, you might actually want to read that," I scoffed. "I'm no biblical scholar, but if my memory serves me correctly, I'm sure there's something in there about infidelity." My words were riddled with sarcasm. Roman hated sarcasm.

He dropped the Bible back in the box. "I asked you to go to counseling," he said. "Several times."

"Why? You're the one who cheated."

"Our marriage was on the rocks before that," he said.

"And you completely pushed it off the cliff," I said. "I told you before we got married that cheating was a deal breaker. You're the idiot who didn't believe me."

"Zenja, don't resort to name-calling."

"Don't try to reprimand me. I'm not your child."

"You're acting like one."

"So now *you're* name-calling." I pointed an accusatory finger at him.

"I didn't call you a child. I said you were acting like one. There's a difference."

"Whatever, Roman," I said, disgusted by yet another argument.

Roman kicked a partially filled box, sending it skidding across the concrete floor of the garage. I wanted to have a temper tantrum of my own and pitch everything he owned to the curb.

Roman was my second husband and the love I'd never thought I'd find again after losing my first husband, Vincent, to pancreatic cancer. The disease had eaten away his body in six months, and I never had time to accept his imminent death. It all happened too fast. Nothing could have prepared me for that grief, and the same was true about this current grief. I'd once heard a woman say she wouldn't wish divorce on her worst enemy. I didn't believe her until now.

Roman flipped off the nearby radio, and the gospel choir on the crackly AM station fell silent. He leaned against the hood of my car and stared at his shiny brown loafers.

"It didn't go as far as you think," Roman reasoned, obviously calmer now. It was a moot point and an excuse he had used since *that* Sunday.

"It went far enough for you to lie to your wife *and* your children," I said. We both knew he was lying.

"Don't bring Zariya and Kyle into this."

"We're a family. They're a part of this by default. Every decision you've made and will make affects them—unless, of course, you're walking out of their lives, too." I stepped over to the radio and turned it back on, then adjusted it until I heard more music than static.

"I wish you'd stop saying I'm walking out on you," Roman said. "It's obvious this is more your decision than it is mine."

"Then why are you leaving?"

"To make you happy," Roman said. "To give us some space while we figure things out." His eyes traveled from my wedge-heeled sandals to my face and then to my crossed arms. I followed his gaze to my left hand.

"Why aren't you wearing your wedding ring?" he asked.

"The better question is, why are you *still* wearing yours?" I countered. It had taken him two months to notice that I wasn't wearing my diamond bands. *Pathetic.* It only strengthened my argument that he paid very little attention to me.

Roman twisted his simple gold band around on his finger until it slipped over his knuckle, then pushed it down inside his pocket. "Satisfied?" he asked.

I shrugged.

"It doesn't change the fact that we're still married," Roman said. "I'm still your husband, and you're still my wife."

"For now."

Roman lifted his hands in surrender, then turned toward the door leading into the house.

"You can pack the rest of your things yourself," I said. "I know you can't take it all at once, but the sooner the better." I hit the button to open the garage door, then dragged an overstuffed trash bag out to the curb for the next morning's pickup. It had been forever since I'd had to touch the trash, but it was one of many things I'd have to get used to doing again. Like sleeping alone.

Two days later, I was curled up in our king-sized bed—in the center of the mattress, instead of over to the right, where I'd slept and had fought for the covers for years. "I need You now more than ever," I prayed. I gave myself permission to cry like a newborn baby and wanted more than anything for God to wrap me in His grace and peace. At least I knew He'd never leave me or forsake me, even if Roman had.

# 1

I'm coming back home."

I hadn't even heard the front door open. I'd just come downstairs to the kitchen, headed out to eat dinner at my favorite Thai restaurant. I escaped there often for time alone, a satisfying meal, and a place to mull over the next steps I would take toward reinventing my life as a single mother of two.

The divorce complaint and civil summons had been delivered to Roman yesterday via certified mail, but today, the envelope was in Roman's hand, the edge of it ripped like it had been opened in a panic and the contents quickly read, then stuffed back inside by shaky hands. Reality had settled in for both of us. I assumed it was the reason for his unannounced return.

"Did you hear me? I'm coming back home," Roman repeated.

I barely heard his words. I didn't know if it was because of the volume of his voice or because my head was crowded with so many thoughts of my own. I knew Roman meant what he said. Even after eleven months of living in separate households, I'd never changed the locks in case he needed to enter the house for an emergency, and he'd never used his key when he knew I was home. Instead, he'd always rung the doorbell and waited on the front porch like a courier. Today, Roman had delivered some unsettling news about his return, and a wave of heat flashed through my body as I thought about a dream I'd had two weeks prior.

Heavy circles rimmed Roman's downcast eyes, and I noticed how the gray hairs in his unshaven beard looked more prominent than before. He looked horrible—not at all like a confident man who'd arrived with intentions of winning back his wife. Maybe he wanted to solicit my sympathy, but it wasn't working. I was leaving for my cruise to the Bahamas the next morning, and I refused to let him ruin my long-awaited vacation.

*Thud!* Roman dropped a purple duffel bag at his feet. It couldn't have held more than one or two days' worth of clothing and a few toiletries. He probably wasn't sure how his proclamation was going to be accepted. If it hadn't been for my dream, this would've been a more chaotic scene. But God had shown me, late in the midnight hour, that this was going to happen. Us standing here. Together. I just hadn't realized it would be so soon. I had awakened from that dream before either of us had spoken a word.

My heart fluttered, but I replied calmly, "You can't just walk in here and tell me you're coming home. That's not your decision."

"Well, whose decision is it?" Roman asked. "I'm making the decision to keep my family together. I want to right the wrong that I've done."

I studied Roman's appearance. Not only could he use a razor but an iron, too. He'd probably slept in those clothes—if he'd slept at all. I picked up the stack of mail I'd left on the counter for him—a credit card bill, a postcard reminder for his dental checkup, the latest issue of *Men's Health*, and, ironically, a manila folder containing another copy of the divorce complaint. I held the stack out to Roman. He pretended to reach for it, then seized the opportunity to grab my arm and pull me against him. I caught my breath as the mail scattered to the floor. My arms fell limp at my sides, refusing to return the strength behind his embrace. Roman was trying to bring me back into his world. Our world. I couldn't let myself slip back in so easily.

"Don't," I said. I wondered if he could feel my heart thumping in my chest. Or was that Roman's heart?

"Don't what?" he asked. "Don't hug you? Don't come back? Don't love you?"

He loosened his grip but still held on to my waist. "I can't *not* hug you. I can't *not* come back. I can't *not* love you."

My words were finally finding their way to my lips. Finally putting themselves together in a way that made sense. "Don't think you can make everything better just by coming home," I said, my voice rising. I started to quiver. I closed my eyes and exhaled a long stream of air to steady my emotions. "This is bad timing. Everything about this is wrong." I twisted out of Roman's grasp and backed away from him.

Roman crouched to pick up the papers at our feet. He paused momentarily when he saw the envelope from my attorney's office, then stood and tossed all of it on the counter. "Let me make it right. Let me try," Roman begged, reaching for my hands. The seconds passed between us slowly, like years.

I'd given up on reconciling. I'd spent the first three months of his absence brooding over everything that had gone wrong. Despite my strong words and confident stance when we argued, I'd seen myself as damaged goods. That was then; this was now. There was a time when I couldn't picture my life without Roman, but now I couldn't imagine my life with him. God had healed my heart, so what was the sense in giving it back to Roman and letting him shatter it again?

I slung my backpack purse over my shoulder and took my keys off the little hook on the refrigerator. I tried to make a graceful exit but ended up tripping over Roman's stupid purple duffel bag. I picked it up and hurled it at him, catching him off guard and making him stumble back a bit against the counter.

"You dropped something," I growled.

"Zenja, please," Roman pleaded.

I turned to look at him. I don't know why. I shouldn't have. I blinked when I thought I saw the hope of a future. *No,* I told myself. *Cheating is a deal breaker.*

Roman had been slumped over earlier, but now he stood confidently in his six-foot, three-inch height. His deep-set eyes looked into me. He'd always hypnotized me with those eyes, and he knew it. Roman wasn't playing fair.

"I know at one time it was hard to live with me, but hasn't it been worse living without me?" he asked with a nervous laugh as I backed toward the door.

At one time, I would've said yes, but that wasn't the case now. I'd mentally shifted from being a married woman to a divorcee, gotten used to climbing in between cold sheets at night, and embraced the right to make the final decision on what to do for dinner.

I couldn't answer Roman, so I escaped out the door, leaving him and the sudden drama he'd brought back into my life behind me. I got in the car, shifted it into gear, and reversed out of the driveway faster than I should have. I waited until I was at the entrance of our subdivision before I pulled over and crumbled in tears.

# 2

"A table for two in the rear," I requested, even though there was only a handful of patrons in the restaurant. By the time I'd ordered a sweet tea for myself and a Sprite for Caprice, I spotted her blowing through the restaurant like a tornado. She still had no idea what was going on; when we'd talked, I'd been so emotional, she hadn't been able to decipher my words.

Minutes later, when Caprice knew the story, the look of worry faded from her face.

I ripped open three packets of sugar and shook them into my tea. I downed a big gulp before I realized it was actually salt I'd added. I sucked my lips in and forced the dreadful taste down my throat. Roman had me all messed up.

"Why did he do this to me? He knew you and I were leaving on the cruise tomorrow. He's not being fair. He's just trying to play with my head."

"From the way you said he looked, I doubt his intentions were to play with your head," Caprice mused. "That man is broken." She signaled our server and requested another tea for me.

"Broken or broke?" I asked her. "Roman's trying to handle two households. Just because he doesn't live with us doesn't mean I let him abandon his financial responsibilities," I reminded her, swirling a fried spring roll around in a pool of sweet-and-sour sauce.

Not only had I also ordered the tempura calamari and coconut soup as appetizers, but I'd ordered the full-sized entrée of ginger chicken and stir-fry vegetables—and had all but scraped my plate clean. The only thing that stopped me was looking at Caprice's half-eaten bowl of lemongrass shrimp salad. I felt like such a glutton.

"I'll tell you like I've always told you—"

"I don't like where this conversation is headed," I interrupted her, checking to make sure I'd picked up sugar this time. "But when has that ever stopped you from speaking your mind?"

"Never," Caprice admitted. "So, you know I've always said your marriage can be reconciled. Even though he did something stupid, my thoughts on that have never changed." She clasped her hands and propped them under her chin.

"No, what he did was more than stupid. Have you forgotten that he tipped out on me? The man everybody thought could nearly walk on water cheated on his wife—*your* best friend. Infidelity is grounds for divorce, and that's not just a woman scorned talking. That's in the Bible."

It wasn't like Caprice didn't know that. She had a passion for marriage and for godly relationships in general. She'd prayed with me until I was able to find a place of forgiveness in my heart for Roman. I could forgive, but I couldn't forget. From all that we'd been through together over the years, Caprice knew that loyalty was high on my list of priorities. Caprice was loyal. That's one of the reasons I was privileged to call her "friend."

"But you don't have to choose divorce," she said, breaking into my thoughts.

"You don't know what it's like to walk in my shoes," I told her.

Caprice looked at me but didn't say a word. She just let the moments pass, like Roman had done. I didn't like the silence because it made me have to think about the options in front of me.

"Maybe Roman wanted to give you some things to consider while you were away. Vacations can be the perfect time to gather your thoughts."

"Well, I'm going to do everything in my power to think about anything and anybody *except* Roman Maxwell. I refuse to let him ruin my vacation *or* my life."

The server reappeared with two Styrofoam containers, but when she noticed that I'd cleared my plate, she left only one, in front of Caprice. Caprice forked the remains of her salad into the container and snapped it closed. I was overwhelmed, while Caprice was calm as ever. I wanted her to join in my Roman-bashing, but that would never happen. She respected her husband and other people's husbands, too.

Caprice rested her chin in her hands again. "Just close your eyes and imagine all the beautiful white sands and transparent blue waters in Nassau," she said, sounding like a Bahamian tour guide. "There's no way you can go there and return as the same woman. You know, a wise man once told me that God lives in the Bahamas."

"Well, it's going to take God Himself to speak to me about Roman while I'm on this cruise," I said, not daring to mention my dream to Caprice. I knew God was speaking then, but I didn't know if I wanted to hear what He had to say.

Without a shred of guilt, I ate the last spring roll on my plate. Food had been my coping mechanism over the last year, and I had eighteen additional pounds to prove it. "This extra weight I'm carrying now wouldn't be so bad if God would let me choose where I wanted it to go," I said, slapping the side of my thigh where last week I'd noticed the expanding cellulite. "Unfortunately that's one choice I didn't get to make."

"You've got bigger choices in life that you need to be focusing on," Caprice said.

"Right," I said, picking up the menu. "Like dessert. I wish they had red velvet cake."

"At a Thai restaurant?" Caprice snatched the menu out of my hands before I could order a second round. "You're getting on a cruise ship for the first time tomorrow. Don't overdo it."

"I hadn't thought about that." I checked my watch. 6:46. "I need to run to the mall to find a couple more sundresses. Want to join me?"

"No, thanks." Caprice pulled her wallet out of her purse and put down enough money to cover both of our meals. "My treat," she insisted when I shoved the money back toward her. "Buy yourself a little something extra. Perhaps some lingerie." She winked. "There's a great sale at Macy's, by the way. I'm headed home to my husband. You should probably go home to yours, too."

~

Roman's car was still in the driveway when I arrived at home after two hours of retail therapy. Even Macy's best sale hadn't cured my anxieties about Roman's return. The only things I had to show for it were one dress that actually fit and two that I promised myself I would be able to wear by the end of the summer. The rest of my clearance finds were accessories—the things every woman can wear, no matter her size.

I parked on my side of the garage, since I'd never taken the time to completely empty Roman's half. He'd always opted to use it as a man cave instead of a shelter for his Volvo. The most prominent items that remained were a worn leather armchair, a multicolored braided rug, and a black trunk that doubled as a coffee table and storage for part of Roman's treasured record collection. Kyle had taken to using the space as a respite when Zariya's teenage hormonal surges were too much to bear. Until now, I hadn't thought much about it, but Roman had probably kept it there to mark his territory. He had every right. Roman Maxwell was the sole name on the deed, since he'd purchased the home years before we'd met. I'd known that I would eventually have to find another home for me and my kids, but I'd tried not to think about it. Now, I had no choice. Coming home to music playing in the house had always meant that Roman was there. I tiptoed up the steps so that my shopping bags wouldn't rustle and announce my arrival before I was ready to face the inevitable. I saw Roman's silhouette move around the guest room at the end of the hall, so I slipped into my bedroom and eased the door closed with a soft click. I spread out my findings on the bed and wondered what Zariya would say about my taste in fashion. She had an opinion on every piece of clothing that touched my body. Just in case I had a change of heart, I kept the tags on the dress I could fit in, and went into the walk-in closet to stuff it inside my single piece of luggage. At Kyle's earlier request, I also packed a photo of him and Zariya so they could go on the cruise, too.

For the past week, my children had been in the safe and capable hands of my parents in New Jersey. Two weeks of their summer break had always been devoted to time with their grandparents, but this year, they'd begged to extend their visit to an entire month. I'd reluctantly agreed. I enjoyed having them around, and they were usually involved in some type of academic camp. That was your summertime fate when you had a mother who was an elementary school vice principal and a father who worked in higher education. I missed them already, but with all that had transpired over the last few hours, I was relieved they weren't here.

Ironically, a few minutes later, my cell phone rang, and the home screen lit with a picture of their smiling faces.

"Are you ready to come home yet?" I asked of whoever was on the other end of the line.

"Umm…well, right now we're at the hospital," Zariya said.

"You're where? Oh, no. What happened?" My legs felt like gelatin. Thank goodness I was already sitting on the closet floor.

"Wait a minute, Mom," Zariya said. There was rustling in the background, muffled voices, and a clanking, as if she'd dropped the phone.

"Zariya! Zariya Rose!" I yelled, hoping she'd hear my voice and remember that she had a frantic mother on the other end.

"Hello?" she finally said. "Sorry, Gemma was trying to—"

"Why are you at the hospital?" I demanded. "What happened?"

"We're here because *your* son thinks he's a flying trapeze artist and tried to swing from some contraption he tied to a tree in the backyard. He fell and broke his arm. I guess there's no future for him at the UniverSoul Circus."

"You've got to be kidding me," I said, relieved that a broken arm was all it was but slightly distressed that I wasn't there to comfort him. I didn't care if he was eight and had outgrown public kisses to his forehead. He was still a Mama's boy at heart, and I knew he'd prefer to be in my arms. Mama, however, was almost 500 miles away. His grandma's arms would have to do. I closed my eyes and slid back into the mountain of shoes on the closet floor.

"Where are Gemma and Grandpa?" I drilled. "No—let me talk to Kyle first."

"They're all in the hospital room with the nurse," Zariya said. "She's about to set Kyle's cast, and he started flipping out like somebody had set him on fire or something. When we first got here, he didn't even want the doctor to touch him. It was so embarrassing. That's why I left the room."

I hoped it hadn't been that bad. I'd have to get a firsthand report from my parents, since Zariya was embarrassed by most things these days. She was a teenager, though, so that was her job. It wouldn't surprise me if *she* was the one overreacting.

"Is everything okay?" Roman's voice startled me.

This time, I was the one who dropped the phone.

"Can you announce yourself next time, please?" I whispered, clutching my chest.

"Sorry. I knocked, but you didn't answer. Are you alright?"

"Yes," I said, showing my annoyance.

Roman was wearing a white tank top and a pair of cotton pajama pants that drooped around his waist because he hadn't bothered to tie the drawstring. He'd shaved and showered. The woodsy scent of his soap and aftershave took over the enclosed space, making me remember what it was like to have a man in the house. But not just any man—my husband.

"Mom? Mom?" The tiny voice far away in New Jersey beckoned me back.

Roman picked up my phone and handed it to me.

"I'm here, Zariya. Not so loud, please. You're at a hospital. Can Gemma come to the phone now?"

"Hospital!" Roman gasped.

I waved a hand to quiet him and shot him the evil eye. "He's okay. Just a broken arm," I said, covering my cell phone's microphone. Roman didn't budge. If only I could snap my fingers and make him disappear.

"Mom, is that Dad? Can I talk to him? What's he doing there this time of night?" Zariya's questions tumbled over each other in excitement.

"It's nothing. He had to pick up some mail since I'm leaving for my cruise in the morning."

"Why couldn't he get it later? Did you take his key? What if there's an emergency?"

Zariya sounded panicky. The thought of me and Roman divorcing was always at the forefront of her mind. She worried about losing another dad. She'd been five when her biological father had passed away, but Roman had never treated her any different than his own flesh and blood.

The fact that Roman still had a key to the house was Zariya's last hope. I knew because I'd read it in her so-called hidden diary, which I took the parental liberty of reading whenever I had the chance. It was stashed in her bottom drawer under the Hello Kitty pajamas she'd long outgrown. My daughter and I were close, but that diary made me privy to information I wouldn't know otherwise: She was self-conscious about her growing breasts and wondered how long she'd have to suffer menstrual cramps. She wondered why one boy in her homeroom—Evan—talked to her only if his friends weren't around. She worried about making drill team next year and had already started thinking about college, when she could move out of the house. Despite all her teenage problems, at least once a week Zariya wrote a short prayer asking God to bring her daddy back home.

I looked up at Roman. He was still watching me, trying to figure out the conversation that was going on. I turned my back to him and pretended to rearrange my shoes.

"Zariya, you're asking too many questions about things that don't concern you," I said. "Tell Gemma to call me as soon as she can. Don't forget. Promise me."

"I promise. She's all shaken up, too. On the way to the hospital, she said you were never going to let us come to New Jersey again. Is that true?"

"No, it's not true." I stood, brushed past Roman, and went into the bathroom. "I need to finish getting ready for my cruise. We'll talk later."

"Tell Dad to call me," Zariya said quickly before hanging up.

I ignored Roman while I tended to the mess in my bathroom. There was a mound of towels in the corner that needed to be washed before morning. The beauty products I'd used to scrub, buff, polish, and shine my skin to Bahamas-ready perfection littered the counters. What I hadn't done myself at home, I'd gotten plucked and waxed at the day spa yesterday.

"Excited about your trip?" Roman had appeared in the doorway.

"Very," I said, my voice more excited than necessary.

"What time are you leaving?"

"Around eight. I'm meeting Caprice at her house."

"How's she doing?"

"*They're* doing great," I said, purposefully including Duane—Caprice's faithful, committed husband, who was still keeping his wife happy. *Think about that, Roman.*

Roman scooped up the dirty towels and left without trying to press any further conversation. I closed the bathroom door as soon as I heard the washing machine begin to fill with water. My legs held strong for a moment, but then they weakened, and I leaned back against the door, sliding down until I reached the cold tile floor. Then I cried. Nine months may have changed a lot about me, but it hadn't changed that I still had love for Roman in my heart.

Why couldn't Roman have just accepted the divorce petition so we could focus on building our separate lives? I was willing to co-parent with him, if that was what he wanted. I spent nearly an hour second-guessing every decision I'd made. Praying. Asking God to change my feelings and to guard my heart.

In the midst of my personal reflections, Mom called. She let me speak to Kyle, assured me that everything was fine with my children, and insisted I carry on with my cruise with no worries.

"I'll come pick them up when I get back," I said.

"Why? A broken arm in New Jersey is the same as a broken arm in North Carolina. I'll keep the rest of his body in one piece," she assured me with a laugh.

"I'll think about it," I said. But unless Roman had left with his purple duffel bag by the time I returned from the Bahamas, I wouldn't be bringing them back to 2412 Whispering Brook Lane. We had too many things to figure out.

"Anything else going on?" Mom pried.

"Nope. I'm packed and getting ready for bed."

I knew Zariya had already told her that Roman was at the house. My daughter was a leaky bucket whenever my mother got ahold of her, and it didn't take long for her to spill everything she knew, or *thought* she knew. My mother was also aware that Roman rarely came over unless he was picking up the children or tending to maintenance around the house.

"Oh." Mom paused. "Okay. Well, call me before you get on that ship. I don't like those things. You're out in the middle of nowhere, with nothing around you but water for as far as the eyes can see. The Titanic isn't the only ship that sank, you know? Did you see on the news about that cruise ship that went down in Germany?"

"It was Italy," I corrected her. "And, yes, I saw it." My mother could be so dramatic. She didn't want me to run track in high school because she thought I'd break my leg. She didn't want me to get my driver's license because she was worried I'd get in a head-on collision with a drunk driver, and if it wasn't for my father's support, I never would've been able to attend college out of state.

"Be careful." *Pause.* "Alright...well, if it's nothing else..." *Pause.*

There was no way she was going to find out what transpired today. Mom was as bad as Caprice when it came to Roman. I'd complained to her once when Roman had been out of town on yet another Friday night, performing with his band, and she'd responded, "At least he's out playing his saxophone and not somewhere with his friends at one of those places that some men frequent. And you know *exactly* what I mean by that. Be grateful. Someone else would be happy to have a man like Roman."

Well, someone else *had* been. I'd seen her face, and she'd looked ecstatic.

"I'll try to call you before we set sail," I said to my mother. "Give Dad and my babies a kiss for me."

Minutes later, I threw back my comforter, slid down under the coolness of the sheets, and closed my eyes. I could still hear Roman's music, though the volume was much lower. He'd come into the bedroom only once since washing the towels, and that had been to ask if there were any dryer sheets. They were in the same place they'd been kept for the last six years, in the storage cabinet directly above the dryer. Roman had lingered like he'd thought I was going to extend him an invitation to get in bed with me. Negative.

As hard as it was to admit, I felt more secure with Roman in the house. I never slept well when I was at home alone, and with my kids away, I'd spent most nights tossing and turning. Tonight, I let a peaceful, comfortable sleep overtake me. I stirred only once—when I sensed Roman's presence. I opened my eyes just enough to see Roman standing in the doorway. *God,* I thought, *what are You doing?*

# 3

I met the morning with green tea and honey, compliments of Roman. When I walked downstairs, I immediately noticed that the suitcase I'd left by the garage door was no longer there.

"I put your bag in the car," Roman said, taking a mug from the cabinet. His half-empty cup of black coffee and a bowl with traces of oatmeal were on the breakfast bar.

"Thanks," I said, feeling refreshed. It was amazing what a good night of restful sleep could do for me.

"I'll drop you off this morning," he offered. He was wearing the same pants from yesterday but had starched and ironed them to perfection.

"I can drive myself," I said, avoiding his gaze. "Really. It's no problem."

"I know you can, but I'll go ahead and take your car to the dealership for an oil change. I saw the reminder card on the refrigerator."

I shrugged my shoulders. "If you insist." I wasn't one to turn down a man's help with things I preferred not to handle anyway. It was one less thing I'd have to tackle on my to-do list when I returned. Roman had already cleaned the refrigerator of an overripe tomato, two containers of expired yogurt, and an open can of ginger ale. He'd also taken out the trash and replaced the bag. I typically kept a clean house, but, being busy getting ready for the cruise, I'd let my weekly cleaning ritual slide. However, from the look of the sparkling countertops, Roman had been the one who'd had the sleepless night. Between getting the house spic-and-span clean and watching me sleep, he should've been exhausted.

I couldn't help but ask him, "So, you're serious about this? You're still going to be here when I get back?"

"Absolutely," Roman affirmed, rinsing out his bowl. "When you get back and forever."

"You can change your address, but it doesn't mean I've changed my mind about us," I said, speaking softly so my words weren't cloaked in anger.

"That's fine," Roman said nonchalantly. He pulled out a small lap tray, placed my food on it, and handed me a napkin.

"Okay," I said, unsure of how to respond.

I took my breakfast of tea and a sesame seed bagel to the front sitting room and posted up in the window seat to watch my neighbors who'd already started their Saturday morning rituals. Across the street, Stan's sprinkler watered his flawless green lawn, and his wife, Barbara, added yet another pop of colorful blooms to the flower bed in front of their house. At the end of the cul-de-sac was the home of Ava Menendez, my neighborhood buddy. Our races had kept us apart for over four years, but an unexpected conversation about God while I was spray-painting two porch planters had brought us together. She had been growing her faith, and I had been attempting to grow petunias. Right now, Ava sat on her patio, watching her two children. Her daughter, Jessica, scribbled in the driveway with sidewalk chalk. In her other hand, she held a banana precariously. One wrong move, and the fruit would become breakfast for the ants. Her son, Chris, was squeezing a tube of yogurt into his mouth.

Ava's attention briefly left her children as she seemed to study the young man walking toward her. Gabe was a neighborhood fixture, though it seemed that no one knew where he actually lived. Every day from dawn to dusk, Gabe circled the streets of our neighborhood. He'd make a U-turn in our cul-de-sac and start his route all over again. Every day the same thing, every day the same clothes—a pair of black shorts and a light blue T-shirt. As fall rolled into winter, he'd add a tattered red sweatshirt, but that was it. Gabe walked, whether sweat rolled down his brow or rain battered his face. Gabe just walked.

The only reason anyone knew his name was because Roman had met him, long before we'd gotten married. One day, Roman had been practicing his trumpet with the garage door open, and Gabe had stopped at the end of the driveway to listen intently. The two of them had talked, and Gabe had revealed his name only when Roman had asked. Once everyone realized he wasn't casing the neighborhood for burglary attempts, they left him alone. Anyone who greeted Gabe received a simple head nod in response. That's just what Jessica and Chris got when they ran to the end of their driveway and emphatically waved at him this morning.

As Gabe rounded in front of Ava's house, she met him with a brown paper bag, which he accepted, as always. He pulled out a banana, peeled it, and polished it off in three big bites. By the time he made it in front of my house, he was gulping orange juice into his stuffed cheeks. But Gabe kept walking, until he paused—and looked in my direction. I waved. He nodded. And then, Gabe showed me something I'd never seen before—his smile—and a beautiful smile it was. Pearly and white.

"I'll be ready after I brush my teeth," I yelled out to Roman, still slightly stunned.

Leaving the bathroom minty fresh, I met Roman outside in my car. On the ride over to Caprice's house, I pretended to read the novel I'd brought along for the flight so I wouldn't have to talk to Roman. The morning traffic flowed easily, and within twenty-five minutes, we pulled into the Mowrys' driveway. The car had barely stopped when I hopped out. Caprice's front door opened, and her sister bounced onto the porch.

"Morning, sunshine," Carmela sang, admiring my bright yellow sundress. "Caprice is looking cute today, too. Y'all are making me jealous. Next time, you won't set sail without me—I can guarantee that." She bounded down the steps like she'd had a double shot of espresso.

Roman got out of the car and set my suitcase on the sidewalk.

"It's no wonder you look so bright and refreshed," Carmela said. "If I had a man like Roman dropping me off this early, I'd have a reason to shine, too. All married and happy. Another reason you and Caprice make me sick. But it's all good, because in due time, I'll be saying, 'Till death do us part.'"

Till the death of what? The death of trust? The death of loyalty? There were plenty of things that could die to bring a marriage to an end, I thought. If Carmela only knew.

Despite the awkward silence between me and Roman, Carmela just wouldn't let it go. "There's nothing like a well-kept woman," she said, her bangles and bracelets tinkling with every flounce and bounce in her step.

Carmela didn't have a clue we were separated. Few people did. My extended family lived far enough away that I didn't have to worry about them, and my mother wouldn't dare share something this private. Weight gain and a job loss, maybe, but never marital problems. My fellow administrators and teachers at the school probably suspected trouble at home, but no one was comfortable enough to approach me about it.

Carmela pushed the button that lifted the carriage to her newly earned pearl white SUV. "I'm taking you guys to the airport since Duane's boss called him into work this morning. Caprice's bag is already in the trunk," she said. "She's inside saying her good-byes. For the fifteenth time."

Roman shoved his hands in his pockets. "I need to talk to Duane," he said. "I'll make sure I ring the doorbell." Then he leaned in toward my face.

A kiss? He couldn't be serious. I turned my head, so that his lips landed on the apple of my cheek. With shoulders slumped, he turned and walked to the porch, where he was met by the happiest married couple of the decade. Duane pulled Caprice into one last embrace, then disappeared into the house with Roman. I could only imagine the conversation about to transpire behind those closed doors.

"Let's go, ladies," Carmela chirped.

Once we were buckled in, she began to back her car into the street. "Roman must be upset that you're going without him, Zenja," she went on. "I could see it all over his face. There's a little jealousy in even the most confident man. I think that's part of the reason I'm still single," she decided.

*And the other part is because you never let a man get a word in edgewise,* I mused to myself. Caprice must've sensed my thoughts because she pulled down the visor and gave me a knowing look in the mirror.

Carmela stopped abruptly. I glanced out the window and saw a car slowly rounding the bend—at least one hundred yards away.

"Really?" Caprice said, peering out the rear window. "At this rate, we'll never make it to the airport."

"Whatever. You don't know how hard I worked to win this car."

"Trust me, we know," Caprice stressed.

The entire Triad area knew Carmela Garrett had hustle. She was more than an entrepreneur in cosmetic sales; she was the kind of go-getter who made me dodge her phone calls. She'd earned a reputation—and not always a good one—for her persistence in her latest business venture. Cosmetics, jewelry, real estate, life insurance, organic juices, luxurious chocolates—Carmela dabbed in it all. Her travel agent business was part of the reason we'd gotten a remarkable deal on our cruise, so, in that respect, I appreciated her drive.

I half listened to Carmela's spiel about how we could make money by teaming up with her to sell a weight-loss drink that had recently hit the market. If I was going to lose weight, it was going to take more than a milkshake supplement. I had enough shaking going on my body as it was—the back of my arms, my thighs, my midsection, and my knees. Whose knees were as chubby as mine?

The traffic whizzed by me as I wondered what Roman was saying to Duane. When Carmela leaned on the horn and slammed the brakes, she snatched me out of my thoughts. She jerked the wheel to the left and barely missed avoiding a rear-end collision with a long sedan. She maneuvered around the car and put down her window. "A turn signal would be nice," she screamed at the elderly man behind the wheel.

I sank back into the seat. *Take me to paradise, please.*

Caprice looked both embarrassed and irritated at her sister's behavior. "As soon as I get back, you're coming with me to volunteer with me at the assisted living home. You're going to be old, too, one of these days. You seem to forget that."

Carmela smacked her lips. "Well, if I'm driving like that, suspend my license and hide my keys." Suddenly she snapped her fingers. "But it might be a good idea to go with you. I have some great vitamins for the elderly. All natural and loaded with calcium."

None of us could keep from laughing. Carmela had a great sense of humor, but that didn't keep her from showing her road rage. I breathed a sigh of relief when I saw a sign for the airport exit. By the time we had checked in, been poked and prodded in security, and boarded the plane, I finally started to relax. "We need this trip," Caprice said, pulling out her itinerary. "Just us, with nobody to worry about but ourselves. Some bonding time."

"Tell me about it," I said, flipping through the safety information card I'd pulled from the seat pocket in front of me.

Caprice ran a highlighter down a list of events. If that was her intended schedule, we weren't going to have a minute to relax. I was going to need a vacation to recover from my vacation.

I slid the papers out of her hand so I could see what I'd gotten myself into. "Zip-lining? Scuba diving?" I shook my head. "These excursions are not for people with young children. I don't need them to cash in on my life insurance policy any earlier than God intended." I handed the papers back. "I'll stick to the activities on the ship, like karaoke."

"That's cool. I can do that, too," she said with equal excitement.

"I'll be better off swimming with the sharks." I laughed and patted her knee. Caprice, an interior designer, was phenomenal at coordinating window treatments and home décor, but she couldn't manage a solid musical note to save her life.

"I wonder what our husbands are talking about," Caprice said, powering down her cell phone. "I'm sure they're still together. I don't know about Roman, but Duane has certainly missed having his buddy around."

"You do that just to get under my skin, don't you?" I adjusted the tiny air vent above my head.

"Do what?" Caprice asked innocently.

"Refer to Roman as my husband."

She stopped and looked at me. "Well, that's what he is."

"On paper," I agreed in a roundabout way. "At least for the next twenty-nine days."

"On paper, in the eyes of God, and in Roman's heart. A man doesn't come back unless he really wants to."

"And regardless of what his wife says or does, he doesn't leave unless he really wants to, either," I added.

"A woman doesn't have to let him back in unless she really wants to. And there's no way she'd let him keep a house key for this long if she didn't intend for him to be able to use it again in the future. Correct me if I'm wrong." Caprice smiled with satisfaction.

"We agreed Roman could keep a key in case of an emergency, or in the event he needed to fix something at the house. He's like a maintenance man."

"Hmm..." Caprice grinned.

"Not *that* kind of maintenance man," I jumped in to say. "Besides, do you really think I could've gotten away with changing the locks?"

"Yes. But don't mind me," Caprice said, slipping her arms through the sleeves of her cardigan. "I just call it like I see it."

The captain announced our departure over the intercom, and we started to taxi to the runway.

"This trip will be a lot better if we don't talk about Roman," I muttered.

Caprice closed her eyes and leaned back against the headrest. "I won't say another word about him."

"Thank you." I popped a piece of gum in my mouth and started chewing to help my ears adjust to the altitude changes, and then I braced for take-off—the part of flying I hated most.

Caprice held out her hand for gum, and I dropped a spearmint stick in her open palm. "Not another word," Caprice murmured under her breath. "I'll just let God do all the talking."

# 4

Since Caprice was the cruise expert, I followed her lead after we claimed our luggage at the Miami International Airport. While she went in search of a nearby kiosk to ask a question of one of the cruise line representatives, I waited in the line for the shuttle bus that would transport us to the cruise ship. That's when I heard my name.

"Zenja?"

I turned around to see a familiar face, but it was one I couldn't immediately place. Had I met him at an educator's conference? His skin looked like it had already been darkened by the Bahamian sun, and his physique appeared to have been carefully chiseled by God Himself. Few women would forget a man like that.

"Dig back to those high-school memories," he said, obviously noticing that my recollection of him wasn't as clear as his memory of me. "Marching Cougars," he added—a hint that pulled memories from twenty years ago back to the surface.

I snapped my fingers. "Drum line? Help me."

"Tuba," he said, puffing out his chest like we were talking about the biggest achievement of his adolescence. The words of our band director must've come to mind because he straightened his back and squared his shoulders. "Lance Freeman."

"Lance?" I was stunned at his transformation. "That *is* you," I said, still incredulous.

"In the flesh," Lance said. "Different man outside but the same man inside."

"Small world," I said. "Are you headed to the Bahamas, too?"

"Yep. I'd swim there if I had to," Lance said.

Once I had the chance to study his features, I realized his almond-shaped eyes and thick eyebrows were still the same, only twenty years ago, they'd been on a face that was round and plump. In high school, his arms had been about as round as the tuba, and he could rest the instrument on the stomach that spilled over his blue polyester pants. Everything that had been soft before looked like steel now. The years had been good to him. Real good. He'd dieted and exercised himself into a chiseled rock of chocolate. And chocolate was my weakness.

My recollection of high school and my stint as a member of the color guard streamed back. I'd developed my share of crushes on those bus rides coming home from away games. Athletes came a dime a dozen, but a boy who could play an instrument was my weakness. Funny how Vincent had barely been able to keep rhythm with the two hands God had given him. But then there was Roman. His musical capability was intrinsic to who he was.

*Stop it,* I told myself. *No thinking about Roman.*

"So, where's Treva?" I asked, looking around for Lance's high-school sweetheart. "I know you two got married."

"Right after college," he confirmed. "And three months ago we divorced."

"Sorry to hear that." I cringed, hating that I'd thrown salt on a fresh wound.

"Don't be," he said. "I like being just what my last name says—a free man. Couldn't be happier."

"That's good to know," I said. His attitude only strengthened my belief that things would be fine with me after my own divorce was finalized. Being happy in life shouldn't be the option; it should be the rule.

Lance and I moved with the crowd as we inched toward the boarding shuttle. Caprice caught my eye and raised her brows with a look that said, *Who is that man breathing down your neck?* I'd noticed that Lance didn't seem to have much regard for personal space, but I didn't mind, because the brother smelled as divine as he looked.

Ignoring Caprice, I caught up on the last twenty or so years since Lance and I had seen each other.

"And you?" he asked. "Married?"

"Separated."

"So, you're in the gray zone," Lance said. "Been there. Any hopes of reconciliation?"

"Not as far as I'm concerned," I said, my heart tightening at my own words.

"Is that your friend over there staring at us?" Lance asked. "Orange-looking dress with the belt."

"Yes," I said. I didn't even need to look at Caprice to confirm.

"She wants you and your husband to work things out, doesn't she?" Lance asked.

"Yes. How did you know?"

"Because she's looking at me like I'm a bull's-eye and she's got a purse full of sharpened arrows."

I sighed. "That's her hope and her prayer," I confessed. "Always easier said than done."

"Well, you should never underestimate the power of a praying woman. My mama used to tell me that all the time," he said, waving at Caprice.

I couldn't see her face, but I could imagine that her expression was less than enthusiastic. I refused to go through a marriage counseling session standing in the shuttle line, so I steered the conversation to a more lighthearted subject—our children. Before long, Caprice joined us.

"This is the most we've ever talked," I joked after Caprice and Lance had been formally introduced. "He was practically married in high school."

Lance tugged at his shirt collar and rubbed his knuckles across his Adam's apple. "Treva did try to hold the reins tight around a brother's neck. Took me years to wrestle that noose off. Hence my 'declaration of independence' cruise."

"You came alone?" Caprice asked.

"Work and play," Lance said. "This cruise is a perk from my company for being one of the top-producing brokers."

"Real estate?"

"Insurance," Lance clarified. He slipped two business cards out of the back pocket of his khaki shorts. "Call me if you want to find the best coverage at the best rates. Auto, life, short-term disability...I do it all." He flipped the cards over as he handed them to us. On the reverse side was a graphic of dumbbells. "I do a little personal training on the side, too," he said.

Caprice handed her card back. "I'm in North Carolina, so—"

"Me, too," Lance said quickly. "I've been in Charlotte for the last ten years. Zenja told me you guys were in Greensboro. I'm there a few times a month. My company has an office there, and I'm partnering with an associate to open a gym that specializes in personal fitness training and boot camps."

"We should get together the next time you're in town," I said, reaching out to squeeze his bicep. "It looks like you know what you're doing, and I sure could use some help tightening some things that have loosened over the years." I was flirting, and I knew it. So did Caprice and Lance.

"It's called gravity, and you look incredible," Caprice interjected. "Nothing a few evening strolls through your neighborhood wouldn't change. You can take a few laps with Gabe."

"I must agree with her," Lance said. "You do look incredible." His eyes drank me in.

The line of cruise passengers started to move freely, and Caprice put her hand on my forearm to nudge me forward. "I thought we'd never get going," she said.

"Let me go catch up with my coworkers," Lance said, looking at me like he was a biscuit and I was a plate of warm gravy. Evidently my small act of flirtation had given him a green light. "We'll catch up on the cruise."

"Definitely," I said.

"We'd better hurry and get on the shuttle with its AC," Caprice said. "Some of us are getting a little too hot."

# 5

Caprice and I settled in near the front of the shuttle. We were seated behind an elderly couple dressed in matching green and yellow floral shirts. They held each other's wrinkled, swollen, arthritic-looking hands with their fingers intertwined as if they'd been that way for fifty years.

"That'll be you and Duane in another few decades," I whispered to Caprice.

She leaned closer and whispered behind shielded mouth, "Minus the shirts. I may be able to make him love me for a lifetime, but I'd never be able to convince him to wear one of those."

"I don't know. You've convinced him to do some pretty crazy things."

Once upon a time, Roman and I had shared fun, spontaneous times as a couple. No matter how busy our weeks, we reserved Thursday nights as our time together. But soon the children's extracurricular activities had filled my calendar, and Roman's band practices had taken priority over our weekly dates. On the weekends, he was nowhere to be found; there was always a gig to be played. We were rarely together. Small things became big things, and irritation grew to resentment. Intimacy waned, not just in the bedroom, but in the degrees of closeness and concern that a married couple was supposed to have for each other. Over time, we ceased being spouses and turned into roommates.

"I'm telling you, we should've done a seven-day cruise," Caprice said, still skimming her itinerary "Next time."

"Let me get through this one first," I said, digging around in my tote and pulling out my arsenal of tricks to combat motion sickness: tablets, acupressure bands, and powdered ginger.

"At least you're prepared," Caprice said, amused yet obviously not surprised.

Lance boarded the bus with the rest of his coworkers. He squeezed my shoulder as he passed.

"He's a little too friendly," Caprice said after a minute. "And he smiles too much. That means he's sneaky."

"He's always smiled like that," I said. "And you can't build an accurate opinion of somebody based on a three-minute conversation."

"Oh, I definitely can," Caprice said.

I glanced over my shoulder. Whatever Lance was saying had captured the full attention of his coworkers. "I wouldn't worry about Lance. He's not out to do any harm."

Caprice wasn't buying it. "He's not out to do any good, either."

I was sucked in to the excitement of the cruise as soon as we boarded the ship, and Caprice and I posed for a picture in front of the stereotypical background photo of a tropical island. I'd always wondered why people bought those cheesy family pictures, but I realized now that it was almost impossible not to get consumed in the entire cruise experience. With our grins spread across our faces, you'd think we'd just won the lottery. My body relaxed, and my soul felt a freeness it hadn't experienced in a long time. If I survived the rocking waves and any emergencies that happened to arise over the next few days, I knew I'd become a regular cruiser.

The ship was like a floating hotel. "Luxurious" was an understatement. A winding staircase of gold was centered in a series of high-end boutiques that sold everything a woman could wish for on dry land. All my fears of being tossed around like the Minnow ship and being deserted on some island with Gilligan and Ginger faded. I fished out my camera and snapped pictures so I could show my mom. It might take a miracle to convince her, but maybe one day she'd change her mind. If only she'd stop watching CNN for the latest cruise-ship catastrophe.

"You've sold me," I said to Caprice on the walk to our cabin. I'd insisted that Carmela book us one in the middle outside after doing some research on which part of the ship was the most balanced.

Caprice unlocked the door, and I followed her inside. Our cabin was about the size of my college dorm room. We stashed our luggage beside the beds, then headed out to the veranda. I'd found my place of solace. At home, I escaped to my newly stained and furnished rear patio, but for the next four days and three nights, I'd simply slide open the glass door near my bedside.

Caprice leaned back against the balcony rail and reclined her head toward the sun. "We're going to have an outstanding time. I can feel it."

"I feel something, too," I said, patting my midsection. "I hope it's not motion sickness."

"We're not even moving." Caprice laughed. "Either you're nervous or it's that Thai food from last night. I told you to slow it down."

"One of these days I'm going to listen to you."

"Thank God. A prayer answered." Caprice slid the veranda door open again. "You might want to find that little survival kit of yours and pop a pill before we get going."

"You're right." I headed inside and swallowed one of the mini motion sickness tablets before rejoining Caprice to relax on the chaise lounges. I tried to stop my mind from wandering to thoughts about Roman. What he was doing? What he was thinking? How and why did he think we were going to work? Was he keeping that other woman on a string in case he realized there was no hope for us? A salty breeze lifted the hair around my face. I tried to inhale peace and exhale worry.

*Clarity, Lord,* I prayed silently. *Give me clarity.* Caprice looked lost in thought, too, and seemed to have found her own place of refuge. Not a word passed between us. Only God was speaking. *Forgive. Restore.*

In a perfect world, Roman and I would've fought through this trial together, and our family would emerge strengthened instead of broken. In a perfect world, *she* would not exist; the two of them never would've been together. In a perfect world, I never would've been alone. But there was no such thing as a perfect world.

"Zenja." My eyes fluttered open to see Caprice standing above me. "I called you three times. I can't believe you didn't hear them blow the horn. We're about to set sail. Let's go to the top deck for the Set Sail Welcome Bash that's on the itinerary." She paused and studied me. "Are you okay?"

"I'm fine," I said, turning away. If Caprice looked into my eyes, she would see right through me. "Still feeling a little woozy, but it'll pass."

"Are you sure? Because we can always just relax in the room."

"Absolutely not," I insisted. "I'd rather get up and move about. My stomach might not agree with my decision later, but I'm actually very hungry. Everyone's been telling me about the buffet spreads on these ships, and I don't plan to miss a single one."

"Don't say I didn't warn you." Caprice claimed the bed that was decorated with a set of towels configured into a swan. "Just be prepared to deal with the consequences."

Little did Caprice know but I was starting to believe my queasy stomach had less to do with my food consumption and more to do with the situation waiting for me when I returned to Greensboro.

We changed into our bathing suits and cover-ups, then headed to the poolside bash. By the time we arrived, most of the lounge chairs were occupied by members of a wedding party. None of them appeared to be a day over twenty-five years old, and their bodies had yet to show the effects of childbirth, gravity, fast food, and genetics. They were all wearing white, including the bride and groom, who differentiated themselves with a veil and a black bow tie. *Oh, to be young and in love,* I thought. *I'd love to see them in ten years. Make that five years. As a matter of fact, I'd like to see how the whole marriage thing is going for them a year from now.*

Caprice made a beeline for the buffet table, and I followed her.

"Aren't they cute?" she said.

"Adorable," I mumbled, letting the sarcasm drip from my words.

"Stop being so cynical," Caprice said.

"Not cynical. Just realistic. I know what it takes to hold a marriage together, and it's more than looking flawless in a bikini and a Speedo."

"Oh, so you do know that marriages can be work?" Caprice raised her eyebrows so high, they nearly touched her hairline. "That's good to know."

I ignored her and focused on finding the shortest buffet line. Caprice and I filled our plates with such delicacies as shrimp, fried Malaga sweet potatoes, seafood salad, and other foods, identified with placards, that I probably wouldn't have tried otherwise. With our plates stacked like Mt. Everest, I spotted Lance a few tables away. He hadn't changed clothes, but he'd unbuttoned his outer shirt to reveal a tank top underneath. He caught me looking. I turned away, feeling myself blush. What woman my age blushed? Probably a woman who hadn't had a man's attention in a while.

The only males who gave me compliments and fought to crowd around my legs were four feet tall, had to be reminded constantly to tie their shoes, and dined in the school cafeteria, where they dipped their fish sticks in ketchup.

Since seating was limited, Caprice and I balanced our plates in our arms until we noticed two sunbathers packing up their things, getting ready to abandon their lounge chairs. We swooped down to claim the prime pieces of real estate.

"I'll definitely have to repent of my gluttony when we get back," I said, my cheeks full of shrimp. I dipped yet another in a pool of butter and cocktail sauce. If all else failed, Lance could help me burn the extra calories. I was sure he wouldn't mind. "I assume that's the only sin you'll have to repent of," Caprice said.

It was like my best friend could read my thoughts. I rolled my eyes, but I was too distracted to come up with a verbal response. I was more into people watching and taking inventory of the various interpretations of "poolside wear." I would never have the confidence to sport some of the attire I was watching on deck.

"Can you believe Duane has already left me three messages?" Caprice mused as she scrolled through the log of missed calls on her cell phone. "It's so sad and so cute at the same time. I mean, I left him with plenty of food and drinks—what more could he want from me?"

I chuckled. "You're talking about the man like he's a puppy and you left out some food and water."

"I can see his little hound dog eyes now," Caprice said. She slurped on her pink lemonade, then smacked her lips like it was the best thing she'd ever tasted. "He'll survive. Absence makes the heart grow fonder."

"Or wander," I said. My eyes fell on Lance again. His eyes were on me. He was circled up with his colleagues but wasn't involved in the conversation at all. He was too busy sending nonverbal vibes in my direction.

Lance. Treva's Lance, as they'd sometimes called him in high school. Even though his divorce was final, I felt like I was flirting with another woman's husband, since Treva was the only one I'd ever seen him with. If there was any couple I would've thought would last forever, it would've been them.

"Is it okay if I return his call?" Caprice asked.

"Nope." I refused to let her break her promise. "You said you'd send Duane a text to let him know we'd arrived but wouldn't call him for at least twenty-four hours. Those were your words, not mine. How quickly you forget."

"I didn't forget," Caprice insisted. "I just thought you'd show me a little mercy."

"God shows mercy."

"Fine," Caprice said, then started typing a text message to her husband instead. A girlish smile spread across her face and grew with every word. I'd been around enough married folks to know that outward expressions of love tended to dwindle after some time. Their sizzle lost its snap, crackle, and pop. But not with Caprice and Duane. He'd chased her from the time he'd offered to pump her gas on the day they'd met, and he was still chasing her. The only difference now was that he didn't have to break a sweat to catch her. God was undoubtedly Caprice's first love, but Duane ran a close second.

I guess that's what Roman's mission was now—to chase me. He'd called me when I was on my way to the upper deck for the party, but I'd sent his call directly to voice mail. I hadn't even listened to his message. The only voices I wanted to hear were those of Zariya and Kyle, and their message had quickly informed me that Roman had called them from the house phone. They had questions, but I didn't have answers. I decided to avoid them for now and give myself time to come up with an excuse to tell my prying mother. No doubt she was on the case, and I wasn't sure if she'd been bold enough to come straight-out and ask Roman. I prayed not.

"Watch my things," Caprice said, dropping her phone in the side pocket of her straw bag.

Caprice couldn't have been more than ten steps away when I noticed Lance heading toward me.

# 6

I see you're enjoying the spread," Lance said, standing over me. "Did you leave anything for anybody else?" He peered at my plate like he was calculating the calories. He didn't have a plate of his own, just a peach-colored beverage with slices of oranges and limes floating at the rim of the glass. I could smell the alcohol.

"It's rude to comment on a woman's plate," I said. "What's the use of going on a cruise if you can't enjoy what they have to offer?"

"Whatever makes you happy," Lance said with a shrug. "But you still have my card, right?"

I slapped him on the shoulder. His hard, chiseled shoulder.

Lance took the liberty of stealing one of the shrimp from my plate and dipping it in cocktail sauce. He took a bite, then nodded his head approvingly.

"You've got something hanging ri-i-i-ight there," I said, using my napkin to dab the lingering red sauce from the small cluster of hairs on his chin.

"Thanks," he said, helping himself to another shrimp. If he sampled one more thing, I was going to offer him the entire plate. I wasn't one for sharing, especially if he started double-dipping in my sauce.

Evidently the look on my face told it all. Lance brushed his hands on the sides of his shorts. He licked his fingertips, definitely eliminating his chances of touching my plate again. Handsome or not, that was nasty. "Maybe I should make my way through that never-ending line," Lance said. "I was running late for my flight, so the only thing I had time for this morning was a protein drink."

"Some things never change," I said. "You were always the last person running for the band bus."

"You don't know how hard it is trying to run in polyester pants with a tuba." He downed the remaining half of his cocktail, shaking the glass so that the alcohol-soaked fruit fell into his mouth.

"You might want to put some food in your stomach before you get carried away," I suggested.

"What's the use of going on a cruise if you can't enjoy what they have to offer?" he teased. "*Everything* they have to offer."

I turned to watch some passersby. Lance was an easy flirt, and I was an easy target. He watched in apparent amusement as the wedding party frolicked from one end of the pool to the other. They volleyed two oversized beach balls personalized with the names Amber and Justin—the bride and groom, I assumed.

"They have no idea," Lance said. "One day, she's going to want to hit his head the same way she's slamming that ball around, and he's going to see that her hormones are just like those beach balls"—he circled his index finger in the air—"bouncing from one end to the other. He'll never know which way they're going to go."

I adjusted my swimsuit cover-up to hide the upper part of my leg, which had somehow managed to escape. Lance didn't even try to pretend he hadn't enjoyed the quick peep show.

"We're not exactly the people to talk about happy marriages right now," I said, beckoning his eyes back up to my face.

"Marriage is a death sentence," Lance said, shaking his head.

"Till death do us part," I quoted.

"Well, my love for Trena died. Does that count?"

"I didn't come on this cruise to talk about my marital woes or anybody else's," I said. "Sometimes it feels like this process is sucking the life out of me."

"It'll get better," Lance said, sincerely. "You'll find someone else to resuscitate you."

*I doubt that,* I thought to myself. I refused to be a forty-something woman who'd been married three times. Maybe I was destined to be alone.

People started shedding their towels and cover-ups and jumping in the water. A puddle began to form beneath my lounge chair from all the splashing.

"Hi, Lance," Caprice said, returning with two more cups of lemonade. "Your coworkers are probably looking for you, and here you are, swarming around Zenja."

Had I not known Caprice, I might have assumed her smile and laugh were genuine, but the way she cut her eyes told a different story.

"What can I say? It's sweet over here," Lance said, stepping back so Caprice could reclaim her seat. Then he held out his hand to take my empty plate. "So, what are you ladies up to tonight?"

"A little bit of this, a little bit of that, I suspect," Caprice replied for both of us. "We've been waiting for this girlfriends' getaway since Christmas."

"Sister to sister, huh? Ain't nothing wrong with that," Lance said, looking only at me. "Maybe I can steal you for a while. It's been a long time."

He slipped on a pair of sunglasses with jet-black lenses. I didn't like that I couldn't see his eyes. I checked my clothes to make sure I wasn't giving him another unintended peep show.

"We'll see," I said.

I was surprised that Caprice didn't respond—not that she had to say a thing for me to know what she was thinking.

But I had some thoughts of my own. I was about to be a divorcee, so who could blame me for having a little innocent fun on the side? It wasn't like I was jumping into bed with the man. I had enough respect for myself and for God not to go there. I even had enough respect for Roman. I may have been an unhappily married woman, but I was still a married woman.

# 7

## ROMAN

Roman walked into his bedroom unsupervised for the first time in months. What he saw caught him off guard. There was no evidence that he'd even existed in Zenja's life. Even their wedding portrait had been replaced by an oversized mirror. The other times when he'd entered the house during her absence, he'd never ventured upstairs. He'd always felt that she probably had a hidden camera somewhere. Zenja would do that—she'd had a nanny cam disguised as a teddy bear when the kids were younger. The last thing he wanted was for her to think he was being a snoop. If she ever caught him, she would never forgive him.

Roman looked at his reflection in the new mirror. *Mirror, mirror on the wall. Who was the dumbest husband of them all?* The bags under his eyes were even more prominent now that he was freshly shaven. He'd lost sleep for weeks, waiting for Zenja to leave on her cruise so that he could return home. He'd purposefully timed it that way. He had to be strategic. He was sure about what God had said to him, but he needed to be careful with Zenja's emotions. The real work would begin in three days, when she would return home and realize that he was still there. He would never give up again. He'd asked God to give Zenja some kind of sign, a dream, anything. But from the look on her face when he'd walked in the door, he didn't think God had granted that request. Yet Roman wasn't deterred; he was determined.

Roman surveyed the room. He opened the drawers of Zenja's armoire. As usual, her clothes were folded and arranged better than a department store display. He picked up a stack of the silky sleeveless shirts that she wore under her work suits. Nothing. He searched each drawer to see if there was a sign that he'd been replaced—a photo; a sentimental gift; a card. Nothing. That was good news.

Roman entered the walk-in closet. At least his side hadn't been completely taken over. Most of it looked to be clothes Zenja had tried on as she packed for the cruise. Roman picked up a red dress he'd bought for her for the Dean's induction ceremony at the University. It had stretch, but not enough to accommodate the fuller hips she'd acquired recently. Not that he was complaining. The curves looked good on her, even though she probably complained about them. He picked up a pair of cargo shorts with the tags still attached. Zenja didn't wear shorts this short. She was too self-conscious about her knees. Most women obsessed about jiggly thighs, wiggly arms, and post-baby stomach paunches, but Zenja was the only woman he knew who didn't like her knees.

His excursion led him to the bathroom, where the smell of her body wash still lingered. She layered her scents, a trick she'd said her aunt had taught her. Body wash, body cream, and then body spray soaked into her skin and lasted all day long. Anything peachy was her scent. Once upon a time, he would cuddle up close to her neck so he could inhale the intoxicating scent after a long day at work. After dinner had always been their special time to connect. Zariya and Kyle would escape to their bedrooms to do their own thing; he and Zenja would escape to theirs. Often, there were kisses and embraces. Other times, she'd read a novel, he an autobiography. Anything as long as they were together.

Roman inhaled deeply. He was home. "Home" wasn't that apartment.

He went down the hall to Zariya's room. She was growing up so fast, already starting to wear lip gloss her mother approved. Roman had come into her life when she was still carrying that raggedy, bald-headed baby doll lovingly named Pinkie. A gift from the hospital where Zariya had been born, Pinkie had been packed in the diaper bag, dragged through airports, brought to church, forgotten in restaurants, and used to wipe runny noses and teary eyes. Over the last year, some of those tears had been the result of relationship troubles between him and Zenja. Zariya was an emotional ball of teenage hormones. Earlier, Roman had made the mistake of calling from the house phone to check on her and Kyle. He should've been more careful. Now he would have to defend himself to Zenja, who was bound to find out soon.

Roman left Zariya's room and went across the hall to Kyle's. It usually looked like a tornado had touched down, but now, surprisingly, it was spotless. His baseball caps hung neatly from hooks on his closet door, his video games were arranged in a tidy stack, and his remote-control cars were lined up in the bottom of his closet. Roman was about to browse through the music on Kyle's digital music player when the doorbell rang.

When he went to the door, Carlos, his neighbor from the end of the cul-de-sac, was standing there, holding two cans and a bag of pretzels.

"Look what the wind blew in," Roman said, joining him on the porch.

"And look what the cat dragged back home," Carlos responded. He handed Roman one of the cans. "Cola. I tried to sneak out with something else to celebrate, but my wife caught me. She said I shouldn't bring a beer over to a church man."

Roman chuckled as he popped the tab on the soda. He took a long gulp, letting the strong carbonation sting the inside of his nose. "This is about as strong a drink as I can stand," he said. "My beer-drinking days are long behind me."

"Well, my beer-drinking days are still in front of me," Carlos said. "But for you, I'll settle for soda."

They sat down on the top step and watched Carlos's children fight over a red kickball. Carlos didn't intervene, even when his son pushed his daughter in the grass. She looked down at the stain on her pink and yellow floral dress, then ran inside, crying. Carlos reached in the bag for a handful of pretzels. "The story of my life. Somebody's always crying over something," he said. "I don't blame you for leaving. Some days, I want to run myself. Wife, kids, money...the problems never stop."

"It doesn't end just because you leave," Roman said. "Leaving can actually be worse."

"Is that why you came back? I've watched you. I figured, after two days, you were back in. But almost a year?" Carlos took a swig of soda. "You never truly left. Picking up the kids. Coming by sometimes to roll the trash cans to the curb. Mowing the grass. You never wanted to leave in the first place. Zenja put you out, didn't she?"

"Yep," Roman confessed.

"How did you let a woman put you out of your *own* house?"

"Long story." Roman used the tip of his shoe to kick a granddaddy long-legs spider to the bottom step.

Carlos and his wife, Ava, had moved to the neighborhood around the same time as Roman. They'd been newlyweds; Roman had still been a bachelor who ordered takeout for dinner every evening. They'd watched each other's houses when the other had been out of town, loaned each other lawn equipment, and given each other jump starts when a car battery had died. They'd even shared their insights on politics. But they hadn't shared their marital problems.

"So, is the old saying true?" Carlos asked. "It's cheaper to keep her?"

Roman crushed his empty soda can between his hands. "Believe me, I've paid a price. And it didn't have anything to do with my bank account."

Carlos steered the conversation away from Roman's issues and over to sports, failed business investments, and his wife's ever-increasing faith in God.

"You make it sound like it's the end of the world," Roman observed.

"Might as well be," Carlos said. "I'm cool with Christmas and Easter, but now she's starting to go to church almost every Sunday. With or without me. And she makes the kids go, too."

"That's not a bad thing," Roman said.

"It's not a necessarily a good thing." Carlos seemed to search for a way to explain himself. "She might change."

"How?"

"Hmm...wearing long dresses, not wanting to listen to the radio, refusing to perform her wifely duties..." Carlos counted each point on a different finger.

"Is that what you think Christian women do—refuse to perform their wifely duties?" Roman mused. "Then why do you think there are all these little Christians walking around?"

Carlos shrugged, then gave a good laugh when he seemed to realize how ridiculous he sounded. "I just don't want her to start acting weird."

Roman slapped his neighbor on the back. "If Ava changes, it'll be for the better. Am I weird? Is my wife weird?"

"*You* moved out of *your* house, so I won't comment on that. But Zenja—she's cool with me. She seems like she can hold her own."

"And that's one of the reasons I love her so much," Roman said. "That's why I'm back here and nowhere else. Zenja pushes me to be a better man."

"Better a better man that a bitter one."

Across the street, Ava appeared on the porch, clutching her daughter's hand. She made her son apologize and hug his sister. At least, it was probably supposed to be a hug. He'd barely lifted his arms.

"It nearly kills him to say he's sorry," Carlos said with a laugh. "Doesn't he know if he'd just say it, both his mama and his sister would be satisfied? It would make his world a whole lot easier."

Ava waved. "Hi, Roman," she called out. "Good to see you."

"You, too," he yelled back. "Like the new cut."

"Thanks," she said, fluffing the sides of her shorter brunette tresses.

"You're making me look bad," Carlos said. "I didn't notice yesterday, and you recognize it right off."

"Take a lesson from your son and apologize."

"I've been saying it and doing it all morning with every pansy in our flower bed." Carlos pointed at the dirt-stained knees of his jeans. "And I'm responsible for dinner tonight, too."

Roman chuckled as he pulled at the stubble that had already started to sprout on his chin. "Make it easy on yourself," he said. "Take the family out to eat, and you might even be able to sleep in your bed tonight instead of on the couch."

Carlos snubbed his nose with his thumb and stood up. "I'll make it back into the bed with my wife before you make it back in with yours."

"If I was a betting man, I'd put some money on that," Roman said, reaching into his back pocket for his wallet. "As a matter of fact, here's fifty. Dinner for the family is on me."

Carlos accepted the bill with no hesitation. "Did God tell you to do that?" he asked sarcastically.

"Sure did."

Carlos slid the money in his back pocket, then picked up their empty soda cans. "You should listen to God more often, man. I've got a boatload of bills that need to be paid by the end of the week. You're more than welcome to come over to the house with your checkbook."

Roman smirked. "I have my own household to take care of. I should be walking in the door with a gift every day for the rest of my life."

Carlos descended the porch steps in long strides, then stopped and turned around. "True. Because if you're lucky, *you'll* wake up to a gift every day, and her name is Zenja. Make that, if you're blessed. See, I can be church man when I want to."

"You'll cross over to the light one of these days," Roman joked. "And I bet Ava will be the one to bring you there."

Roman slapped palms with Carlos before his neighbor ran back across the street.

*Blessed*. Carlos couldn't have said it better. And Roman couldn't wait to wake up every morning with Zenja in his arms.

# 8

## ROMAN

Roman rolled to the middle of the bed in the master bedroom. Now he understood why Zenja had always wanted to buy 500-thread-count sheets and invest in the best mattress their money could buy. Small things made a huge difference. This bed slept nothing like the rough cotton sheets and lumpy mattress he'd been enduring in his one-bedroom apartment. That mattress and all the linens would go straight to the dumpster on Monday.

*I need my wife here,* Roman thought. Her skin, her touch, her soft snore when she was asleep...Roman missed it all. He folded a pillow in half and propped it behind his head, then turned the television on and scrolled through the guide. He selected one of the nature channels. It was a segment on how the female praying mantis and the female black widow spider devour the male during or after mating.

"That's the last thing I need to watch," he muttered, switching the channel. He found a more suitable show on the History Channel and soon was so relaxed that he almost didn't answer the phone when it rang. He did glance at the caller ID, though, and saw that it was his mother. He knew the routine. If he didn't answer now, she would keep calling until he did.

"Hey, baby," his mother said. Her voice sounded tired, but then again, it always did.

"Hey, Lovie," he said, leaning over the edge of the bed to open the drawer of Zenja's nightstand. It was the one place he'd forgotten to check during his earlier inspection.

"Did I catch you at a bad time?" she asked.

"No," he said. "Just relaxing a little."

"No need to relax. It's after nine—you might as well go to sleep. You probably need some rest. Aren't you teaching this summer?"

"I'm co-teaching a class with another instructor, but it meets only three times a week."

"Do you think you'd be able to squeeze in some time down here with me next week and let the other teacher cover the class?"

Roman had known that, sooner or later, Lovie would come back around to begging him to come home to South Carolina. Shamefully, it wasn't a place that he visited often enough, but there were two people in his life who had made it so difficult in the past—his father and Zenja.

If it wasn't for Lovie, he'd probably never take that ride down I-85 South. Roman could never convince her to come back to North Carolina with him. She was a prisoner in her own home, and his father ruled the house with an iron fist from the brown recliner in the living room—a throne that he barely fit in and could hardly lift himself out of.

Zenja tolerated Roman's father, but having her in the same space as Lovie was like putting two betta fish in the same bowl. Someone was going to get ripped to shreds.

"Is there anything wrong?" Roman asked Lovie.

"Your dad..."

Roman could only imagine how that sentence would finish: "*Your dad is sick. Your dad is drunk. Your dad won't take his meds. Your dad misses you.*" He would believe all but the last of those statements.

"...is acting angrier than usual," Lovie said, her voice dropping to a whisper. "Last night he threw a plate at me."

Roman flung the covers off his body. "Pop did *what?*"

"He wouldn't have done it if he wasn't in so much pain," Lovie reasoned. She was always justifying his father's rage.

"That's no reason, Lovie." Roman felt his head pulsate with anger.

"How would you like it if you couldn't do anything for yourself? That's a hard thing for a man to accept."

Roman refused to get drawn into this perpetual conversation. "I'll pick you up so you can come to Greensboro for a day or two. I'll rent you a nice hotel room where you can relax."

Lovie sighed. "And what's your father supposed to do? I can't leave him here alone. I just want to see my son's face."

Roman had too much on his plate to think about even a one-day trip to South Carolina, but he hated to refuse his mother's request. Lovie didn't ask for much—just his love and emotional support—so that was what he gave her. It was his duty, as her only living son. He tried to support his parents financially whenever he had money to spare, but his father always made Lovie refuse the occasional checks for $200, calling them "handouts." Roman called them a "hand-up."

"I can't come next week, but I'll come tomorrow, Lovie," Roman conceded, even though he'd planned on going to church. He threw his size-thirteen feet over the edge of the bed. Even the pillow-top mattress couldn't make him comfortable now. "But I can't stay for more than the day. I need to get back home and take care of some business."

"I can't wait to see you, Son," Lovie gushed. "I love you."

And it was only Roman's love for his mother that had his car pulling into the driveway at his parents' home on Rosebush Lane the next morning. Before going inside, he stalled with one last phone call. He hadn't been able to reach Dr. Morrow last night and hadn't wanted to call too early this morning.

"Roman?" Dr. Morrow answered. "Headed out the door to church already?"

"Actually, I'm in South Carolina to check on my mother."

The lighthearted tone in the pastor's voice turned serious. "Is everything alright?"

"Everything's fine, but I need to reschedule the counseling session we had set for later today. Needless to say, I won't be able to make it."

"So, you'll call me again when you get back in town?" Dr. Morrow asked. "I can meet you during the week, if it's more convenient."

Roman couldn't set a definite appointment date off the top of his head. Last night, he'd made a list of things he needed to do this week, but he'd left it on the nightstand. It had always been Zenja's job to keep him organized. She'd set up the calendar on his smartphone and would send him reminders via text message. His meeting with Dr. Morrow was of the utmost priority, so he'd make the necessary changes to his schedule.

At Duane's suggestion, Roman had started solo marriage counseling sessions two weeks ago. Dr. Morrow oversaw couples' counseling at the church Caprice and Duane attended, and talking to him had already proved beneficial to Roman. Men understood each other; married men, even more so. Zenja had outright refused to seek counseling when she'd first uncovered Roman's affair, but that didn't mean she couldn't reap the benefits of the work he'd been putting in.

"I'll get back to you later tonight," Roman said when he noticed his mother peering at him from behind the curtain in the kitchen window.

"Looking forward to hearing from you, man," Dr. Morrow said. "Now go take care of your mama. That's what sons are for."

Roman stepped out onto the cracked pavement of the driveway and walked across the dry patches of dirt where grass should've been growing. His father had decided that having a smaller yard would require less upkeep. Eventually, less care had changed to no care at all.

Roman hated this house and everything it represented. His father insisted they had moved here because it was a family property that had been passed down for several generations. However, Roman knew the true reason: his father had wanted to escape Roman's childhood home and all the memories of his baby brother, Joshua. Moving to another house may have changed their address, but it hadn't changed what had happened. Roman longed to return to the place where he and Joshua would build makeshift forts out of sheets of scrap metal, jump their bikes over homemade ramps, and take weekly rides on Friday afternoons to the convenience store for nacho chips and grape sodas.

Roman guessed all things had worked out for the good in the end. Pop's growing health problems would've made it hard to maneuver in a two-story home with no handicap accessibility. But this house had the size and stability of cardboard box—a leaky cardboard box, from what Lovie said of their recent roof problems.

When Lovie swung open the door, the hinges squeaked like they'd never been oiled. "Are you losing weight, Roman?" she asked by way of greeting.

Roman laughed. "I guess that's better than you saying I've gained weight." He kissed his mother on the forehead. "Good morning."

"I bet Zenja has you stressed out, doesn't she?" Lovie fussed. "That woman is trying to put you through the wringer. I can tell. I bet she's trying to get child support for her kids and alimony for herself. When are you going to file for divorce? And, for heaven's sake, when are you going to move back into *your* house?"

*And the drama begins,* Roman thought to himself. Now wasn't the time to tell Lovie that he had already moved back home.

Little did his mother know, but the last thing Zenja needed was his money. The life insurance policy from her first husband had done more than put him in the ground; it would supplement her income for a few years, if need be. And though Zenja stressed the importance of high grades and extracurricular activities to her children, in hopes that they would earn plenty of scholarship money for college, she had enough in their trust funds to pay for their undergraduate degrees—and then some.

"I don't smell any breakfast cooking," Roman said. The best way to deal with Lovie was to change the subject.

"You know I fixed you breakfast," she said. "I had to scrounge up what I could, but I think I did a pretty good job."

"I'm sure it's fine, Lovie. Anything is better than an empty stomach."

His stomach grumbled at his first whiff of bacon and fried apples. He knew well the smell of the country breakfast. He also recognized the stench of alcohol and liniment, courtesy of his father's drinking habits and achy muscles. Roman bypassed the den and went straight into the kitchen when he saw that his father wasn't in his usual spot. He could hear him grunting and bumping around in the hallway bathroom.

Lovie fixed Roman a plate of grits, fried apples, homemade buttermilk biscuits with honey, and a stack of bacon. His mama knew how to make it with the perfect crunch. She poured orange juice in a glass tumbler with slices of citrus fruit painted on the sides. She'd had those same glasses for years. They'd started out as a set of twelve, but over the years, they'd been dropped by the clumsy hands of Roman or his brother, or thrown by the angry hands of his father.

"So, your dad's been in quite the rut lately," she whispered. "I know he's acting out because of the time of year."

*First it's because of his physical pain; now it's the time of the year,* Roman thought. He bowed his head and said grace—the only type of prayer in their home when he'd been growing up—and then chomped down on a strip of bacon. He didn't see what the summer season had to do with his father's behavior. Pop had an issue every season of the year.

Lovie eyed him as if waiting for a response. When he didn't say anything, she added, "You know, tomorrow is the anniversary of the day your brother died. Your dad marked it on the calendar with a little X."

"Like it's a cause for celebration," Roman glowered. "So basically, he plans ahead to be miserable."

Roman's thoughts had been so occupied with everything in his life that the anniversary of Joshua's death hadn't crossed his mind. But he couldn't bring his brother back to life, no matter how much his father hated or blamed him.

"You know, people with depression—"

"Who told you Pop was depressed?" Roman interrupted her. "He's never been formally diagnosed."

"But I live with him every day," Lovie said. "A blind man could see it."

"And a blind man could also see that he's bitter and angry, and that he drinks because he wants to make everybody else suffer with him—namely, you."

When Roman heard the bathroom door open, he knew Lovie was done with the conversation. He was fine with that. They'd been exchanging the same rhetoric since the day Roman had backed out of the driveway in his beat-up Toyota Corolla and driven to Greensboro to attend North Carolina A&T State University. He'd had a secondhand Yamaha keyboard in the trunk and a stack of his clothes, still on their hangers, in the backseat. The day he'd left for college was also the anniversary of Joshua's death. As much as it had hurt, Roman had needed to keep pushing forward. He had to live his life, because Joshua couldn't live his.

*Push. Push. Push.*

*The water from Roman's drenched swimming trunks ran down his legs and dripped onto his feet as he watched Uncle Doug furiously pump his brother's chest. The steady pressure seemed too rough for Joshua's skinny frame, but they were desperate for the breath to return to his body. Tears rolled down Roman's face, and the more he rubbed his eyes, the more the pool chlorine burned them.*

*The jovial sounds of the family reunion immediately silenced into fear when everyone realized one of the children had been pulled out of the water. Joshua's body was limp, and his brown skin had turned blue. God had muted the sounds around them, too. The birds lost their voices, the squirrels ceased their scurrying, and the bees quit their buzzing.*

*"One...two...three..." Uncle Doug counted before he blew another round of air into Joshua's chest. He repeated the cycle again and again until the ambulance arrived.*

# 9

# ROMAN

*Lovie fell to her knees and tapped Joshua's face, lightly at first. Then she slapped him like he'd fainted and she was trying to jostle him back to his senses.*

*"Joshua," she said. "Baby, wake up. Open your eyes and look at Lovie," she pleaded.*

*"Joshua!" Pop bellowed. Until then, he'd been in apparent shock. He was fully clothed but wet from jumping in the water to retrieve his youngest son from the deep end of the pool. He had swum back to the edge, making panicked cries for help, and had gingerly laid Joshua in the grassy area beyond the concrete.*

*The pain and fear in Pop's voice shook the world around them. Then he turned an enraged face to Roman and started yelling at him. To Roman's ears, it sounded like his father was screaming underwater.*

*"What happened? I told you to watch him. You couldn't watch him for five minutes?"*

*Roman didn't have an answer. At seven years old, he didn't fully realize the danger of water for two boys who could barely swim. They had been having the time of their lives with the rest of their cousins, who all were supposed to watch over one another. If you couldn't swim well, you weren't supposed to go beyond the white and blue floaters bobbing in the middle of the water, separating the shallow end from the deep end.*

*"I said, what happened?" Pop gripped Roman's arm and gave it a painful jerk, as if trying to shake an answer out of him. Roman's body was limp like a doll in his father's hand.*

*"Thomas, let the boy go." Uncle Tip came to Roman's rescue and did his best to calm Pop down. All Roman could do was watch. He watched his brother's lifeless body until the paramedics covered it with a white sheet and pushed the gurney into the back of the ambulance.*

The week until the funeral had passed in slow agony. Roman hadn't been able to keep food in his stomach, and Lovie had cried every second of the day. Roman hadn't spoken to anyone until a week after they'd lowered his brother into the ground. He'd lost his words but found his music.

Since Joshua's death, he hadn't experienced tangible grief until he'd realized his marriage was falling apart. It weighed heavily on Roman's soul, but the burden had lightened since he'd returned home. God was going to fix his mess.

"Lovie!" Pop's voice wasn't nearly as strong as it used to be, but it was still stern, in between his frequent gasps and grunts.

Roman scraped the last bit of cinnamon apples out of his bowl with his spoon.

"Yes?" Lovie stood like she'd been summoned.

"Who is that you're talking to?"

Lovie glanced at the door leading to the hallway, then looked back to Roman.

Roman pushed away from the table and walked the three steps to the hallway entry. "Pop." He nodded his head with the simple acknowledgment.

"Pop" was the right name for his father, considering that was what it looked like he was about to do. Roman was taken aback at his appearance. His face was overinflated like a blowfish, and his eyes were a jaundiced yellow. Even though his health had been on a gradual decline for years, it was still disheartening to see him like this. Pop was a man who'd done little with his life except slowly poison it with anger, resentment, and alcohol.

Roman had once heard it said that a boy needed to look no further than his father to see how his life would be.

*I pray this isn't my reflection.*

Pop didn't even look Roman in the eye. "Help me get to my chair," he puffed.

*What about a "Hello, Son"?* Roman thought. *"Good to see you"?* No. That would never happen.

Pop put all his weight on Roman while they slid the distance to his brown recliner. He fell back into the chair, picked up the remote control from the mini fridge that doubled as an end table, and started flipping through the television channels. Lovie took a seat beside Roman on the couch, and they let the television program fill the space where a conversation should have been.

Roman stared at the photos on the wall that chronicled their lives. In the photos before the drowning, their entire family had been in the picture. Joshua was always clowning around or looking somewhere else besides at the camera. In most of the pictures taken after his death, Pop was absent. Lovie's was the only face lit up with parental pride in Roman's graduation picture. Roman was smiling, too, but only because he'd been about to escape—finally.

It was nearly unbearable for Roman to sit and watch every second click on the clock. He'd come here to placate his mother, but he had a long list of other things he could be doing. Half an hour passed before Pop said another word.

"Moved back into your house yet?"

Roman noticed an oxygen tank in the corner of the room. It sounded like Pop desperately needed it.

"Almost."

Lovie pressed her hand to her chest. "So, they finally moved out? I think that's the best thing for you both. You'll find another wife in no time."

"I'm not looking for another wife," Roman said. "Zenja is my wife."

"Why, Roman? Just tell me, why?"

"Because I love her. I love my family, and I want us to be together." Roman picked up a bottle—one of Pop's numerous prescription medications. Roman couldn't even pronounce the name of those yellow horse pills. "Do you need to pick up any of Pop's meds?" he offered. At this point, Roman would do anything for a breath of fresh air.

Lovie sighed. Pop laughed. Roman wanted to hit I-85 and head north, but he'd been at the house less time than it had taken him to drive there. Besides, Lovie needed the company.

Few people came by the house anymore. Pop didn't like visitors, and most people couldn't stand to watch while Lovie endured his verbal abuse. Lovie's closest friend, Queen, had become immune to Pop's rants and would visit occasionally to play checkers or Scrabble, or to wash and curl Lovie's hair.

Roman, however, was never up for playing games, and he rarely stayed at his parents' past six o'clock. Lovie always tried to force them to be one happy family. Maybe they would be, if that equation didn't include his father.

At precisely 5:30, Lovie walked Roman back to his car and waited until he was buckled in before handing him the dinner she'd prepared for him. She'd packed a plastic container so full of veggie lasagna that the lid had barely closed. In another container that had once held whipped cream, she'd stuffed two ears of corn atop a garden salad.

"When are you coming back to visit us?" Lovie asked.

"I can't say for sure," Roman said. He needed to have a good reason to come back again before his normally scheduled trips in October and the first week of December. He usually visited alone because of the strained relationship between Zenja and Lovie. Even Kyle and Zariya opted out of coming along, because even though Lovie treated them with courtesy, she'd never shown them grandmotherly love.

"We enjoyed your company," Lovie said.

"No, *you* enjoyed my company," Roman corrected her. "Pop wouldn't care if he never saw me again."

"That's not true," Love insisted.

"It is. I've accepted it; you might as well accept it, too."

"I will never accept it. I know the man that I married, and I know the kind of son I raised," Lovie said, her voice firm. "I've done the best that I could, and I won't stop until things are right. Even if it kills me."

"Lovie, don't say that."

"That's what I feel," she said. "And that's what I mean."

Lovie leaned inside the car, gripped Roman under the chin, and pulled his head toward her so she could kiss his forehead. Then, without warning, she smacked his crown. "You're two of the most stubborn men I know."

Roman rubbed the center of his head.

"But I still love you." She smiled and backed away from the car.

"Is that how you show your love?" Roman teased.

"There's nothing wrong with a little thump on the head every now and then. Maybe it'll knock some sense into you."

Roman shifted the car into reverse. "You should try that on your husband," he said. "Bye. Love you."

Maybe someday, he'd cure the yearning in her heart for reconciliation between the two most important men in her life. Perhaps one day, Roman would mend the breach...as soon as he mended his marriage. First things first.

Roman rode back to Greensboro in silence. He needed to be with his thoughts. He needed to pray and hear God's voice. He needed assurance that although Zenja had not returned his call from yesterday, God was working on her heart. Roman was thankful that she'd taken the vacation with Caprice—her most faithful friend and a steady voice of reason in Zenja's ear. His wife was in good hands.

# 10

I couldn't have connected with Lance last night, even if I'd wanted to—and, trust me, I'd wanted to. My first night at sea was dizzying. Even now, I felt nauseated just thinking about it. A nearby storm had created rough seas that rocked the cruise ship, and my stomach wasn't happy about it. I was beyond miserable and constantly heard my mother's voice of warning. By nine thirty last night, I was almost ready to jump off the ship and doggie paddle my way back to the Miami shore. My well-stocked motion sickness kit hadn't been of much help. I'd finally had to resort to going to the ship's infirmary for a shot so deep in my hip muscle, the nurse on board advised me my hip might be sore for the next two days.

When I opened my eyes this morning, I was relieved to find my equilibrium rebalanced. I swept blush across my cheeks so my face wouldn't reveal the rough night I'd endured. Caprice returned from breakfast with a warm bowl of grits and two bananas for me. I frowned at the bland meal, even though I knew I needed it.

"You might not thank me, but your stomach will," Caprice said, passing me a peeled banana. "Why did that feel like déjà vu?"

"I'm sorry you had to play nurse last night," I apologized. I picked up the damp washcloth I'd been using all morning and pressed it against the back of my neck.

"That's what friends are for," she said. "It was a pretty rough night for a lot of people, from what I overheard at breakfast. The captain avoided as much of the storm as he could."

"I knew we shouldn't have booked our trip during hurricane season." I shook my head. "You know I hate storms. They didn't even give us any storm safety precautions." Suddenly I felt vulnerable to the wide-open waters.

"It's still early in the season. We'll be fine. Jesus walked on the water in a storm," Caprice reminded me.

"That's Jesus," I said. "I'm Zenja Diane Maxwell."

Caprice slid the veranda door open, and the sounds of the ocean and the cruisers below us drifted into our room. I didn't want to spend all day in the cabin when everybody else was ready to take full advantage of the island.

"You should probably skip Jet Skiing this morning," Caprice said.

"Definitely," I agreed. "My book and I will be fine by the pool. And if that fails, there are tons of things to do on the ship to keep me entertained. I'll meet you for a late lunch, and we'll go adventuring later."

Caprice tried without success to fold two of the unused hand towels back into the swan shapes they had been in when we'd first arrived. Her twisting and tucking resulted in something that looked more like a mangled snake. "I think I'll stick to folding my towels like normal people."

I laughed. "Me, too."

"So, a late lunch? Sounds like a plan." Caprice opened her suitcase and pulled out a one-piece aqua bathing suit that would make her blend in with the rippling waters of the Atlantic. "I forgot my swimming cap," she discovered after a couple of minutes unfolding and refolding sundresses and tank tops. "Do you have one?"

"In the very bottom of my bag," I said, scooping a spoonful of grits out of my bowl.

"Good, because I'm not trying to fuss with my hair." Caprice reached under my carefully rolled clothes and found more than my swim cap. She handed me a stack of cards tied with a satin bow.

"From the look on your face, you didn't know you had these," she said, smiling from ear to ear.

"Not at all," I said, puzzled. There were four envelopes, each of them a different shade of pastel. One quick pull of the deep purple ribbon released the knot and revealed Roman's unmistakable handwriting on the front of each one.

*My Wife*, the first one read. I flipped to the second one. *My Love*. The third: *My Life*. And, finally, the fourth: *My Everything*. Each envelope indicated the day I should open it. I'd already missed opening yesterday's. Writing was Roman's modus operandi. His messages of love and apology alike flowed better on paper than they did from his lips. I'd had a plastic bin of cards and notes at home to prove it—until I chased down the garbage man and gotten rid of it about two months ago. Roman's handwritten apologies were now keeping company with flies in a landfill.

Caprice picked up the swim cap and her backpack. "I know you don't want an audience while you read your cards," she said, backing out of the door. Her regret was obvious. Caprice was a hopeless romantic. But she had promised not to say anything about Roman. "I'll see you later."

I took the first two envelopes out onto the veranda and pulled a chair closer to the railing. I felt like I was about to have an emotional conversation with Roman when, in fact, we were waters apart. I propped my feet on the railing and ripped open the first envelope. It was an anniversary card, dated February 14. Neither Roman nor I had called the other that day. Instead, I'd ordered pizza and wings with the kids, then faked a migraine, so they wouldn't disturb me, and went upstairs to cry myself to sleep.

I closed the card and slid it back inside the envelope. For me, it was proof that Roman had been thinking about me on our anniversary and probably hadn't been enjoying *that* night with someone else.

I opened the envelope marked *My Love*. On the inside left, Roman had written Scriptures from the Song of Solomon—poetry in its own right. He ended the selections with Song of Solomon 6:3: *"I am my beloved's, and my beloved is mine."*

My emotions took ahold of me. Or was it God who was trying to wrap me in His protective arms? I was supposed to be frolicking in the crystal waters and shopping for useless souvenirs, not crying about Roman. God had found me in the middle of the Atlantic. I bet it was Caprice's fault. She probably did some serious praying on the veranda before I even cracked my eyes open this morning. I stuffed the second card back in its envelope and stood to look over the railing and peer down at the deck below.

Lance was the last person on my mind but the first person in my line of vision. He seemed to be enjoying his role as center of attention in a group of people down by the pool. Within five minutes, I'd put on a sundress, sandals, and sunglasses so I could head down to the pool myself. I tucked Roman's cards back beneath the items in my bag where Caprice had discovered them. I'd always been taught to have a backup plan in case things didn't go the way I intended. I wondered if that included having a backup man, too.

# 11

Goodness, girl. You've just changed my day," Lance said when he saw me. He left the side of his coworker, who was too engrossed in trying to discreetly snap photos of the bathing beauties beside the poolside to notice, and sat down in a lounge chair.

"Thank you," I said, then reclined in the chair two down from him. I pretended that reading my novel was my top priority.

Lance wore a pair of black swimming trunks with neon green stripes down the sides. The only thing on his chest was a thin silver chain and a cross pendant, which dangled between his well-defined pectorals. Something was terribly wrong with this picture. I wasn't the kind of woman who usually gawked at a man, so I wanted to believe I was distracted by his necklace instead of his body. "How have I changed your day?" I finally asked.

"You're the best-looking woman I've seen since I opened my eyes," Lance said.

"You're reaching real deep for a compliment."

"How deep do I have to reach to get you to spend the day with me? That is, if your chaperone isn't keeping an eye on you."

"If you're talking about Caprice, she's off Jet Skiing. I had a rough night, so I'm taking it easy until later."

"You, too?" Lance chuckled. "But I think mine had more to do with the number of drinks I had yesterday. I probably celebrated my declaration of independence a little too much."

"I tried to warn you," I said. "That's why you need to stay away from that stuff. It's bad for your health."

"So are fried chicken, loads of pork, and TV dinners; so, since I don't eat any of that mess, I figure a tasty beverage every now and then never hurt anybody."

I folded my legs underneath my dress and opened my book to the page marked by my cruise itinerary. I could tell by the tightness in my thighs that I wasn't going to be able to hold this position very long. It was cute but nowhere near practical for a woman who hadn't given flexibility a thought over the last five years. "So, what are your plans after your toast to independence wears off?" I asked.

Lance made his pectoral muscles jump.

*Show-off*, I thought. At least it was a nice show.

"After I grab a bite to eat, I'm going over to the Atlantis to kick back on the beach...maybe do a little shopping...no definite plans. At home, I'm always on somebody else's schedule, so I'll let the day dictate itself." He snapped a white towel out of his back pocket and laid it across his head to shield his eyes from the sun. "When I'm on vacation, I'm the only one in charge of my schedule."

"I couldn't agree more," I said. This summer was going to be different from the past thirteen years. My time. My terms. During the school year, it was a constant cycle of staff meetings, career development workshops, teacher gripes, problem students, and more meetings to figure out what to meet about at the next meeting. On these blue seas, it was all about me.

"So, tell me, are you the adventurous type?" I asked Lance.

"I'm adventurous in my own way," Lance replied. "You remember those band trips."

"I don't remember much about you back then, other than your being wrapped up with Treva."

Lance seemed a little annoyed by my statement. I guess he didn't find it as funny as I did. "You promise not to mention my ex-wife, and I won't talk about your *current* husband. Let's cut the conversation right here." With his hand, he made a slicing motion across his neck.

"Deal," I agreed.

Lance offered me a hand up from the lounge chair. "So, are you in?"

"Why not?" I accepted his assistance as gracefully as I could. As I slipped my fingers into his grasp, I was thankful I had him to help steady me while I uncurled my numb pretzel legs from under me. "But I've already eaten."

"Well, watch me eat," he said, "and then we'll go over to the Atlantis. I need to be with somebody who doesn't have as much hair on her legs and arms as I do." He leaned down and ran his hand up and down my calf muscle. "See? That's what I mean."

I slapped his back. "You're so crazy. Keep your hands to yourself."

"I'll try," Lance said, "but I never make promises I can't keep. Do you need to get anything from your room?"

"Nope. I'm wearing my bathing suit under here," I said.

Lance looked at me like he wished he had X-ray vision. "I didn't get a chance to see you in it yesterday," he said. "You had everything covered except your arms and feet."

"That's the point of a cover-up—to cover up everything you want to hide."

"I can't imagine you'd have anything to be ashamed of."

"That's great," I said. "We'll leave everything to your imagination."

Lance walked over to the chair where he'd left his shirt, slid his arms into the sleeves, but didn't button it up. He said something to his colleague, who subsequently paused in taking pictures so he could look my way. I waved, unsure how to respond to the sly look on his face.

"You ready?" Lance asked me, taking my hand again. He gave it a slight squeeze, as if to indicate that he wasn't going to let go. And I wasn't about to make him.

"Sure am," I said, convincing myself to enjoy the moment without any guilt. I thought about that Sunday when I'd seen Roman with *her*. I decided that spending this Sunday with Lance didn't seem like such a bad idea.

"You seem tense," Lance said, rubbing his hand up and down my arm. "Don't worry. You're in good hands."

~

I stared at the endless waters rippling across the horizon. The tide crept in and circled around my ankles as I dug my toes into the sand. I'd needed the escape. I'd needed to leave reality behind.

"This is so much better than lying out by the pool," I said.

Lance snapped his towel against the slight breeze and spread it out in the sand. "Throw me your towel," he said.

I tossed it to him, then went about searching for seashells that had been smoothed to perfection by the ocean waves. Zariya loved walking the beach and collecting shells. Some of her favorite vacations were the trips we'd taken to Myrtle Beach.

"Does anyone ever do anything with those things?" Lance said once I'd joined him. He'd laid our towels side-by-side and dumped the contents of his bag: three bottles of water, his shades, his wallet, a pack of spearmint gum, and a tube of SPF 50 sunscreen.

"My daughter decorated a shoe box with some seashells once, but that was years ago. Mostly we pick them up for the memories, just like everybody else."

"There are lots of other memories to be made at a beach," Lance said, stripping off his shirt again.

The only places I'd seen abs like Lance's were in magazines, and I was sure all those had been airbrushed. Lance had more ripples than the ocean, and there wasn't anything fake about them. I tried to pretend I wasn't mesmerized, but my awe must've shown on my face.

"Yes, they're real," Lance said, rubbing his shirt across his stomach. "And I can wash clothes on them, too."

I laughed. "I bet you could."

Lance uncapped his sunscreen and smeared it in thick white layers over his arms, legs, chest, and face. He handed the bottle to me, and I started to do the same. "Could you hit my back for me first?" he asked. He positioned himself in front of me and leaned back on his elbows until he was practically in my lap.

*I'm not doing anything wrong,* I reasoned. *Helping a friend with his suntan lotion is nothing compared to what Roman—* No. I wasn't going to think about Roman. I willed myself not to remember our happier times as a family, even as I watched a couple and their two children throwing bread cubes in the air for the seagulls. Their daughter squealed in delight as the birds swooped down to catch their treats in midair. The husband and wife stopped to share a tender kiss before running after their children, who'd taken off ahead of them. I sighed internally. It had been a long time since I'd been kissed.

That was no longer my life. No use daydreaming about it. "So, what about *my* shoulders?" I asked.

Lance got up so that we could trade places. "I'll do your entire body if you want me to."

I laughed. "There's no need for all that. I'm already breaking my first rule because I told you to keep your hands to yourself."

"I don't remember that rule," Lance said as he moved the strap of my sundress so that it dropped down off my shoulder.

"Selective memory," I said. "Most men have that."

Lance ignored my comment and got to work. It felt like he was applying massage oil instead of suntan lotion, and I let myself relax under his care. It had been even longer since I'd been caressed. This was crazy. It was wrong. But for once in my adult life, I was choosing *not* to play it safe.

Lance and I stretched out beneath the perfectly blue, cloudless sky. We reminisced about being teenagers in the eighties and marveled at the way our separate lives had brought us both from New Jersey and down the East Coast to North Carolina.

"Let's go in the water," Lance suggested.

"Okay," I agreed, "but I'm not going out far."

"Why? Can't you swim?"

"Probably better than you," I boasted as I stood and shook the sand from my clothes. I also knotted my dress at my knees so that it wouldn't get drenched in the water.

"Don't tell me it's because you don't want to get your hair wet," Lance said.

"Okay then, I won't," I replied.

"Not wanting to get your hair wet is a sorry excuse. Why would you waste all God's creation standing on the shore?" With that, Lance turned and jogged toward the ocean.

I didn't care how Lance teased me. Not only didn't I want to get my clothes and hair soaking wet, but I didn't want to be the person a jellyfish or shark chose for lunch. I tiptoed into the water until it pooled around my calves. Lance waded out in the water till it was waist deep, then swam out about another ten feet. Around me, the gleeful squeals of the family I'd watched earlier floated over the sounds of the seagulls and the ocean waves. After a few minutes, Lance made his way back to me, glistening wet.

He shook his head, and beads of water flew from his face. "Come on," he coaxed me. "Walk out just a little further."

"No, this is far enough," I said.

"Fine. You're making me do this," he said, before lifting me in his arms and running deeper into the water.

"Stop it!" I screamed. I tried to fight back, but he had such a tight grip on me that the more I thrashed, the more I increased my chances of making myself fall into the water. I gripped Lance's neck. "You're going to regret this."

"And what are you going to do?" Lance asked. He dipped down onto his knees, sending me underwater.

I emerged with soaked bangs covering my eyes.

"I wouldn't threaten me again if I were you," he warned with a devious smile. He set me down on my feet and let his arms slide to my waist. "I told you, there are better memories to make at the beach than picking up seashells."

"Memories like what?" I said, trying to catch my breath. My heartbeat quickened as Lance leaned into me. Closer. Until our lips almost touched. *Almost*. I turned my face away from him and pushed against the water as my body buoyed farther away from the shore. I had to remind myself that I was a married woman. For now.

# 12

Caprice had just stepped out of the shower when I returned from the beach with Lance. The timing couldn't have been better, since I wanted nothing more than to stand under a heavy stream of warm water. I smelled like the Bahamas sun, salty ocean water, and perspiration. Caprice stared at me like she could smell the guilt on me instead. I'd lost track of time and missed our lunch together.

"Looks like you're feeling better," she said, rubbing a towel across her freshly shampooed hair. I guess she hadn't succeeded in preserving her hairdo.

"Vitamin D," I said, shaking my sandals over the trash can. Sand still clung between my toes and to the rest of my body, and after more than three hours in the sun, I'd tanned enough to make the lines of my sandal straps visible on the tops of my feet. "How were your excursions?" I asked, trying to deflect her suspicions.

"Amazing." She combed mousse through her hair and slicked it back. "The only thing missing was Duane. He would've loved it. We definitely have to do a couples' cruise next time."

I didn't utter a word but turned on the shower instead.

"So, what did you find to get into?" Caprice asked, trying to sound indifferent.

"I went to over to the beach at the Atlantis. Took my book. Relaxed. Searched for some seashells. Found a couple of cute souvenirs for the kids."

Of course, I left out everything that she didn't need to know. I didn't want the judgment or the criticism.

"I was hoping you weren't out swimming with the sharks while I was swimming with the dolphins," Caprice said as I reached my hand into the shower to check the temperature of the water. The steam was already starting to cloud the mirror.

"No sharks," I said. I pushed the bathroom door almost closed, leaving only a small crack, then slid my sundress from my shoulders, letting it puddle around my ankles. "I'm starving."

"Me, too," Caprice called out. "I decided to wait for you instead of going to eat as soon as I got back. The sun drained my energy."

"I know the feeling." The sand between my toes loosened and washed down the drain as soon as I stepped into the shower. I rubbed soap between my palms until I'd worked up a sudsy lather. "We'll both feel better after we eat. I think I can handle more than a banana now."

"So, what's on for tonight?" Caprice asked. I could tell she was standing directly outside the bathroom. "Are we still going to karaoke?"

"Only if you promise not to sing," I teased. "You know you can take things to another level of embarrassing."

I could tell by the chill that brushed my body that Caprice had opened the door wider. She snickered. "That's your personal problem. I'm not embarrassed at all. But if it'll make you feel better, I won't sing a word."

"Fine," I said, not believing her for a second. "Now close the door. You're letting out the good steam, and I'm trying to purify my skin."

Caprice lingered for a moment. "Do you have something else you want to tell me about?"

"Yes," I answered innocently. "Next time, use some spray before you come out. It smells horrible in here."

"Whatever." She finally closed the door.

I needed Caprice to tell me when my latest hair color wasn't working or if my shorts exposed too much of my chubby knees. I wanted her to let me know if I'd overreacted by grounding Zariya or been too lenient with Kyle. But I already knew what she would say about my day out with Lance. She'd tell me that I shouldn't have massaged sunscreen into the firm, mountainous muscles of his back, and that I definitely shouldn't have agreed to let him return the favor. She'd say that we shouldn't have waded together in the Atlantic, and that I shouldn't have let him fall asleep afterward with his head in my lap. She'd tell me that I had a husband at home who could pick me up and swirl me through the waters. Caprice would voice the very reprimand God had been whispering in my heart.

The woman on the karaoke stage was singing Gloria Gaynor's "I Will Survive." She'd earn points for enthusiasm, even though she sounded like a wounded cat. Compared to her, Caprice wasn't all that bad. The room was dark, lit only by some recessed lights in the ceiling and a single spotlight centered onstage. I peered through the darkness, looking for Lance. It had been a little over twenty-four hours since we were standing in the shuttle line and six hours since we'd frolicked in the ocean like a scene from a romance novel. It didn't make sense that I was already smitten over a man I hadn't seen in twenty-four years.

"There's a table right up front," Caprice said. She started walking in that direction before I could object.

After a slight hesitation, I followed. The closer we were to the action, the sooner she would start to feel that she'd miraculously acquired a musical ear.

The charming host took the stage again and got the crowd riled up. He easily could have been a performer on Broadway, with his carefully molded hair, makeup-buffed face, and overexaggerated movements. "And tonight, as a special surprise, the karaoke winner gets one grand!" He fanned a stack of bills in the air.

The crowd screamed so loud that I could barely hear what Caprice was saying. I leaned closer to her. "What?"

"Are you sure you don't want me to sing? I mean, it *is* a thousand dollars. Shopping money. I'll split it with you."

I laughed. "Do you really think you can buy my integrity with five hundred dollars?"

"We'll probably never see these people again in our lives," Caprice reasoned. "What's the use of being on a cruise if we're not going to have fun? You said that yourself."

Yes, I did. And I'd definitely had fun all day.

"Do it. Just do it," I said, reaching forward to pat down a strand of hair on her temple that had a mind of its own. I consented only because $500 would cover the remaining item I needed for my renovated deck. An outdoor chandelier would lend the perfect ambiance.

"Make me proud," I yelled as Caprice shimmied toward the stage, giving people high fives along the way. The other contestants lining up didn't have half the confidence Caprice had. Or the magnetism. An hour later, I walked out of the room $500 richer, thinking about all the evenings I would spend in my serene backyard escape.

"Didn't I tell you?" Caprice said. She threw her arm around me, and we sashayed down the hall like the lifelong friends we were. Eighty percent of the other contestants had lungs built for running the octaves, but Caprice had been the best performer by far.

"What's next?" I asked. "The night's still young, and I need to make up for being sick yesterday evening."

"We'll find something," Caprice said. "There's no lack of entertainment." She rubbed her bare arms when we walked out to the balcony. "Let me go up to the room and grab a sweater. It's a little chilly, and you know how cold-natured I am. Do you need anything?"

"I'm fine," I said. "I'll stay right here and wait for you."

I leaned against the railing and admired the beauty of the sky, trying to make sense of the groups of stars scattered across the expanse. Zariya and Kyle were expert stargazers who could spot every constellation, but I didn't know Andromeda from Canis Major, no matter how many times they pointed them out to me.

"What are you thinking about?" Lance's voice jolted me out of my reverie.

"Constellations," I said, turning slightly as he joined me at the railing.

He reached over and squeezed my shoulder, then let his hand slide to the middle of my back, where it rested for a moment. "I thought you might say you were thinking about me."

I didn't answer.

"I've been thinking about you."

How did he expect me to respond to that?

"If you're into constellations, you must be into astrological signs," he continued. "I'm a Scorpio. What about you?

"Pisces," I said, "which means nothing. I'm not into constellations like that, and I definitely don't put stock in astrology." I took a deep breath. "Please don't tell me you look at horoscopes."

"Every now and then. I don't plan my life by them, but I've found them to be pretty accurate. Scorpios, in case you didn't know, can be charismatic and passionate."

I turned toward him. "Is that so?"

Lance answered with his lips. His mouth met mine, hesitantly at first, as if giving me a chance to pull away. I didn't. It had been almost a year since I'd been kissed, and even longer since I'd been kissed like *that*. No reserve. All passion. I disregarded the people passing by and lost myself until someone called my name. I sucked in my breath and pulled away from him, preparing to face Caprice. When I whirled around, my friend was nowhere in sight, yet she was the only person who could've called my name, especially with such authority. It couldn't have been Lance; he'd been too busy performing mouth-to-mouth.

"What's wrong?" Lance asked, running his hand along my spine.

"Someone called my name."

"I didn't hear it."

"I heard it."

Lance took a step back. "I'm sorry. I shouldn't have done that."

"You're right, you shouldn't have. And I shouldn't have, either."

Covering my lips with my fingertips, I turned and sought the source of the voice that had shaken me up. The taste of Lance's lips lingered on mine. How could something feel so right *and* so wrong at the same time?

# 13

## ROMAN

Roman stretched his arms above his head until he felt the knot in his neck loosen. His shoulders and back still ached, but that was what he got for sleeping on the couch last night. When he'd awakened at three in the morning, he'd been too exhausted to crawl upstairs to the master bedroom, where he planned on sleeping until Zenja was back in town.

*What I wouldn't do for one of Zenja's massages right now,* Roman thought. He'd never needed to visit a massage therapist when he'd had his wife to work out the knots and kinks buried deep in his muscles. By the time he finished moving all his belongings out of the apartment, he would probably need some ice packs and a heating pad, too. At least Duane was there to help him with the larger items.

"I'm just thankful to have a brother who's still on my side," Roman told his friend.

"Never left it," Duane said. "You might've been able to ignore my calls, but God didn't ignore my prayers for you. Let me tell you, you've had a brother on his knees for a while."

"So that's why you're walking like that." Roman gave his friend a playful punch in the shoulder, then lifted one of the boxes from the sidewalk and slid it onto the bed of the moving truck.

Until Roman's affair, he and Zenja had shared a close friendship with Duane and Caprice. He'd had little contact with Duane in the months since he and Zenja had separated, but when he'd called to ask for a marriage counselor recommendation, their brotherhood had been quickly reestablished.

"It's official now," Duane said, bending at the knees to protect his back. "Once you turn in those keys to the apartment complex, your temporary stint as a single man is over."

The two men grunted as they carried the wooden dresser up the ramp.

"I never felt like a single man," Roman said. "I felt like a married man who'd made a mistake—a huge mistake." He huffed as he set the dresser down. "Now it's the beginning of something new, but I feel like I'm putting myself on the front lines of a war zone."

"It is a war zone. You're fighting for your marriage. It's do or die trying." Duane's facial expression was as serious as his statement.

"I've been dying for months without my family. Keeping Zariya and Kyle on some weekends wasn't enough."

Roman jumped off the back of the truck and immediately regretted it. He felt and heard his knees crack. He was too young to have so many aches and pains. When he'd signed the lease on the apartment, he hadn't realized that climbing up three flights of steps every day would reveal just how out of shape he actually was. It didn't help that an old knee injury from intramural basketball reared its ugly head every now and then.

Roman and Duane grabbed the straps on either side of the rolling door and pulled it down until the latches caught with a loud slam. The sound set off a chain reaction of barking from the two Chihuahuas that lived on the first floor. Roman wouldn't miss them. The rascals had once attacked his ankles for no reason.

"Closure," Duane said.

"Closing this chapter," Roman agreed. "And I'm not looking back on it." He lifted his arms and rolled his shoulders. "It's not a part of my life that I'm proud of."

"And you shouldn't be. Shame comes with it, but forgiveness does, too."

"God's forgiveness came easy," Roman said. "Forgiving myself and gaining Zenja's forgiveness, however, is a work in progress."

"Things didn't come apart overnight, so don't expect for things to be put back together in a day," Duane reminded him. "Sometimes, when things look like they're falling apart, they might actually be falling into place."

Roman wiped his forearm across his sweaty brow. The days prior had seen comfortable afternoons in the low seventies, but today, the temperature had spiked into the upper eighties. Sticky. Thunderstorm weather. Zenja hated storms.

They trudged up the stairs to the apartment, which was almost empty, except for his keyboard case and stand, a pizza box, a cooler of perishables from the refrigerator, and a black trash bag.

"When things look like they're falling apart, they might actually be falling into place," Roman repeated. "Nice slogan for a T-shirt."

"Then put it on and wear it well, my brother. It's the life you have right now."

Duane was telling the truth. Roman stuffed his mouth with the last piece of chicken supreme pizza they'd had delivered for lunch. They'd ordered two grape sodas, too, in memory of his brother, Joshua. Duane was the only brother he had now.

"Having my wife and kids back will be worth it, even if it takes a miracle."

"God specializes in those," Duane said. "You'll be fine. You know what they say: What doesn't kill you makes you stronger. Keep the faith, man."

"Do you have a slogan for everything?" Roman joked.

"Blame it on Caprice. She's got me watching too many TV psychologists and life coaches. Unless it's football season, she controls the remote, so I'm always forced to suffer through other people's problems."

"Better somebody else's problems than your own."

"We all have our share," Duane said. "Some are just bigger than others."

"Don't remind me." Roman eased down to the floor and stretched out on the apartment-grade carpet. It was nothing like the plush rugs at home. "Man, my faith isn't the only thing that needs to get stronger. My back does, too." He winced.

"As a friend, I should tell you that you might want to hit the gym." Duane grinned. "Your midsection is spreading."

Roman hit his stomach like a drum. "Are you trying to tell me I'm getting fat?"

"I didn't say that; you did," Duane replied. "Zenja can love you for being a real man, but she can love you for your muscles, too."

"Ain't nothing but more for her to love," Roman smiled. He knew that stress eating over the last year had given him a gut, but after a couple of months of regular workouts on the treadmill and backing off from fast food, he'd be back where he needed to be.

"I'll get to it sooner or later," Roman said, turning on his side to find relief from his back pain. He grunted.

"I might be your boy, but I draw the line at carrying you piggyback down those stairs when it's time to leave." Duane leaned against the wall and slid down to the floor. "You're on your own."

"Man, I'm so happy to be getting out of this place, I'll crawl. I might even roll down the stairs. You just don't know. Being single again isn't for me. Once you've known married life with a good woman, you can't imagine it any other way."

A tap on the open door silenced their conversation. Roman assumed it was the woman from the leasing office, stopping in to inspect the apartment. But the woman standing in the doorway was the last person he wanted to see.

# 14

## ROMAN

Jewel looked around the empty apartment, letting her gaze rove slowly, as if she were mentally placing the furniture where it had once been. "You're going back to your wife? I didn't think you would."

Roman bolted forward to a sitting position, forgetting for the moment that he'd even had back pain. He looked at Duane, and even though his friend had never seen Jewel before, it was obvious that he knew who the visitor was. Duane stood and cleared his throat but didn't leave, to Roman's relief.

"Hello," she said, cheerfully, though Roman could tell by the uneasy expression on her face that she was slightly uncomfortable. She probably hadn't expected him to have company.

"How are you?" Duane asked as a halfhearted courtesy. His words revealed no emotion, neither a welcoming hand nor a cold shoulder. He hadn't given Jewel the reaction most men did when she entered a room. Men gawked. They whistled. Many turned their heads in admiration when their wives or girlfriends weren't watching. Jewel was attractive, but it wasn't that she was the most beautiful woman they'd ever seen; it was that she knew how to carry and accentuate what God had given her.

"You shouldn't be here," Roman said. He didn't even stand to greet her, and he hoped that his actions would speak for him. What they'd had was over; it had ended nearly as quickly as it had started. Jewel had pretended to accept it, even though Roman had always known that she wanted more than he was willing and able to give. After two short months together, Jewel had seen a future for them, while Roman had seen only their sin.

"I was riding by and saw the moving truck. Something told me it was you, and then I saw that horrible TV armoire on the curb. I hope you're leaving it there for the trash pickup."

"Okay, so now you've seen me," Roman said. "And, yes, I've gone back home to my family."

Jewel stole a quick glance at Duane. "Do you think we can talk in private?"

"No," they both answered.

Jewel looked shocked when the refusal struck her from both directions. She turned her back on Duane, trying to block him out, but he wasn't having it. He left his spot in the corner of the room and moved to the kitchenette area, in full view. Then he wrung water out of a mop and started sweeping it across the laminate floor in slow, even strokes.

Jewel walked back over to Roman and knelt down in front of him. "All I want is to know that you're happy," she whispered. "You're my friend. I'm concerned about you."

"Don't be." Roman stood, his voice rising at the same time. "And whatever friendship we had is over."

Jewel looked up at him. "Just like that?"

"You keep popping up, acting like I haven't been telling you the same thing for months," he said between gritted teeth. He beat his fist into his palm in frustration. "It's annoying. No, actually, it's downright crazy."

He got up, walked over to the door, and opened it wider, leaving a chasm of space for Jewel to pass through. She dropped her head a moment before standing to her feet, then glanced around the empty room again.

Roman didn't know what she was looking for. If she wanted the scented candles she'd placed throughout his apartment when he'd first moved in, or the aloe vera plant she'd bought and placed on the windowsill after he'd burned his wrist frying pork chops, then she'd have to dive in the dumpster out back to find them. There was nothing else for her to claim. Despite Jewel's attempts, Roman had never let her keep so much as a pair of footies at his apartment. Once, she'd left a pair of gold hoop earrings on the counter, and Roman had hidden them in his bottom dresser door until she'd returned three days later. What if Zenja had visited him unexpectedly? What if the children questioned him about another woman?

"My number has been the same for years, and I don't plan on changing it anytime soon," Jewel said as she retreated. "Call me if you ever need to talk."

Roman didn't waste time listening to her footsteps trot down the flights of steps. The slam of the apartment door echoed through the empty space. He grabbed the mop from Duane's grip and started his own deliberate strokes across the floor. Whatever did or didn't happen between him and Zenja, Jewel would never become Mrs. Maxwell. She was caring and decent, but she wasn't wife material. At least, not for him. She would only be a reminder of his sin. And besides, a woman who cheated *with* him was likely to cheat *on* him. Hypocritical, he knew.

"Interesting," Duane finally said.

"And she tried to play the 'I'm here as your friend' card." Roman dropped the mop and found his comfortable place on the floor again.

"She knows what she's doing, I guarantee that," Duane said. He walked to the window overlooking the parking lot and peered outside.

"Is she still out there?" Roman asked. "She drives a silver sports car."

"Parked right behind the truck," Duane confirmed. "She's either crying or planning your demise."

Roman tapped his fingertips on either side of his chest like he was playing his keyboard. "I don't think revenge is her kind of thing."

"That's what they all say," Duane said. "I don't mean to dredge up old stuff, and once we leave this apartment, we don't ever have to talk about her again. But I've always wondered...how did you two meet in the first place?"

# 15

# ROMAN

*Twelve months prior*

*Brad must've spent a fortune on this,* Roman thought as he drove into the entrance of the Grandover Resort for his colleague's wedding. For six months, he'd been listening to Brad, another instructor in the music department, complain about the wedding expenses and the 250 guests his fiancée had insisted they invite. This wasn't the courthouse ceremony officiated by a justice of the peace and the backyard reception for fifty Roman and Zenja had enjoyed. No wonder Brad brown-bagged his lunch every day. Roman walked into the Grandover Resort without his wife on his arm. As usual, Zenja was busy meeting the emotional needs of everybody but him. She'd complained that his band practices and playing gigs were taking precedence over quality time with his family. But now that he'd given that up, she still hadn't put him first. Nothing was ever enough.

Since Kyle's stomach virus had him down for the second day in a row, Roman had agreed to take Zariya to tumbling practice that morning so Zenja could give her son a mother's attention. However, by the afternoon, Kyle was holding in his food from both ends and was up playing video games. That was why Roman had taken the initiative to call a sitter. Wasn't that what Zenja had said she wanted? Initiative on his part so they could spend time together?

Roman had never thought Zenja would refuse to leave Kyle with a sitter for even a few hours. He got it—they'd had a scare five years ago, when Zariya had developed appendicitis. But Kyle's stomach bug clearly wasn't that serious. So, they had argued, and Roman had left. He never had his wife to himself.

As soon as Roman found a seat, the ceremonial music announcing the beginning of the wedding began. Brad's nuptials included all the pomp and circumstance usually associated with weddings planned by brides who had been living and breathing for that very moment. There were twelve bridesmaids, twelve groomsmen, and a mother of the bride who sashayed down the aisle like she wanted to steal the spotlight. Roman could tell Brad was trying to hold his composure when his future wife first rounded the corner, but Brad's tears fell unrestricted before she made it halfway up the center aisle.

Another colleague sitting beside Roman nudged his arm, and Roman nodded in silent agreement. Brad would never hear the end of it.

The ceremony was just like Roman liked them—quick and to the point. Everybody knew the best part of a wedding was the reception, anyway. Roman was herded with the other guests into the adjoining ballroom, where he spied a table in the back corner that hadn't yet been claimed. Pretty soon, he had been joined by two teenage boys who were wrapped up in watching for girls in revealing party dresses.

"Is this seat taken?"

Roman turned at the female voice.

The woman didn't wait for him to answer but pulled out the chair and slid down beside him. He saw her try to discreetly slide her feet out of her strappy sandals, glittery pink toenails and all. Her perfume, though not overwhelming, floated under his nose. She wore just enough to accent her femininity but not enough to announce her arrival.

"I'm surprised they don't have assigned seats," she remarked. "I bet that was the groom's doing. There's always a seating chart at productions like this."

Roman could see why she had called it a production. He'd noticed a wedding planner walking around and whispering directions into the mouthpiece of her headset.

"Are you as hungry as I am?" the woman asked.

"Starving," Roman admitted.

"I think I saw servers coming around with hors d'oeuvres."

"Good to know," Roman said. He tried to keep his eyes elsewhere in the room instead of being engaged in conversation with her, but she didn't seem to mind making small talk to pass the time.

"How do you know the happy couple?" she asked before taking a sip of her iced tea.

"I work with Brad," Roman said.

"And I work with Sarah. Well, used to. They eliminated my position last month."

"What kind of work do you do?"

"Marketing full-time, but I do some artist management on the side for bands on independent labels. I actually manage the band that's playing now." She nodded toward the stage.

"Really? I was admiring their style. They've got some real talent." Now she was talking about something worth listening to.

"They're one of the best." She took another sip of tea, then opted for her water instead. "I help musicians showcase their talents in the community and get paid for pursuing their passion. Nothing wrong with getting paid to do what you love."

Roman was impressed. Greensboro and the rest of the Triad area had some local venues and opportunities for a showcase every now and then, but not enough to get the exposure he wanted. All the hot spots already had their regulars.

"Well, you're talking to somebody who plays for the passion without making too much money," Roman said. "Not enough worth counting."

She smirked. "All money is worth counting."

"You're right. I take that back."

She fingered the charm at the end of her necklace, and Roman noticed that it was a musical symbol—a treble clef, to be exact.

"But I don't have the time right now, anyway. Wife. Two kids."

"A person will always make time to do what they really want to do and make time for who they want to. There's never really a balance. Somebody or something will always get the short end of the stick."

"True," Roman said, signaling a server who was passing by with a tray of appetizers.

"Crab cakes—my favorite," the woman said when the waiter finally made it past the voracious teens.

Roman held up a hand. "I'm allergic to seafood."

"That's too bad," she said. "Shrimp étouffée, oysters, crawfish boils...if it's in the ocean, you can bet I've tried it at least once. It's the Louisiana girl in me."

"Well..." Roman paused. "I don't even know your name."

"Jewel."

"Well, Jewel from Louisiana, I don't think my wife wants me coming home with lips swollen to half the size of my head."

"Definitely don't want to mess up that face," Jewel said with a wink.

Roman and Jewel eased into comfortable conversation as everyone at the reception seemed to loosen up. Evidently the open bar helped. Roman wasn't a drinker—never had been. He'd seen the effect of alcohol on his father, and after Zenja told him about her downward spiral following the death of her first husband, they had made a pact never to bring the stuff in the house. But when Jewel brought him a glass of champagne for the toasts, he didn't turn it down. It wasn't a big deal. It wasn't like he was sitting on the front porch tossing back a beer with Carlos. This wedding was cause for celebration, and Jewel even managed to drag him to the dance floor as many as three times. In his head, Roman was as smooth as Fred Astaire, but he wasn't that confident with his moves in front of other people.

"That band is truly phenomenal," Roman said when he and Jewel returned to the table. He loosened his tie, unfastened the top button of his shirt, and took long gulps of water until his glass was empty.

Jewel slid her chair closer to his and leaned over to talk to him above the music. He tried to keep his eyes on the mole above her lips instead of letting them drift down to where her treble-clef charm dangled. As if she knew his inner struggle, she clasped it between her thumb and forefinger and played with it.

"We should exchange numbers in case you decide you want to start performing around town again," Jewel suggested as the evening drew to a close. She gathered her long hair at the nape of her neck, twisted it, and somehow got it to stay in place. "Your best marketing is word of mouth. It's all about being connected to the right people."

Roman logged her number in his cell phone under J.P., for Jewel Perry. A week passed, and although he'd thought about her several times, he never called.

But Jewel eventually did.

Roman's time with Jewel was exciting and different, unlike the monotonous routine of his predictable daily life. At first, Roman was always looking over his shoulder, but his apprehension soon waned. What he had with Jewel was like quicksand, only he didn't discover that until he tried to fight his way out—after Zenja discovered them together.

The pain in Zenja's eyes was a look he'd never forget. From that moment, he knew that none of the secret phone calls, text messages, or visits with Jewel had been worth it. The words Zenja had said to him the day she'd packed his belongings were still etched in his memory: *"You got what you wanted, but you lost what you had."*

It was the escape he'd really wanted, not Jewel.

The leasing office manager never showed up, so Roman locked the apartment door, then slid the key in a small envelope to leave in the drop box. The office would perform the walk-through later and mail him a check for the amount of his security deposit. He'd already planned to use it to do something special for Zenja. A peace offering, if there was such a thing. The cards he'd hidden for her to open during her cruise had been written straight from his heart. He wanted her to know that she was constantly on his mind. He prayed he was in her thoughts, too.

# 16

When can I see you again?" Lance asked.

The cruise ship would dock at the Miami port early tomorrow morning, and Lance and I had found a dark cove on the lower deck where we could be alone. He wrapped me in his arms to shield me from the ocean breeze, and I leaned back against his chest. I just wanted to be held.

"That's up to you," I said. "You'll have to call me whenever you come to town."

"You wouldn't come to Charlotte to see me?" he asked, pressing his cheek against mine. The scruff of his five o'clock shadow pricked my skin, and I tilted my head out of the way. Apparently he took that as an invitation to kiss my neck.

"No," I protested. "My mama didn't raise me that way." But my voice sounded like a purr. What was coming over me? "If a man is interested in you, he's the one who's supposed to do the chasing."

"Good for Mama," Lance said. "She taught you well."

"I tend to think so," I said.

Lance kissed my neck again. My knees nearly buckled. "In the meantime, good luck with your own declaration of independence," he said. "You'll be better off without your husband, take it from me."

Why did he have to go there? Why did he have to put Roman in my head when I'd done a decent job all this time pretending that he didn't exist? I'd even thrown away the cards he'd slipped into my suitcase, never having bothered to open the last two.

"I tend to believe you might be biased," I said.

"Not biased, just experienced." Lance turned me around so that we were face-to-face. "I'm experienced in other things, too," he whispered in my ear. "Come to my room. We don't have to walk there together; I'll give you the extra key."

"I can't do that," I said, my mouth suddenly dry.

"Why? Afraid your chaperone will catch you? You're a grown woman."

"Exactly," I said. "And I make grown-woman decisions. I can't let my body make those decisions for me."

"You don't want to leave this cruise with any regrets," Lance said, still trying to convince me to make that walk to the fourth level.

I'd already taken it further than I'd intended. The first kiss after karaoke had led to three more, each one more intimate than the last. I was tiptoeing into dangerous territory. No matter how much I wished the night would never end, with its perfect full moon and ocean breeze enveloping me, reality would set in the next morning: Lance and I would go our separate ways. He'd live as a bachelor, and I'd live in limbo between what my heart wanted and what my mind said I should do. Whenever I reached a crossroads in life, I'd seek Caprice's advice. Of course, in this situation, I couldn't.

Caprice and I met during our senior year at Bennett College and became instant friends. We've talked from dusk until dawn. We've defended each other from gossip and bailed each other out of trouble. We dedicated our lives to the Lord in our mid-twenties at the same church, and she stayed close by my side, even when her passion for God's Word burned high, while I was merely straddling the fence. When I watched the funeral director close Vincent's casket, my mother held my right hand; Caprice gripped my left. She cuddled and swaddled my children on the day they were born, even though she has never been able to conceive her own. I've told her everything, but I couldn't tell her about the times I spent with Lance. Before they'd been tossed in the trash, I'd purposefully let her see me tuck Roman's cards into my tote bag and told her I was going on a late-night stroll to think, when I was really going for another stolen moment with Lance. It was the first lie I ever told her.

I never made it to Lance's room that last night. Instead, I spent the last waking hours of the cruise with my best friend and met the next morning's sunrise on the veranda outside of my room. As the sun climbed above the horizon, I whispered a one-sentence prayer: "Your will be done, God."

Caprice rolled down the ramp toward the shuttle taking us back to the airport. "That was over way too quick," she pouted. "Next time, we'll do seven days, or even ten. Maybe we'll spring for going somewhere a little more exotic, like the Mediterranean."

"I have to admit, I did have a great time," I said. "It was nothing like I thought it would be. And my mother will be glad to know that I didn't have to fight for a life jacket or go to the bathroom in a poopie bag even once."

Lance was already off board, and I immediately spotted him wearing a ridiculous-looking straw hat that he'd bought from CocoCay Island.

"You ladies look like you enjoyed your cruise. Rejuvenated," Lance said when he met us at the end of the ramp. He and I were both acting like we'd never spent a minute together.

"We feel it, too," Caprice agreed. Her face glowed with a natural, sun-kissed tint.

"You two are beyond beautiful," Lance said, "but when you want your bodies to feel as good as they look, don't forget to give me a call. I'll be up your way in a couple of weeks if you want to schedule a personal training session. Of course, I'm still working out the particulars, but I'm sure things will fall into place." He'd slipped into his salesmen pitch, still trying to cover our indiscretions.

"I'll keep that in mind," Caprice said, though I could tell she didn't mean it. She reached for her buzzing cell phone. "That's Duane calling. He couldn't wait for me to get on dry land." She shook her head as she stepped away to answer the phone. She was as eager to see her husband as he was to see her.

"Don't get to Charlotte and pretend like you never knew me," I said to Lance. "I could use some training."

"Do I get to choose what kind of training?" he asked. I saw him glance quickly at Caprice, to see if her antennae were pointed in our direction.

"You have my number," I said, before Lance was summoned back to his group of coworkers. "You know what to do with it."

"Keep those lips warm for me," he said.

I did want to see Lance again, and not just for his personal fitness training. The mere thought of squats, lunges, crunches, and exercise balls made my muscles ache, and I hadn't done a single rep. I'd been promising myself for years to make health and fitness a priority. Forty was supposed to be my big birthday year to reveal a new and improved body, but that was two years ago. Better late than never.

When we landed in Greensboro, I was still wondering if Lance would actually call. The pilot had announced that we'd caught a tailwind that pushed the plane back to NC in record time. This could only be God's doing. He'd rushed me back home to Roman.

Duane was waiting for us at baggage claim, and he swept Caprice into his arms as soon as she was within reach. He kissed her with no reservations about who was watching.

"Whew," Caprice said, flustered. "I should go away more often."

"No, you shouldn't. Not unless you're taking me with you."

"Next time," Caprice promised. "To the Mediterranean."

"Or we can take Friday Night Love to the seas," Duane said.

"Friday Night Love? What's that?" I asked.

"You remember the couples' ministry I was telling you about?" Caprice said as Duane carried our bags toward the covered parking area.

"Vaguely," I admitted. "I probably subconsciously blocked it out. I'm missing one half a couple."

"Not anymore," Caprice said. "I think you and Roman would enjoy yourselves."

"Hold it right there," I said, opening the back passenger door of their sedan. "I don't even know how I'm going to handle this whole Roman situation. I couldn't do anything about it while I was on the cruise, but now it's a different story."

"And Roman still wants to be a part of it," Duane added.

It surprised me that he'd said a word. Duane was an inner processor—he took it all in but rarely offered his opinion or insight unless we drilled him for it. At least, that was usually the case when it came to conversations between Caprice and me.

"I'm sure he poured his heart out to you," I said. "But it's more complicated than that. You're on the outside looking in."

"True," Duane said, slipping his parking voucher into the prepaid slot.

*"True"*? That was all he had to say? I'm sure he had more than that to say to Roman. Undoubtedly he'd convinced his friend to hang in there until the end. He had Roman's back, and he didn't have to tell me that for me to know it.

I'd become quickly agitated. There I was, thinking about Roman again, when I would have rather been engaged in mindless chatter about how Caprice had had to play nurse my first night on board, how she'd convinced me to go zip-lining, how our cooking class had turned into a disaster, and how crazy we'd been to participate in a volleyball tournament with an overzealous bridal party.

I watched the highway signs leading back to Highway 64 whiz past.

"Roman and I hung out Monday night after I helped him move the rest of his stuff back in," Duane finally said after I'd ridden in silence for several minutes.

"So, he's really moving back in. He wasn't bluffing."

"Not bluffing at all," Duane affirmed. "That apartment is probably cleaner than the day he moved in. He said he was coming home, and he brought his furniture *and* his heart with him."

I slumped in the backseat. "Can I stay with you guys tonight?" I asked this half-jokingly, even though I would've gladly taken the ride to their house, had they agreed.

"Not a chance," Duane said. "I haven't seen my wife in four days."

"Okay, okay," I said. "You don't have to say another word. I get the point."

When Duane pulled into my driveway, I was still mentally rehearsing the rant I was going to unleash on Roman.

"I can't believe you're going to leave me here," I said to Caprice while Duane unloaded my luggage and the two bags of useless souvenirs I'd bought for the kids. I'd hoped Roman would be at work, but he was piddling around *my* garage, sidestepping all the junk he called furniture. "I feel sick," I said, watching him.

"It's your nerves. You'll be fine." Caprice turned around in her seat to get a better look at me. "All your emotions are bundled up inside. Just remember he's your husband, not a stranger."

"I don't know Roman anymore. He's not the man I married."

"None of us are the people we were when we first got married. We should be grateful for that."

"But we should be *better* people." My feet throbbed. My head throbbed. My heart throbbed.

"I think Roman's probably a better man after this," Caprice said.

I couldn't believe her. Once again, she was acting like Roman's infidelity wasn't a big deal. I unstrapped my sandals, which felt as if they were cutting off the circulation in my ankles. I hesitated before opening the car door. When I stepped out, Caprice was waiting with her arms open wide. She squeezed me in an embrace, probably an attempt to transfer some of her strength, grace, and faith.

"You'll be fine," she assured me again.

"Only if he stays on his side of the house, and I stay on mine," I said. "How are we supposed to cohabit with all these issues between us?"

"This isn't just about living arrangements," Caprice said. She pointed skyward. "Take it to the throne. Pray, pray, and pray some more."

# 17

Not only were my feet like bricks, but my legs felt weighted with concrete as I headed toward the house, wading through the emotions that made me dread going inside. I walked past Roman like he was as insignificant as a piece of his furniture. Furniture that by no stretch of the imagination would be staying in *my* garage.

Duane honked the car horn and Caprice waved good-bye just as I closed the door leading from the garage into the kitchen. I rinsed out a glass from the dishwasher and filled it with filtered tap water from the sink. It quenched my thirst and moistened my dry throat. I noticed two arrangements of tulips on the kitchen table. I love tulips; in fact, I prefer them over every other flower. To me, roses are overrated. Smitten teenage boys give them to their high-school sweethearts, beauty pageant queens are draped with them, and they're hustled at every city corner on Valentine's Day. But tulips have always moved me. My heart filled with joy, not because Roman had given to me, but simply because I appreciated their beauty. Beside the vase was yet another card.

Roman came inside then, and even though I didn't want to acknowledge him, I turned around to face the conversation I'd been dreading since I set sail from the Miami coast.

"I don't think this is going to work out," I said calmly. So much for the rant I'd prepared. "This is too much, too soon. We should accept that it's over."

Roman washed his grungy hands at my kitchen sink. I hated that.

"I know it's not over," he said. "I won't accept that."

"You accepted it when you walked out."

"Why do you keep throwing that in my face when you know it's not how it happened? *You* packed up my stuff. *You* wanted me to leave, so I left. I was trying to make things easier on Zariya and Kyle because our home was too explosive. But I didn't expect the arrangement to go on for this long. Two, maybe three, months—until you cooled off."

"There are a lot of things I didn't expect, either," I said, growing more irritated by the second. I hated rehashing old arguments. "And just so you know, I'm still heated. When your husband cheats on you, you can't just 'cool off.'"

Roman flicked the water off his hands, and my eyes dared him to use my dishcloth to dry them. He opted for a paper towel but left it on the counter instead of dropping it in the trash can. *Men*. It didn't take them long to fall back into old habits.

I propped my elbows on the bar and rested my forehead in my hands. "I can't fathom why you're doing this right now. It doesn't make sense." All the joy, fun, and excitement I'd experienced on the cruise had seeped out of me. My life was deflating, my ship sinking.

"What happened to divorce not being an option? That came from your own mouth before we even got married," Roman had the nerve to say.

"What happened to being faithful?" I shot back. "That came from *your* own mouth."

"I didn't mean for it to happen. I love you. It's you I want. I've said it a thousand times, and I'll say it a thousand times more. I'll say it, and I'll show you, from today until the last breath leaves my body."

Then Roman started to cry. There had been few times in our life together that I'd seen him weep with such pain, and the last time had been at the funeral of his college friend three years ago. Roman didn't try to hide his emotions. He wanted me to see his brokenness, to feel it, maybe to cry with him. But I couldn't. I'd shed enough of my own tears when he hadn't been there to hold me. My bed pillows had been soaked with despair and saturated with questions, like what I had done to drive him into the arms of someone else.

I'd left the calming waters of the Bahamas and returned home to turbulent seas. I picked up Roman's dirty paper towel and the card he'd left with the tulips and threw them both in the trash. Roman didn't make a move to rescue the envelope as it joined a half-eaten frozen meal, a blackened banana peel, and an empty can of ginger ale.

"And just so you know, those other cards you gave me are probably floating somewhere in the ocean." I wanted to convince both of us that his words didn't matter. I stopped and peered into his eyes. "I deserve better than what you gave me," I said.

"And that's why I'm here—because I want to be the man to give it to you." Roman wiped his eyes with his hands, but the pain remained on his face. "Please, Zenja. Please give me that chance."

# 18

## ROMAN

Roman hadn't meant to cry like a baby in front of Zenja, but what was done was done. His emotions had erupted like a volcano, and he couldn't have smothered them if he'd wanted to. His vision had been blurry, just like the words he'd intended to say.

He waited until Zenja went upstairs, then dug his card out of the trash can. He wiped it off with his shirttail and slid it inside the drawer where they'd always kept their latest paid bills.

Roman wanted to fix things. He wanted Zenja to look at him and see his sincerity instead of his mistakes. He wanted to hold her and not have her resist. He wanted to be with her in a way that was sacred between a husband and wife. Undefiled. Roman held fast to his faith that it would be that way again soon.

*Weeping may endure for a night, but joy comes in the morning,* he thought as he went upstairs to change his shirt. *When will my daybreak come?*

Zenja needed her space, and Roman could respect that. Hence his decision not to move any of his items back into their bedroom but to stack his boxes in the guest room, instead. It felt claustrophobic, but it would have to do for now.

Roman tested his freshly laundered shirts that he'd hung inside the closet and, finding them dry, yanked a short-sleeved polo off a hanger and pulled it over his head. "It's gonna get better," he said aloud. "It's gonna get better."

Yes, he was talking to himself again. He took the Scriptures and the advice from Dr. Morrow seriously. If life and death were in the power of the tongue, as the Bible said, he was going to direct his power to restore life to his marriage. "Zenja will desire me and me alone as her husband. God will be glorified in our marriage. Our lives and our love for each other will flourish like never before," he proclaimed.

Roman decided to go for a drive to clear his head and bring back something for lunch and dinner so that Zenja wouldn't have to worry about making something to eat. He would stop by her favorite Thai joint and order enough food for a mini buffet. He glanced down the hallway. Zenja had closed the bedroom door. Shut him out.

He grabbed his keys, wallet, and cell phone from the basket near the fridge and headed outside, still thinking about special things he could do for Zenja. She hadn't seemed impressed with the tulips, and he now knew what she'd thought about those cards. He loved her, and what was love if he didn't put it into action in a way that spoke her language?

As Roman was driving, his cell phone rang, interrupting his thoughts about Zenja. He looked at the screen. *Jewel.* He'd deleted her contact information but recognized the number. *Unbelievable.* He hit the button to send her to voice mail. Before her visit two days ago, they hadn't spoken in at least a month. The last time they'd talked, she'd called to see if he was interested in playing his saxophone for an event at an art gallery. Of course, he'd declined. Before then, it had been even longer since they'd been in contact. He'd run into her on a late-night trip to the drugstore to pick up drops for his itchy, runny eyes.

"How are you?" she'd said when she'd found him inspecting the relief symptoms on the back of each box. "Wow," she'd added, wincing slightly when he'd looked up at her. "Allergies have you and everybody else."

"Doesn't look as bad as it feels," he'd said, reading the box for the drops that promised instant relief.

"Sorry. That's pretty bad."

"Could be worse, I guess." He'd made his final choice while she'd pretended to peruse the nearly empty shelves next to him. "Take care of yourself," Roman had said before walking away, ready to make a beeline for the registers.

Jewel had touched his arm as he'd walked by, gripping it softly to stop him. "Is that what you're doing? Taking care of yourself? Or is your wife taking care of you?" There had been hope in her eyes.

"Look, Jewel. Whatever is happening with my life or my wife is none of your business. It doesn't matter who's taking care of me. If it ends up being my wife, all the better."

Jewel had tried to reason with him and, at the same time, plant seeds of doubt in his head. "If she even *lets* you come home, it doesn't mean things are going to change." She'd squeezed his forearm.

"A chance I'll take," Roman had said, wrenching his arm from her grip. He'd pulled a handkerchief out of his pocket and pressed it against his left eye.

"You know what they say—when a woman's fed up, there's nothing you can do about it. I think she's fed up. She's never once asked you to come back home. Unless it's about your children, she doesn't even call you. Those are your own words."

Roman had regretted confiding in her to the extent that he had. He'd given her just the words to use to shake his confidence. *Be careful about revealing your marital problems to someone of the opposite sex.* He'd heard that warning in premarital counseling years ago, but hindsight was twenty-twenty. Roman had clutched his eye drops and a bottle of 24-hour allergy medicine and walked away.

"I hope you believe in miracles," Jewel had said, "because that's what you're going to need."

Well, Roman did believe in miracles. Then and especially now. And above all else, He believed in God.

His cell rang again, and for the third time he ignored Jewel's call. A minute later, his phone buzzed, alerting him to a new text message. Roman glanced at it, hoping it was Zenja asking him to come home. If it was, he'd break every traffic rule to get there.

But it wasn't Zenja.

Roman pounded the steering wheel in frustration. "Why is she doing this?" he growled between clenched teeth. He wasn't just angry with Jewel, he was angry with himself.

Thinkn abt u. Wish u were here.

Roman was going to text a reply, but he must have pressed "call," because the next thing he heard was Jewel's voice.

"So, you were thinking about me, too?" she purred. "You should come by tonight. I'll be home around seven."

"Look, Jewel," he yelled, tightening his grip on the steering wheel. "You need to stop this foolishness. I won't let you sabotage my—"

*CRASH!*

# 19

# ROMAN

A strong force smashed into his vehicle on the driver's side, throwing Roman's car into a spin. Metal crunched. Horns honked. The air bag exploded into his face, and a burning sensation seared his face and arms. Something cut his lower neck and collarbone, causing him to scream in agony.

"Sir, are you okay?" The man's question was accompanied by a fist pounding on the car roof. Roman's sight was too blurred to make out his features, but he could tell that the face was fully bearded and that the man wore sunglasses so big, they made him look like a human fly.

Roman tried to answer "Yes," but moans were all that rose from his throat. His head throbbed, and the entire left side of his body ached. The man continued talking as he tried to yank open the door. Roman attempted to assist him, but he didn't have the strength to do much. His shattered window looked like crumpled aluminum foil, but it hadn't fallen in.

"The door's jammed," Roman heard the man say. Voices moved to the passenger side, and Roman felt the car sway as people tried to open the door.

"Man, this one's stuck, too."

"Sit tight. We'll get you out of there. Help is on the way," said the fly man.

Roman used his right hand to unlatch his seat belt, releasing the pressure from his chest and midsection. He felt less restricted and soon noticed that his racing heartbeat had begun to slow. He inhaled deeply and took deliberate breaths to calm himself down.

*God is my refuge and strength, a very present help in trouble,* Roman thought. *And, God, this is trouble.*

Roman ran his hand along the front of his neck to the place where his collarbone stung. Warm blood stained his fingers. He grimaced. He didn't like blood, not even his own. He leaned back against the headrest. At least he was alive. Carefully, gently, he moved his other limbs. His left wrist was sore, but nothing seemed broken.

"Close your eyes!" the voice screamed.

When he opened them, the passenger window had crumbled into a thousand pieces that looked like a pool of fake crystals on the seat beside him.

The fly-man stuck his head through the open window, then pushed up his shades to reveal a pair of eyes that were unbelievably deep and green on a man whose skin was as dark as a cup of coffee without cream and sugar.

"Do you think it's okay if we move you?" he asked Roman.

"I think so," Roman said, leery. "I don't think anything is broken, but maybe I should stay put until help comes."

"I was trying to get you out in case the car blew up or something."

Roman hadn't noticed any fumes, but now he wasn't so sure. Was that gas he smelled? Was he about to make Zenja a widow yet again? Roman was relieved when he heard sirens approaching. The wailing grew louder until it sounded like it was right outside the car, and then it stopped. Flashing red and blue lights had joined the glare of the sunshine.

"I'll step back and let the professionals do their job," the fly-man said. "Seems these days the Good Samaritan is always the one to get sued." He looked down at the pool of glass on the seat.

"Don't worry about it," Roman said, trying to smile. "It's only a car. I'm just glad it wasn't me."

"Are you sure?"

"That's what insurance is for."

"Stay strong, buddy," the fly man said, relieved. "That guy ran the red light like he was blind. With all the chaos and other cars blaring their horns, I'm surprised you didn't see him." He shook his head. "But it can happen like that." He snapped his fingers. "I'll give the police officers my contact information."

"I appreciate your help. I didn't catch your name."

"They call me Fly."

It figured. "Thanks, Fly," Roman said.

A paramedic appeared behind Fly. "Thank you, sir. We'll take it from here," the man said, then looked in on Roman. He couldn't have been more than two years out of high school. "You'll be fine, sir. The fire department will pry open the door so we can get you to the hospital."

"Alright," Roman said. As he waited for the professionals to do their job, he turned his body carefully to look for his cell phone but didn't see it anywhere. He tried not to move too much, in case the adrenaline pumping through his body had masked any major injuries that would only get worse if he jarred the areas.

Even though Roman felt capable, the EMTs refused to let him walk to the ambulance after they had dislodged him from the wreckage. It was the first opportunity he'd had to survey the damage to his car and to the two other vehicles involved in the crash. Neither of them had sustained nearly as much damage as his car. It was probably totaled. He silently thanked God for sparing his life.

"My cell phone is still in the car," Roman told the paramedic who was checking his vitals. "Can someone try to find it for me?"

The paramedic nodded. "I found a cell phone and umbrella. I'll get them in just a minute." His nose was buried in his clipboard. Roman may have needed to go the hospital, but it looked like this dude was due to see the eye doctor. "Is there anything else you're missing?" the man asked him.

"Nothing important," Roman said, thankful that he'd cleaned his trunk earlier that day of all his papers from work. "I wanted to get a picture of the car."

"I don't blame you," the youngster said. "I can't believe you walked away with what looks like only some cuts and bruises from the air bag." He slid the blood pressure cuff off Roman's arm. "You might want to call someone to meet you at the hospital."

Roman nodded. "I'll call my wife."

# 20

Roman's best bet was to make himself scarce for the night. I breathed a sigh of relief when I walked in the bedroom and realized he hadn't tried to force his way back into my space. Everything in the bedroom was just as I had left it. "God, You're really going to have to help me with this."

It was ludicrous to think I could keep a man out of his own home. Roman hadn't missed a mortgage payment, even after he'd moved out. I didn't know how he managed to pay both his apartment rent and the house mortgage, but I assumed he'd dipped into his personal savings. We kept a joint savings account, which neither of us touched, but we'd each kept a separate stash of cash in case of an emergency. He'd started the habit since his first job in high school because his father refused to give him money for anything other than essentials, like food and, on occasion, clothes.

With little to do besides unpack, I was suddenly in the mood to snoop. I checked the driveway again for Roman's car, then went into the guest room to pick through his items. I wasn't sure what I was looking for; I just knew I didn't want to find something that would send me reeling.

I could tell that Roman had hastily thrown the comforter on the bed; his bed-making skills had always been comparable to Kyle's. I restrained myself from smoothing the bedding and tucking the corners because I didn't want my housecleaning pickiness to give me away.

*The alarm*, I thought.

I ran downstairs to arm the system since I didn't know if Roman would be away for ten minutes or two hours. This way, when he returned, I'd have a few extra seconds to place things back in order and slip out of the room. I was a master at investigating in Zariya's room without her noticing, and I knew I could pull it off with Roman, too.

I started at the top of a stack of his blue storage containers. It held most of his khaki pants and bow ties. The second was full of some of his class material. The third was a box of the bills and other junk mail he'd amassed while he was away. I picked up a handful of envelopes and flipped through electric bills, rent receipts, and some paperwork from the dean of the school. I was nearly at the point of taking off my sleuthing hat when I came upon a card the size of a small thank-you note. The handwriting was a woman's, and it wasn't mine or his mother's easily identifiable chicken scratch.

They say if you go looking for something, you'll find it. And I did. My blood boiled. I felt the tension and betrayal like it was happening for the first time. Who was this woman with no qualms about writing notes to a married man? I knew that she knew about us—his wife and two children. I had known by the look on her face the first and only time I'd seen her.

It was a Sunday, of all days. After a Spirit-filled worship service at church, Zariya and Kyle had begged me to let them spend the rest of the day with Caprice and Duane. Their godparents spoiled them to the point that they'd set up a bedroom for them at their house and had enough luxuries at their home that my kids didn't have to take anything else but the clothes on their backs whenever they visited. Duane had promised to grill ribs—his specialty—with the secret sauce for Kyle, and Caprice and Zariya planned to experiment baking cupcakes inside waffle cones.

I promised to join them in the evening for dinner, then left the wannabe chefs to whip up their meals while I trekked an hour and a half away to Charlotte for some early-afternoon retail therapy. I was elated to have the energy and time to do some shopping alone. The children were in good hands. Roman had skipped church so he could practice all day on campus for an upcoming concert hosted by the music department. Without my family members huffing and puffing in boredom outside the dressing room, I could try on and model as many outfits as I wanted.

By the end of my excursion, I'd found two pairs of slacks that fit impeccably, six flattering blouses, and two dresses. Satisfied with my finds, I was headed toward the parking lot when a stylish mannequin in a men's clothing store window caught my attention. Actually, it was the bow tie that turned my head. It was nerdy-looking with red and blue diagonal stripes—truly Roman's style. Buying it for him would be my way of apologizing for being a nag; his words, not mine. I thought it would be nice to plan a Thursday night date and give him the gift at dinner. We'd been drifting apart. Far apart. I was only three steps inside the doorway when I heard a woman call "Roman!" Instinctively, I turned. I'd never met or heard of another man with the same name as my husband, and the name had rolled out of her mouth with a flirty giggle. I stopped and took a deep breath as I followed the sound with my eyes. Roman was standing near the front counter. The woman ran her hand down his spine and settled just above his belt. I knew I hadn't heard wrong when Roman told me that morning, "Babe, I'm meeting with the jazz ensemble today to practice for their concert. I'll catch up this evening. Call me if you need me."

So I did just that. I called his cell phone and watched him unclip it from his belt.

He stepped away from the woman and wandered to a rack of belts near the center of the store.

"Hey," I said, trying to keep my voice from trembling with rage.

"What's up?" he asked. I could hear the rush in his voice and watched him turn his back toward the woman lingering at the front.

"Just checking in. Do you want me and the kids to drop by and bring you lunch?"

"No, I'm good," he lied. "We ordered pizza and wings. That should tide me over until later, but thanks for asking."

I started walking in his direction, keeping him distracted with useless chatter while I watched him squirm behind those belts. Anyone else would have seen those belts as accessories, but at that moment, I saw them as weapons. I paused at the counter to assess the woman who was with my husband. Like most women, she couldn't have graced the cover of a magazine without some professional airbrushing and photo editing, but most men probably considered her beautiful. I didn't care what she looked like. She was with my husband.

"Well, Roman," I said, "call your wife and children when you finish buying this blue and green plaid tie. The red and blue one in the window would look much better on you. Trust me. Your wife knows these kinds of things."

The woman didn't budge. I believe she was as shocked as Roman. He'd turned around and was headed toward me. I wasn't about to air my dirty laundry in public or give the sales associates in the clothing store something to gossip about the rest of the week. I moved as quickly as my weak legs would allow, brushing past the clothing racks to get away from Roman so that the other woman wouldn't see me fall apart.

Sundays were supposed to be the best day of the week, but my encounter changed that.

I tore the note I'd found into pieces so small that I couldn't rip them anymore. I stood, snapped the lid back on the container I'd been rummaging through, and put everything back in place. Emotionally, I wasn't ready for this. For the last twenty minutes, my cell phone and then the house line had been ringing repeatedly with calls from Roman. I'd ignored them all. If he wanted to talk to me about our marriage—or the lack thereof—he'd have to wait until he came back home.

Another five minutes passed before Roman enlisted the help of Caprice and Duane to contact me. I was furious.

"Hello?" I said, trying to remember my best friends weren't the source of my frustration.

"Zenja," said Caprice. "Roman has been trying to call you."

"I know. And now he has *you* on bended knee for *him*. I hate that he had to—"

"Roman's at Wesley Long Hospital. We're on our way now. We'll meet you there."

# 21

What?" Fear rose in my throat.

"He's been in an accident." Caprice's voice was calm, which helped to settle my panic somewhat. "He said he's only bruised and cut up, but the car was a complete loss. It was so mangled that the fire department had to cut him out."

Guilt washed over me. I never knew what people meant when they said the blood rushed out of their face, but I believed it was happening to me. I slipped on a pair of flip-flops and dashed out the door.

Twenty minutes later, I swerved into the hospital parking lot. I was already frazzled, and it didn't help that the hospital's recent expansion made it difficult to know which way to go. I followed the signs that read "Emergency Room," found a place to park, and ran inside. I spotted Caprice and Duane sitting in the waiting room. Their eyes were on each other, while everyone else, looking tired and frustrated, was fixed on the television in the corner. "Roman's fine," Caprice assured me. "They gave him some pain meds, so he's resting. He'll be happy to see you."

"Quite the welcome-home gift," I said, relaxing now that I knew his state. I shook my head. First Kyle's broken arm, now Roman. "You guys go home," I told her. "I can handle everything from here."

A smile spread across Duane's face. "We're leaving Roman here in fairly good condition. Don't do anything to put him in critical condition."

Caprice jabbed him with her elbow. "She wouldn't do something crazy like that." Her eyebrows almost met at the top when she looked at me. "Would you?"

"Let's just say I won't do anything that would land me in jail."

"That's a deal," Duane said. He helped me into my cardigan after noticing me rub my arms, which were covered in goose bumps. I walked him and Caprice to the end of the hallway, delaying my visit to room 23, where Roman was resting. Several minutes later, I tapped on his door, then stuck my head inside. He roused and tried to see who was coming in. His right eye fluttered open, but there was little he could do with the left bruised eye. Caprice and Duane had said he was in good condition, but to me, it looked like he'd gotten in a fight with a bulldog and lost.

I stood at the foot of the bed. "So this is what you do to get my attention?"

He grunted. I think it was supposed to be a laugh, but he was so woozy from the medication, I couldn't tell. It hurt just looking at him.

"Thanks for coming," he mumbled.

It was hard for me to keep an attitude with Roman when he truly looked pitiful. He'd been known to exaggerate his symptoms of illnesses or injury to elicit sympathy from me, but this was real. *Poor thing.*

I pulled a chair to the corner of the room and used the TV remote attached to the hospital bed to change the channel from the news to *Family Feud*. Then my stomach started to grumble loudly.

"Hungry?" asked the nurse who'd just come in to check Roman's bandages and take his vitals. She offered me a granola bar from the pocket of her scrubs.

"That's okay," I said. I would need a lot more than that. "Is the cafeteria open?"

The nurse looked at her watch. "Yes," she said. "And the food is good, believe it or not. They've got hot food, a deli, and a salad bar. Almost anything you have a taste for."

"Is it okay if I bring something back here?" I asked.

"I won't tell if you won't," the nurse said, then gestured at my oversized purse. "You could put that to good use."

"Gotcha," I said.

Roman cleared his throat as if fighting hard to speak. "Can you get me something, too?" He lifted his hand and lightly touched the cut under his Adam's apple, then tried, unsuccessfully, to reach for the thin blanket lying in a jumble at his feet. I spread it out and tucked it under his sides like a cocoon. Before I could step away, he caught my hand and squeezed it weakly. I waited a moment before sliding it out of his grasp. His eyes opened and closed as if in slow motion as the pain medicine pulled him back toward sleep. "I'm so sore."

"Get some rest," I said. "I'll bring you something."

Lucky Roman had medications to numb his pain. I didn't. I hated that I cared. What was I doing here? I'd dashed out of my house when I was supposed to be avoiding him. *God, why is this happening?*

I left the room at the same time as the nurse, then waited for her to drop her clipboard in the plastic file bin hanging on his door.

"Quick question," I whispered. "He won't need long-term care or anything, will he?"

She gave me a slightly amused look, then said, "Oh, no. He's bruised and battered but seems fine overall. I did notice that his blood pressure was a little high, but I'll monitor it over the next hour or so and see what the doctor says."

"Okay, great. Thanks for your help."

"Either way, he'll need to take it easy for a few days," the nurse added. "I suggest having some heating pads around because after you've been in a car accident, it can take days for some of the pain to rear its head. He may also have some neck and back discomfort."

"Alright," I said.

The nurse must have caught me rolling my eyes. "One of those days?"

I'd seen her wedding ring, so I knew she'd understand when I said, "One of those years."

I found my way to the cafeteria and quickly realized it wasn't as impressive as the nurse had indicated. Compared to other hospitals, I guess it was, but I was coming off a cruise and was spoiled from having had shrimp, flank steak, and other delicacies at my fingertips for four days. Somehow chicken fingers with honey mustard dip didn't measure up. I bought them anyway and carried my tray to an empty table in the dining area instead of sneaking my food back to the room.

Before returning to Roman, I called my children. They deserved to know what was going on. Zariya's phone was always attached to her ear, so I wasn't surprised that she answered before the second ring.

"Hi, sweetheart," I sang. "I'm back home."

"How was your cruise?" she asked. "I know you and Auntie Caprice had fun. I'm jealous."

"No need to be," I said. "You'll have your turn soon enough."

"Next year?" Zariya asked hopefully.

"No promises, but we'll see."

"I know what that means. It's a nice way to say no."

"That's not true," I insisted. But it was my way of delaying an answer in hopes that she'd find something else to obsess about. I'd need to come up with another strategy. The older Zariya got, the quicker she caught on to my parenting tricks.

"I can hear Gemma fussing," I said. "What's going on now?"

"Grandpa is always doing something to set her off. I think he does it on purpose," Zariya said. "That's how you and Dad will probably act when you get old. I'm so glad he's home now. You don't how much I've prayed for him to come back."

*Actually, I do,* I thought. *I know that and then some.* I couldn't wait to get my hands on her diary when she got back home so I could read about what had really happened in New Jersey. Then my thoughts snapped to what Zariya had said.

"Don't concern yourself about whether your Dad is staying home," I told her. I'd totally forgotten about Roman's slick move of calling my parents from my house phone. He rarely even touched the home phone, since we received more calls from telemarketers on the land line than we did from friends and family.

"I'm sure about it, Mom. I had a dream. I knew it was going to happen sooner or later, but I didn't want to say anything to you."

*A dream? Zariya, too?*

"Plus, Dad told me," Zariya said.

Heat flared in my face. He should've consulted me before saying something like that. "Your dad really said that?" I asked.

"Yes. He said he wanted us to really pray for our family. All of us. He made Kyle get on the phone and he prayed with us, too. Both me and Kyle were crying, and you know Kyle's not the sentimental type. Most of the time he acts so unconcerned about stuff, at least on the outside. We wanted to come home, but Gemma said you two needed to have some time alone."

Great. Now my mom was in on it.

"Mom," Zariya said, barely stopping to take a breath, "having faith is real to me now. I believed it even when I couldn't see it, and now it's happening."

How was I supposed to respond? I considered every word that I could say to her. The last thing I wanted to do was crush Zariya's confidence and faith in God.

"Baby, I don't want you to dwell on what's going on between me and your dad right now," I finally said. "These are adult matters, and you shouldn't be worried about what's going to happen."

"But Mom, I'm not worried." She spoke with such confidence. "Remember what Pastor Hunter used to make us say at the end of each church service? 'God said it. I believe it. That settles it.'"

Tears tried to pool in the corners of my eyes, but I fought them back. I decided to put off telling the children about Roman's accident until tomorrow. I didn't want Zariya to have to deal with my emotions or her own. She and Kyle had never learned the reason why Roman and I had separated. Even though it would've been easy for me to smear Roman's name, their love for their father was more important than seeking vengeance to salve my wounded pride.

"Put Gemma on the phone, please, sweetheart," I said. "I'll call you back again tomorrow, okay? I'm pooped."

"Alright, Mom. I love you and miss you so much."

"Miss you and love you, too."

My mother was on the phone in the next beat. "Zenja?"

"Mom, I really don't want to talk about what *you* want to talk about right now," I said before she could get started. "Things aren't like they seem."

"Well, how are they? Because it seems to me—"

"Please, Mom," I said, sternly but with respect. "Is Zariya in the room?"

"No. She went to the kitchen to dig around in the refrigerator, like she always does. You're going to have to keep an eye on her eating habits. You know you went through your chunky phase when you were about that age."

"Do you always have to remind me? I don't need a chubby-girl flashback," I said, easily recalling the years I'd been teased for my chipmunk cheeks and double chin. But the summer that my dad had made Mom stop buying cheese puffs and moon pies for snacks, the fat melted away and revealed a womanly body underneath. The same boys who had hassled me during eighth grade didn't look at me the same during my freshman year of high school.

"But back to the reason I called. Don't let the kids know, but I'm with Roman at the hospital. He was in a car accident, but he's fine. I'm sure they'll send him home tonight."

"Are you sure he's not just lovesick?" Mom teased.

"Bad time for a joke," I said. "And I'm sure that's not the case."

"I'm glad he's alright and that he's home so you can take care of him."

She just had to slip in her clever remarks when she could. First one, then another.

"The sooner he's up and running, the better," she went on. "When the children come home, you all can be one big happy family again. God knows you haven't been the same since he's been gone."

"A matter of opinion," I finally responded. "And you're right, I haven't been the same. I've been better."

"Like you said, a matter of opinion."

Mom dropped the subject and started giving me her weekly briefing on both her and Dad's sides of the family. In the meantime, I went back to the deli area and bought a chicken salad croissant for Roman. I picked up a package of mustard, even though I thought the combination was disgusting. Roman loved mustard on anything made with bread. Then, instead of immediately heading back to his room, I detoured to the front entrance of the hospital.

Outside, it seemed much later than three o'clock with the way the gray rain clouds shielded the sun and skies. The humidity in the air was so thick that it didn't take long for me to perspire. I suffered in silence while Mom complained about the pile of dirty socks that Dad kept in the corner on his side of the bed. Same story, different day. Daddy's socks hadn't made it to the hamper in forty-five years.

Mom still would've been complaining about Dad's habit for another five minutes if a phone number with a Charlotte area code hadn't popped up on my screen. *Lance*. I rushed her off the line with a promise to update her on Roman and me the next time I called back. It worked.

I switched calls. "You just couldn't wait, could you?"

"No, I couldn't. I want to see you tomorrow."

"Tomorrow?" Surprisingly, I panicked. I hadn't thought about Lance popping in to spend time with me so soon. Where could we go? I knew too many people—teachers, students, parents, families, church members—to be frolicking around town with another man. Word would spread fast.

"I had some good news when I got home," Lance went on. "That business partner I was telling you about found an existing gym that he's going to buy out, and he's looking for some hands-on investors. I'm going for it. I know a good opportunity when I see one, so I'm driving up tomorrow to check it out."

"Shouldn't you be conducting business instead of worrying about seeing me?" I said, trying to postpone our visit for at least another two weeks.

"My man wants to assess my personal training style and fitness knowledge, and I was hoping you could help me demonstrate my skills."

I looked down at my stomach bulge. "Don't you think you need someone who's already in shape?"

"He's checking out my skills, not your physique," Lance said. "Even though, I have to admit, it would be pretty hard not to get caught up with you."

I walked back inside the hospital when fat raindrops started to pelt my forehead. "You don't have to butter me up—I'll do it," I said, too quickly. Without thinking. "What's your business partner's name?"

"Drew."

*Drew*. Good. I'd never heard of him. Lance gave me the address, and we planned to meet around a quarter to five the next afternoon. At least I'd have time to find something athletic to wear that didn't make me look like a sausage roll. That meant that spandex or anything similar was out of the question.

I stifled a yawn.

"Go to bed. Sleep does the body good," Lance said. "Besides, it's been an adventurous few days." He paused. "And nights."

The memories of our stolen moments and late-night embraces made me feel a twinge of guilt. I brushed it away.

"Hopefully I'll get into bed sometime soon," I said. "It's been drama since I walked in my front door."

"Wanna talk about it?"

"Absolutely not." I didn't want to talk about it, much less face it. But I had to. So, I pushed Lance to the back burner, humbled myself, and sat in the lobby for a few minutes before I took Roman his chicken salad sandwich with the nasty mustard.

# 22

## ROMAN

Roman was hungry, tired, and in pain. Thank God he'd come out of the accident nearly unscathed, but his muscles were beginning to ache. His heart was aching, too—and it wasn't from his heightened blood pressure the nurse had questioned him about. His heart ached for his wife. He wanted to see joy when he looked into Zenja's eyes. Instead, he saw uncertainty.

Roman twisted slowly to his left side, finding that his body had stiffened. The nurse said it was from the sudden impact and assured him that the pain would diminish after a few days. On top of everything else on his plate this summer, he'd have to fit in some visits to his chiropractor. He was past due for adjustments, anyway.

Roman raised the back of the hospital bed until he was sitting upright. He flipped through the local channels, stopping when he saw the weather alert ticker scrolling across the bottom of the screen. They needed to get home before the brunt of the thunderstorms rolled through. Zenja didn't even like being inside the safety of the house during a thunderstorm, much less driving through one. He was ready to go, too. He'd been poked and prodded too many times already. He wanted to get his discharge papers and go home to bed. Their bed. The one in their bedroom. A man could dream, couldn't he?

When he'd left the house, all Roman had wanted to do was give Zenja some space and bring home a meal for her. And now this... Once again, Jewel had wrecked his life.

Zenja would be furious if she knew. Although she'd trashed the card he'd given her, at least she'd found it in her heart to come see about him. That meant something. He'd hold on to what little signs he had.

Roman closed his eyes. He didn't bother opening them when the door clicked open and then shut. He wished the nurses would leave him alone. The tap of high heels approached his bed. Those weren't nurse clogs.

Roman cracked open his eyelids.

*Jewel?* He blinked, sure that the pain medication was causing hallucinations.

Jewel reached out and stroked his forehead with the back of her hand. Roman lifted his arm to smack it away but immediately regretted it as pain seared through his left side.

"Get out," Roman hissed. This woman was in the same hospital as his wife. Was she crazy?

"I heard the accident. I heard everything," Jewel said, her voice shaking. Lines of tension creased her forehead, and her eyes begin to water. "The crash...the commotion... I was listening and calling your name, but you didn't respond. I'm sorry. I shouldn't have been trying to get in touch with you. I just felt like we needed to talk."

"No, you shouldn't have tried to get in touch with me, and no, we don't need to talk. Not now. Not ever. My wife is here. Get out."

Jewel glanced at the door. "I know. I saw her. She's in the lobby talking on the phone."

"So you're a stalker now?"

Jewel looked offended. "No. I'm a concerned friend. I didn't let Zenja see me."

"Don't use my wife's name."

"Well, what would you rather I call her?"

"Nothing. Keep both of our names out of your mouth."

"You're unbelievable, you know that?"

*No, this situation is what's unbelievable,* Roman thought. He wouldn't entertain Jewel with a conversation. The more he gave her, the more she'd try to take.

"You need to leave. And leave now," Roman stated. He carefully maneuvered his legs over the edge of the bed.

"Do you need help?" Jewel offered.

"No. I need you to leave." How had she found his room, anyway? Wasn't there such a thing as patient confidentiality?

There was a quick knock before the door opened. Jewel stepped back. Roman held his breath. A nurse with hair like puffy white cotton balls entered. "I didn't mean to interrupt," she said. "I'm the nurse taking over. I'll be out of your way in just a second." She wrote her name on the dry-erase board on the wall, then rummaged through one of the cabinets for some supplies.

"I apologize again," the nurse said, looking at Jewel. "I didn't know you were Mr. Maxwell's wife. I thought I saw someone else come out of the room. Sometimes these exam room doors all start to look alike."

"My wife? She's not my wife." Roman clenched his fists, then stretched his fingers. His left wrist ached. "And I already asked her to leave. Three times."

The nurse's eyebrows lifted in perfect question marks.

"I didn't say I was his wife," Jewel said, backpedaling. "I said I was looking for his wife."

The nurse shook her head adamantly. "No, that's not what you told me."

"Maybe you misunderstood me," Jewel said.

"No, I didn't." The nurse looked at her with an accusing eye.

Jewel looked at Roman like she expected him to save her. Roman was content to watch the scene unfold.

"I better get going," Jewel said.

"I think that's a good idea," the nurse said, gripping her stethoscope by the earpieces. "Because I can and will call security."

Jewel retreated, but not without slicing Roman with a nasty look. She stomped out the room.

Once Jewel had left, the nurse came over to adjust Roman's pillows. "Do you think I need to call security?" she asked, her eyes wide open. "I don't mind."

"I'm good," Roman said. He held up the remote control by the bedside. "But I'll buzz you if there's a problem."

"You can buzz even if there's not a problem." She winked at Roman. She'd transformed from protective mother hen to cougar in one breath.

Roman smiled. He'd seen his reflection in the mirror—his bruised face; the cuts across his shoulder and neck from the seat belt. His upper body was wrapped like a mummy, but Betty Lowe, RN, didn't seem to care. She was old enough to be his mother, and they both knew it.

"I don't think my wife would appreciate that," Roman joked.

Nurse Lowe propped her hands on her hips. "Neither would my husband," she laughed. "If you think you look bad now, that's nothing compared to how you'd look once John Lowe got ahold of you."

"John doesn't have to worry about me," Roman said, shifting his weight to his right side. "You seem like a handful, and Lord knows I don't need anything else to deal with."

"It's none of my business who comes in this room and why, as long as the safety of you and the other patients isn't compromised," Nurse Lowe said. She paused. "Whatever it is, God will work it out. I'm a living witness. I'm a two-time breast cancer survivor; God delivered my daughter from alcoholism; and my husband pulled through triple-bypass heart surgery. And that's just in the last six years. Can't nobody tell me what God can't do."

Nurse Lowe pulled a notepad out of the pocket of her scrubs and started scribbling something. "All you need is a good Scripture to stand on. Man might lie, but God never will. He holds true to His Word." She tore off the paper and handed it to Roman.

*The Lord will perfect that which concerns me; Your mercy, O Lord, endures forever; do not forsake the works of Your hands.* Psalm 138:8

"I like that," Roman said. "Thank you for letting God use you as a vessel."

"That's why I'm here," Nurse Lowe said. She took the paper from Roman, folded it, and slipped it into his shoe. "You stand on that Scripture. If you ask God for something, and it's in accordance with His Word, He'll do it for you. I can tell you're a man of faith, but sometimes we all need a reminder that God is in control."

Roman had no choice but to believe it. His small request of God right now was that Jewel would make it out of the hospital without crossing paths with Zenja.

Nurse Lowe poured him a glass of water from the plastic pitcher by his bedside. "I promise they'll get you out of here sooner rather than later."

"I hope so. My wife hates storms," he said, glancing at the TV. The thunderstorm warning still flashed across the screen.

"I do, too," she said.

The door opened again, and Roman and Nurse Lowe turned. Zenja entered the room, and Roman heard Nurse Lowe's sigh of relief. If Zenja had seen Jewel, she wasn't showing it. Roman was thankful they hadn't crossed paths today, and he prayed they never would.

# 23

I tried to decipher the expression on Roman's face when I walked into his room. It looked like panic morphed into relief. Strangely, the nurse was looking at me the same way.

"Is everything alright?" I asked. I handed Roman his chicken salad croissant.

"Yeah," he said. He looked at me, glanced at the hospital door, and then eyed me again. "Shaken up. In a little pain."

"Still? Even with the meds?"

"Not as bad as earlier," Roman said, biting the mustard packet open with his teeth. He squeezed every ounce onto his sandwich, then took a bite that was too large for his mouth.

The nurse tiptoed out of the room and closed the door behind her.

"They said we should be able to leave soon," Roman said.

I rolled my eyes. "In hospital terms, that means at least another two hours." There were better things I could be doing with my time. Like sleeping. Or going to my favorite home décor boutique, now that I was $500 richer thanks to Caprice.

"If you want to go, I'll call you when I'm discharged," Roman said, obviously noticing my impatience.

That sounded like the perfect plan—until the meteorologist on Channel 2 interrupted with a weather report. The map of our region was covered in red, orange, and yellow, signifying a line of severe thunderstorms and tornado watches.

I settled into the rock-hard chair in the corner. "No rush now."

Roman adjusted his body to face me. The bruise under his left eye had darkened slightly in the last hour, and the puffiness looked like it was probably sore to the touch. "I hate to put you through all this trouble," he said.

"Lying in the hospital after a car accident is trouble, not going to get a sandwich." Before I knew what came over me, I had stood, walked over to his bedside, and used the tip of my pinkie to press the area under his eye. Roman blinked but didn't grimace. He grabbed my hand, entwined his fingers with mine, and looked at me with a love I knew was real. Again, Roman had asked for forgiveness without saying a word. But when I looked at his face, I didn't see him alone; I saw him *and* her. Had Roman gazed into her eyes in the same way?

I pulled my hand away, grabbed my purse, and dashed out the door, then walked as fast as I could to the bank of elevators. When I reached the lobby, I went from a walk to almost a full run to my car. A steady rhythm of raindrops pounded my forehead as I sloshed through the puddles that had formed in the parking lot. I fumbled around for my keys, pressed "unlock," and yanked open the door. I crumpled into the driver's seat and shed my soggy flip-flops.

My mind was moving too fast, and my body matched its pace. I threw the gear shift in reverse and was so frazzled that I nearly slammed into a silver sports car that was passing by my blind spot. I honked my horn in apology. The car slowed to a crawl, and I prepared myself for a verbal lashing from whoever was behind the tinted windows. After making a brief stop, the car zoomed out of the lot like the driver had something to prove.

The near accident gave me a moment to calm myself down. I pulled back into the parking space and turned off the ignition. I wrung my hands together, not just trying to squeeze out the jitters but to get rid of the warmth that I'd felt from Roman's touch. So quick and unassuming, it had sent more through my body than any of Lance's kisses. I couldn't let Roman touch me again.

I'd wrongly assumed that I had returned home to my bedroom untouched, because last night, I was wrapped up in the comforter *and* the scent of Roman. Undoubtedly, he'd taken the liberty of sleeping in the master bedroom during my trip. I'm convinced that was the reason I dreamed about him all night. The next day, I stayed out of Roman's way as much as I could. I awakened early to fix his meals and iron his clothes so he wouldn't have a reason to ask me for anything. Thankfully, the help he needed was minimal. Most of the morning, he lounged on the living-room couch with the TV remote, a bag of trail mix, a bottle of acetaminophen, and a heating pad within reach. By the afternoon, he seemed bored with channel surfing and apparently felt good enough to go to the garage and set up his keyboard.

"I'm headed out," I told Roman. I'd found him pecking away at the keys with one hand. Even then, he still sounded as good as most keyboardists playing with all ten fingers. "Do you need anything while I'm out?"

"I don't think so. How long will you be?" He surveyed my newly purchased hot pink and navy blue workout attire. He'd been icing the area under his eye for most of the day, so the swelling had diminished significantly. Still, I couldn't quite tell if he was squinting from pain or from assessing my outfit.

"I'm not sure. I'm going for some exercise. My day is pretty much open, so I wasn't going to rush back."

"You joined a gym?" Roman asked, eyeing my new tennis shoes.

There was no way I was going to wear a perfectly coordinated outfit with the same pair of shoes I used for doing yard work. I was definitely a gym newbie, and even though I looked the part, I knew I probably couldn't jog from my driveway to the end of the street without suffering cardiac arrest.

"I decided to work with a trainer," I told him. "What can I say? Seeing all those beautiful bodies on the cruise inspired me."

"Is Caprice going with you?" Roman asked, now seeming to find more interest in my schedule for the day than in his instruments.

"No."

"You're going alone?" He tapped the middle C key repeatedly.

"Why all the questions? I'm going to the gym. There's no reason for Caprice to go with me."

"Just wondering."

"Oh." I guess that was it. Funny how the tables had turned. Roman hated being questioned—it was one of his things. Daddy had a thing about piling his dirty socks in the room, and Roman had a thing about feeling like he was under police interrogation.

I grabbed two bottles of water from the extra refrigerator in the garage, then opened the freezer and took out one of the five plastic storage bags filled with ice. I tossed it on the couch beside him.

"So, you have everything you need for now, right?" I confirmed.

"Not everything," Roman said. "I don't have you."

I ignored him because I was too focused on going to see my vacation crush. Reality kept slapping me in the face. I reminded myself again: Cheating was a deal breaker.

In my car, I checked my hair in the review mirror. I'd had to salvage my curls after getting pelted by the rain yesterday, but I didn't want to put in too much effort, only to sweat it out again. I could tell Roman was following my every move, so I let him watch and wonder. I could only imagine what he was thinking when I pulled out my lip liner and lipstick and painted on the perfect mouth.

I tooted my horn good-bye as I set out to meet Lance. I slowed when I noticed Ava's minivan rounding the corner. She rolled down her window and flashed the brightest set of teeth I'd ever seen.

"Hello, chica," she said.

"Love the new 'do. What's up?" I asked, admiring her beautiful bronze tone and exotic look. Even on her "worst day," Ava looked radiant without even trying. And it seemed that the closer she grew to God, the more stunning she looked. God had a way of doing that.

"Thanks," she said, fluffing the sides of her shiny black tresses. She pointed at me. "It looks like we have some catching up to do," Ava said. "Carlos was on your doorstep as soon as he had the chance. You didn't tell me all this was going on."

I shrugged. "That's because I didn't know. You weren't the only one who was surprised."

"The only One who wasn't surprised is God." She looked in the rearview mirror at the ruckus her children were causing in the backseat. "Christopher has made a mess of himself, so I need to get to the house." She tossed her hands in the air. "If it's not one thing, it's another."

I smiled. "It'll get better. Before you know it, Christopher will be sixteen and begging to take his driver's license test so he can take girls on dates. These are the easy times."

"Oh, really? I can't imagine how it could get worse. Jessica is starting to ask questions that I have no idea how to answer," Ava said, seeming relieved about the prospect of getting some things off her chest.

"We'll talk tomorrow morning for sure," I said. "I'll bring over some raspberry zinger tea. We have tons of catching up to do." I waved, then pulled away to head for downtown Greensboro.

Only one day had passed since I'd seen Lance, yet I crossed my fingers and hoped that he still looked as appealing as he had on the cruise. I prayed my eyes and judgment hadn't been influenced by motion sickness, starry nights, and the Bahamian sunlight.

I walked into the warehouse that had been transformed into an intimidating obstacle course. Lance was at the far end of the gym, and as I drew closer, I knew my eyes hadn't deceived me. He was every bit as fine on dry land. Lance grunted through another set of repetitions on a piece of equipment that worked his legs. His lean muscles flexed from his ankles to the tops of his thighs. Dressed in a black tank and gym shorts, he apparently intended to show every muscle he'd worked hard to cultivate.

"Is this going to be a gym or a training base for the military?" I asked, setting my duffel bag on a nearby shelf. I looked around at the weight machines, punching bags, rock climbing walls, and ropes courses. This was exercise at another level.

"Impressive, right?" he said, puffing out his chest like he'd already signed on to join the business. "It's a money maker *and* a body maker."

"All I see is pain," I said, taking a closer look at the contraptions around me.

"That's good, too," Lance said. "Pain is weakness leaving the body."

A man wearing a Nike T-shirt and a pair of baggy gray sweatpants appeared out of nowhere. His shoulders were draped with a bundle of jump ropes, and he carried two small medicine balls under each arm.

"You didn't tell me the lady joining you was going to be this gorgeous," he said. He set down the equipment and held out his hand. "Drew."

"Zenja," I said, wishing he'd wiped his sweaty palm.

"Beautiful name for a beautiful woman," Drew said.

Lance grabbed my waist from behind and propped his chin on my shoulder. "How many times are you going to tell her how beautiful she is?

Can't you come up with some better words? Like 'breathtaking'? 'Stunning'? 'Lovely'?"

Lance's lips brushed against my neck. I elbowed his gut, and he folded slightly. In the dark, in the Bahamas—that was one thing. In the middle of the day, ten miles from my home—that was another.

"We'll hurry this up so you two can get to whatever it is you want to do," Drew said.

"Don't mind him," I said, pulling my shirt down over my backside. "He's misbehaving."

"One of my favorite things to do," Lance said. "But you're right. Let's get to business."

After a brief warm-up, we dove into action. Lance started off with a full body analysis, which included measuring my BMI to find my body fat percentage. He pinched my fatty love handles with a skin fold caliper, assessed my metabolic age, and completed other measurements on his never-ending list. Lance definitely knew his stuff, but I hated to be the guinea pig he used it on.

"This is embarrassing," I whispered when Drew stepped away to answer a call from his son.

"If you want results, you have to know where you're starting from," Lance said, caressing my back.

"Not here," I whispered.

"Then where?" Lance said.

"Nowhere. I'm here to help you show what a phenomenal addition you'd make as a business partner. That's all."

"That's not all," Lance said. "You're here because you wanted to see me. You could've said no just as easily."

Lance was right, and now that I was there, I felt more uncomfortable the longer I stayed. But since I'd committed to the session, I worked the entire time, giving it all that I had. Lance impressed me with his knowledge of all things fitness, and I could tell he'd inked the deal with Drew, too.

"I better get going," I said after a while. I wiped my face and neck with a hand towel. "My body is already starting to ache. You worked out muscles I didn't even know I had."

"There's still more left," Lance said, rubbing the side of my arm.

"You just don't give up, do you?" I asked.

"Not easily," he boasted. "It's not my way." He handed me another bottle of water, since I'd guzzled all mine a long time ago.

I dug around in my duffel bag for my car keys and phone. Roman had called twice, and Kyle had texted me a picture of the graffiti-looking artwork covering his arm cast.

"I really need to go," I said. "When are you headed back to Charlotte?"

"In a couple of hours, unless you give me a reason to stay."

"I can't do that. Not this time," I said. "It's complicated."

Lance walked me to the front of the gym. "Next time?"

"Maybe."

"That's right—you told me you like to be pursued," he said, propping his foot on a stack of exercise mats.

"When the timing is right," I said.

"No time like the present."

"Presently, the only thing I want to do is soak in a warm bath with Epsom salt."

"I can run your bathwater," Lance offered.

"I can handle it," I said, laughing.

Lance walked up to me until he'd pinned me to the wall like a high-school girlfriend against a hallway locker. "Drew's in the office," he whispered with his lips against my hair. "Relax."

My heart pounded in my chest. "I'm hot and sweaty," I said, brushing my wet bangs to the side.

"That's perfect," Lance said.

But that was the problem. It wasn't perfect.

Lance pecked my lips. He waited for me to respond, and when I didn't, he pressed his mouth to mine until I gave way. I tried to recapture those nights on the cruise. Nothing.

I was no better than Roman. I'd already committed adultery in my heart. Until my divorce was finalized, I couldn't let this thing with Lance continue.

"I'm still a married woman," I protested, pushing him off me.

"You were still a married woman on the cruise, but that didn't stop you."

"I was wrong. And confused. I still am."

Lance took a small step backward, but not far enough for me to reclaim my personal space.

"You're scared, and that's okay," he said. "You're a woman with morals, so you feel like you're cheating on your husband. But if you wanted to be with him, you probably could be. If you wanted to remain his wife, I'm sure you would've reconciled by now." He lifted my hand and pressed my palm against his lips. "Take it from me—days without him will get easier. You'll see."

My phone vibrated, and I looked at the screen. It was Roman. How convenient. How like God.

# 24

I walked in the house and dropped my keys on the kitchen counter, glad to be out of the rainy weather. If it wasn't for the fact that I was sticky and sweaty, I would've crawled into my bed and pretended that the rest of the world didn't exist.

I looked out the bay window in the living room. As long as the rain sprinkled peacefully, I was fine. But that wouldn't last. The gray-black clouds looming a few miles away were predicted to bring severe weather in our direction again. Last night, the heaviest thunderstorms had avoided my side of town, and this evening I prayed for another shift of the wind.

Roman strolled into the room. "How was your workout?" He joined me at the window to watch the clouds. Thick. Low. Ominous.

"Excruciating," I said, half lost in thought. I glanced at him. "How are you feeling?"

"Stiff. I forgot to call the chiropractor's office before they closed. I need to get in there before my back starts feeling worse."

"Make sure you keep a record of all your visits," I advised him. "You may need to arrange for them to get reimbursed by the other guy's insurance company. Have the ambulance chasers started calling you yet?"

"Four already. It's amazing how they can track you down."

Roman touched the side of my wet, stringy hair. "Keep this up, and you'll be the same size you were when I met you." He quickly added, "Not that you don't look great now."

I didn't respond much to Roman's attempt at conversation because I didn't trust myself. My emotions were schizophrenic.

He left the window, but I watched his reflection. He picked up a photograph of the family taken on our wedding day. I was about twenty-five pounds thinner, and Roman didn't have half the gray hair he had now. The children gripped us from both sides—Zariya attached to my hip, Kyle clamped to Roman's.

Roman blew the dust off the glass and frame. He looked up and caught me staring at his reflection in the window, so I turned my attention back to the storm clouds, now moving across the sky like a slow oil spill. This would be a nasty one. My grandmother could always sense a storm's approach, even when there were no clouds. There was a change in the air, and the birds always flew in the opposite direction. God, she'd say, was working His business. On days like today, I wished He'd work His business elsewhere.

It hadn't always been this way with me and storms. I'd grown up a latchkey kid two days a week, when there was no one at home to supervise what I watched on television. One day, I was sucked into a television special on tornadoes. One minute, a small town in Mississippi was standing, and the next minute, it was completely flattened. I'd been terrified of storms ever since.

I pulled the curtains closed and decided to head up to my room to shower before the thunder and lightning began.

"I'm going to jump in the shower," I told Roman.

"Would you like me to fix you something to eat?"

"No thanks," I said. "I'll just grab a banana and some yogurt. Missing a meal won't hurt. Since you've noticed my weight gain and all."

"I've noticed it," Roman said, trailing behind me to the bottom of the stairway. "And I've noticed that it's landed in all the right places."

I took my time going up the stairs so that Roman could take in all that he'd put in jeopardy. I knew without looking back that he was watching me ascend every one of the eighteen steps. With each upward move, I wondered why I wished he'd follow me. *Lance. Roman. Lance. Roman.*

I went into my bedroom and turned on the news. Severe thunderstorm and tornado watches were in effect in my county until past midnight, which meant I'd get little sleep. I went into the closet to find my emergency flashlights, then put them under my bed before I took the quickest shower known to man.

~

The thunder boomed so loudly and with such force that it shook the walls of the house. I jolted upright in bed and felt a catch in my neck. I'd dozed off leaning against a stack of pillows, but the pain was nothing compared to my anxiety. The lights flickered once, and before I had time to react, they flashed brightly, the television buzzed, and then everything went black. I crawled off the bed and peeked through the blinds. The rain blew so hard that it swirled across the ground. Roman hadn't brought our garbage can or recycling bin inside, and now they were rolling toward Carlos and Ava's. A limb from the oak tree in the side yard snapped as if God had thumped it with His pinkie finger.

The bedroom door opened, and a wide shaft of white light landed on me. "Are you okay?" Roman asked.

"No, not all," I said with trembling voice. I reached for my flashlight and joined its glow with his.

"Tornado warnings in the county and all around," he said. "One already touched down in Alamance County. Things could calm down before they come this way, but just in case, you better come downstairs."

Roman didn't have to tell me twice. In fact, I was out the door before him, but not before snatching two ultra-cushiony pillows from my bed. I padded down the carpeted steps, guided by my flashlight, even though I could've found my way in pitch blackness.

The thunder shook the house again, and I nearly fell to my knees. Roman grabbed my arm and steadied me until we reached the sunken den area. It was the lowest part of the house.

"Our next home has to have a basement," I said.

As if someone had hit a mute button to the sky, the roaring and howling ceased. The winds had stilled. "This isn't good," I said. "It's not good." Before I finished my sentence, I heard tornado sirens in the distance. The alarm should've sounded in time to give people sufficient notice to take cover, but it hadn't. Soon the siren was drowned out by screeching and grunting unlike anything I'd ever heard before. It sounded like an approaching train, just like people said it did. And there was nothing I could do to stop it.

Roman jerked my arm and pulled me toward the half bath, where we could be better shielded. My feet tumbled over each other as they tried to keep up with his long legs. He pushed me onto the floor, then threw one of my pillows on top of me. I felt the weight of his body land on mine as we balled ourselves up in the space between the toilet and the pedestal sink.

"God, please don't let us die," I cried. I thought about my children and was relieved for once that they weren't in my arms. Two minutes from now, we could be dead. I tried to keep myself from thinking about my death, but I couldn't.

I called on God more in the next thirty seconds than I'd probably ever done over my entire lifetime. A Scripture I'd read recently surfaced in my heart—a promise that God would satisfy me with long life. I pleaded with Him. Forty-two years wasn't long at all.

Roman strapped himself on top of me, but I could still feel the walls breathing. I prayed they wouldn't peel away, leaving us to be thrown through the air like rag dolls. My biggest nightmare was brewing over my house. Somewhere, the tornado was ripping apart houses and, possibly, lives.

In my panic, I hadn't noticed that Roman hadn't moved.

"Roman!" I thought I screamed, but after I said his name again, I realized it had been more of a panicked whisper. I tried lifting my shoulders to rouse him, but he tightened his hold around me.

"Stay down," he yelled. "Stay down."

"Is it over?"

"I love you, Zenja," he said. "Baby, I love you."

"Don't say that," I begged. It sounded too much like the words of a dying man. We couldn't die. Not right now. Not like this. Not when I was feeling the exact same thing. I swallowed the lump in my throat. This moment might be the last chance I had to say those three words to another human being. To Roman.

"I love you," I answered back. I felt the words. And the peace that overtook me when I spoke them was stronger than the fear I felt huddled in the downstairs half bath. I prayed this didn't mean that my days on this earth were almost through.

"I think it's over," Roman said.

"Are you sure?" My body and my voice trembled. I didn't know how much time had passed.

Roman shifted and struggled to his feet. I could tell from his grunts that forcing his body to fit into such a tiny space had exacerbated his pain. He lifted the pillow that had buffered my body, and helped me to my feet. My legs were like gelatin, partly because they'd been folded into a fetal position, partly because Roman had held me with such passion and protection. He held on to me; I held on to him.

"We made it," Roman whispered.

I exhaled long and hard. Never had I been so thankful for the breath in my body. "I thought it was the end," I admitted.

Roman shook his head. "I never thought we'd die. We have too much to live for."

He cracked the bathroom door open, and we both stopped to listen. Silence. Breeze.

"I feel the wind," I said.

"Me, too," Roman said. He opened the door wider, and we cautiously walked out. Glass crunched under our feet, blown in from the broken patio doors. Two of the plants that lived in the shade of the awning were now in the hallway. They were waterlogged and surrounded by muddy potting soil.

I was too stunned to speak. My house had been ransacked by the violent winds, rain, and sleet. I followed Roman through the dirt and damage, wiping tears as I stepped over crumbled pieces of sheetrock. The damage wasn't as harsh as I had expected, but it was still disturbing to see the back end of the house looking as if someone had shaken it up like a snow globe. Two or three days of work from an expert contractor could piece things back together, but I didn't know if that would be the same for the rest of the neighborhood or the city.

"It's not as bad as I thought," Roman said. He picked up one of the outside deck chairs that had blown into the den and landed with one leg in the fireplace. "God is good."

We'd survived.

Distant sirens broke through the quiet of our stunned silence. Roman and I ran for the front door and surveyed the chaos outside.

# 25

My heart wasn't ready. Misery, astonishment, and panic hung over the air like the clouds of doom that had blown through our city. Doors flung open one by one as neighbors ran toward each other, weeping. Before the storm, neighborhood conversations had been about local politics, the weather, the ongoing highway construction on Business 85, or what we used to fertilize our yards. But the tornado had immediately formed us into a tight-knit family.

Our huge oak trees leaned precariously against the power lines the way the frightened wives leaned on their husbands. The men stood tall, trying to be strong, but, like Roman, their emotions were just as disheveled as the women's. The darkness was spotted with the circular glow of flashlights like huge eyes. They beamed in every direction as everyone assessed the destruction. The ferocious funnel cloud had randomly picked which roofs to peel away, what trees to uproot, and whose automobiles to overturn.

My breath caught when I realized just how blessed Roman and I had been. On our end of the street, Carlos and Ava's house had suffered the most destruction. It was nearly flattened, except for the frame on the left side. "God help us all," I whispered. I felt like I would hyperventilate as my hands covered my mouth in disbelief. Besides on TV, I'd never seen such a horrific scene. Witnessing it on a widescreen television was absolutely nothing in comparison to seeing it in living color. I prayed it was the last time I'd experience a disaster of this magnitude.

We'd started to run toward the cul-de-sac when Carlos emerged from the rubble and ruins of his house, his face covered in a mixture of grayish mud, crumbled drywall, and trickling rain. He carried Jessica and Chris in the groove of each arm. The children, clinging to his neck, were shaking and crying, but Carlos's wails drowned them out.

"Ava, Ava, Ava," he pleaded at the sky.

Barbara, our neighbor two doors down, and I ran to Carlos and lifted the children from his arms. He released them reluctantly.

"I tried to protect her," Carlos yelled. His voice held such terror that it sent tremors through my body. "I tried, I tried, but Ava kept yelling for me to protect her babies. She held my leg," he panted. "She tried to hold on."

I looked down at Carlos's bare feet, marred by scratch lines from Ava's nails as she desperately clung to him, trying to save her life. Blood trickled from the streaks of torn flesh.

"We'll find her," I managed to say without breaking down.

Carlos ran in dizzying circles up and down the street until he was back in front of what was left of his house. "Roman!" Carlos screamed. "Help me, my brother."

Despite his own pain, Roman found the strength to help Carlos lift an armoire. Nothing. They hoisted other furniture: a set of kitchen cabinets. Clothes. A section of the stairwell. No Ava.

Carlos sprinted down the street, still calling for his wife. The other men followed suit, walking around tree trunks, hoisting debris, and listening for the slightest response.

We all knew that Ava could be three feet away or three miles away, yet the neighborhood men looked for her with the same resolve and urgency as they would their own wives.

"Let's take the kids inside," I said to Barbara, then started for my house.

"I want my mommy," Jessica squealed.

I pushed her wet hair out of her face and kissed her soiled cheek. I didn't want to tell her that we'd find her mommy. I couldn't bring myself to tell her that we'd see her in a few minutes or that she would be fine. I didn't want to make promises to a seven-year-old that I couldn't keep.

Barbara and I kept the children on the first floor, since I didn't know how stable the upstairs was. It would be difficult for any of us to assess our properties until daybreak. I took a washcloth out of the dryer and dampened it with warm, soapy water in the bathroom. Minutes ago, this very spot had been my fallout shelter. Minutes ago, my friend and confidante had been holding on to her husband for dear life. Now we had no idea where she was.

I let the tears flow freely from my eyes, but I didn't allow the wails that were building up in my chest to escape my mouth.

"I'm going to run upstairs to get some clothes for the kids," I called out to Barbara. I needed a minute to get myself together.

"Be careful," she said.

Upstairs looked untouched, but I wouldn't truly know until morning. I shone my flashlight in front of me as I climbed the stairs to Zariya's room and grabbed two T-shirts from her bottom dresser drawer. I rushed back downstairs to find that Barbara had already peeled off the kids' wet and soiled clothes. I passed her the washcloth, and she wiped their faces, arms, and hands.

I'd never known it was possible to have an entire conversation without saying one word, but that's what Barbara and I did. Our eyes said it all. Our careful attention to Ava's children said even more.

"I want Mommy," Christopher whined.

"I'm hungry," Jessica whispered. "Mommy said she'd make us popcorn after the storm was over."

"Well," I said, standing, "I don't think I have popcorn, but I may have some chips."

Barbara touched my arm. I noticed her eyes were moist now. "I'll find something," she said.

I sensed that she needed a chance to let *her* tears escape. She stepped gingerly around the debris in the living room and made her way down the hall to the kitchen. I heard her open the pantry door. Shortly she returned with chips, a banana, and two juice boxes. We fed the children in a vain attempt to distract them from reality.

"God, help us," I said again. Clearly, those were the only words my mind could put together. *God, let them find Ava. Please let them find Ava.*

Jessica scooted over closer to Chris and wrapped her arm around him. I was used to watching them bicker and tease each other, and this rare display of sisterly love was an encouragement to me as I prayed for a miracle on Whispering Brook Lane.

I went into the front room—out of view and earshot of the children—so I could check the progress of the search party outside. Carlos was nearly inconsolable; Barbara's husband, Stan, and Roman had draped his arms over their shoulders to hold him upright. His grief was overwhelming.

Suddenly a thin shaft of light pushed through the clouds, making everyone stop with the searching to admire God's splendor. It pulled me out onto the front porch, where my gaze followed everyone else's.

I caught my breath at the sight. My prayer shouldn't have been just that Ava would be found. It should've been that she would be found alive.

Ava's lifeless body was draped across Gabe's strong arms. He carried her effortlessly toward the crowd of neighbors, most of whom looked away, as if not wanting to be the first to see her up close. I, however, couldn't bring myself to look anywhere else. As usual, Gabe didn't speak a word, and he never changed the cadence of his gait. He pushed his way through our newly formed family until he reached the place where Roman and Stan had sat Carlos down on the curb. Gabe placed Ava in his outstretched arms and then, in the most compassionate gesture I'd ever seen, kissed the top of Carlos's head.

The wail that had been lodged in my chest passed to Carlos.

The whole neighborhood cried. Ava was gone—her body in her husband's arms, her spirit in God's. That was the only thing that bought me comfort.

I eased back inside the house and closed the door. Ava's children were oblivious that God had called their mother home. They'd never have Ava for another Mother's Day, school play, or soccer practice; she wouldn't be there for their commencement ceremonies or wedding days. I'd never be able to call her for new recipes or ask her to keep an eye on the house while we were out of town. We'd never get to have that conversation over a cup of raspberry zinger tea.

I found Barbara clinging to my living-room curtains. "I don't know what to do," she whispered. She wrung her wrinkled hands so severely, I thought she'd twist the skin right off them. Then she wiped them across her splotchy red face.

"Pray," I answered without a second thought. "It's the only thing we can do at a time like this."

We reached for each other simultaneously, and Barbara's hands trembled in mine as I led us in prayer.

"God, we don't know what to do," I prayed honestly. "We're thankful to be alive, but we've lost a friend; a husband has lost his wife, and two children have lost their mother. You know what we don't know and can see what we can't see. We need peace like never before. We need wisdom like never before. And even when we don't understand Your ways, we have to trust in You. Help us to trust in You. Amen."

"Amen," Barbara sighed.

I kept Jessica and Chris preoccupied with board games and my stash of arts and craft supplies. Jessica was counting out play money when her father rode away with her mother's body in the back of the ambulance. Carlos's brother and sister-in-law picked up the children nearly an hour later, but the shaken couple was so lost in their own grief, I didn't know how they'd handle delivering the news to the children. Jessica had already poured out a barrage of questions that neither Barbara nor I had answered directly.

"You're exhausted," Roman said to me around two o'clock in the morning. Our entire downstairs was lit with candles that I'd stocked in our emergency kit and with battery-powered flashlights from the garage. "You've done all you can do for the night. I've walked around upstairs, and it's safe in the bedroom. Why don't you go to bed? Get some sleep?"

"I don't know if I can sleep."

"Then get some rest."

I propped the broom against the pantry door and took his advice. "Exhausted" wasn't the right word. I lit candles in the bathroom to be able to see enough to wash off before retiring to bed. I reached for my cell phone and tried to find a comfortable position. The chaos had distracted my aching body, but now I was fully aware of every muscle Lance had pushed to the max. I'd missed six cell phone calls from my parents and children, so I called them to calm their fears. I wanted nothing more than to snuggle with Zariya and Kyle, even if that would mean constantly kicking Kyle's cold feet away from me or overlooking Zariya's tendency to grind her teeth at night. I couldn't imagine my life without them, and I especially couldn't imagine their life without me. Yet that was reality for Ava's children. With prayer, love, and help, Jessica and Chris would learn to live without her.

The house was quiet enough for me to follow the movements of Roman and Stan. The men had paired off to work on boarding up broken windows and hanging plastic sheets and tarps across other openings. With Roman's injured wrist and sore left side, I know he was grateful for the help. They went in and out of the garage door several times. As I began to doze off, I heard the pounding, the rustle of plastic, and more pounding.

Deep sleep evaded me. My cell phone still had enough power to last until morning, so I checked it for the time. 3:47. Water ran in the hall bathroom for some time before Roman retreated to the guest room. I curled up on the right side of the bed instead of in the middle, like I'd been doing for almost a year.

I waited and waited some more, but Roman never came. I flipped over on my stomach and caught a cramp in my left calf muscle. I massaged it out until the hallway went completely dark. Roman had blown out the candles in the guest room and turned in for the night.

My heart sank. Tonight I'd told Roman that I loved him, and my heart believed it. But my heart had felt a lot of things in the past that had taken me down the wrong road. My heart could make me do some foolish things, like getting up ten minutes later and walking down the dim hallway carrying a single lit candle.

Roman was lying on his back with his hands folded behind his head. I watched him until my eyes adjusted to the darkness. The room's solar-powered night-light shed a soft amber glow in the room. His eyes were closed, but he must've sensed my presence because he said, "Zenja?"

"Hi," I said.

"Are you okay?" He sat up quickly, like he was ready to tackle whatever assignment I was going to give him. Double-check the downstairs locks? Find the weather radio? But no. There was nothing for him to take care of. Nothing but me.

"I'm fine," I said. "Did you finish up downstairs?"

"We did enough to keep animals from looking for a place to sleep," he said. "It'll be fine until we get going in the morning. I'll head to the hardware store, along with every other person in town."

"I'll go with you," I volunteered. "We'll have to look at replacing the door."

Roman eased onto his right side. "Whatever you want to do," he said. "I can take care of it. It's no problem."

"It's no problem for me, either," I said. "You probably still need to take it easy, so I'll drive."

"That'll work," Roman said, rotating his left shoulder. "I might have gone overboard tonight, but the adrenaline made me push myself. This is like a bad dream."

I took one cautious step into the room, then another, until I was seated on the edge of the bed. "This has been a crazy two days, hasn't it?"

"Tell me about it," Roman agreed. "But plenty of people go through worse. You just have to keep pressing through."

I took a deep breath. "Is that what we're supposed to do? Keep pressing through? I'm talking about *us*," I specified. "Our marriage. Our family."

My question made him more alert. He sat up and joined me on the side of the bed.

"I'm here because I want to keep pressing," Roman said. "I made a decision to love you, and I didn't stay true to the covenant we'd made. I was misled by my feelings, but a person's feelings don't always speak the truth."

"So, when I felt like punching you or running you over with the car, that was all a lie?" I asked.

He chuckled. "A lie if I've ever heard one." He raked his fingers over the top of his hair.

"What about right now, when I feel like I want you to come back to our bed? Are my feelings lying now, too?"

Roman turned toward me and took the candle from my hand. The light danced across the walls, casting our shadows on the ceiling. "Now you're making me rethink my theory," he said. "Sometimes your feelings can shout the truth loud and clear."

At those words, I stood and walked out of the room, knowing he'd follow me.

# 26

## ROMAN

Roman didn't have to wonder whether it was right. When he slid under the covers beside Zenja, he knew that everything he'd prayed for was about to start happening. He nestled in close to her back and rested his hand comfortably in the crook of her hip. Her skin felt softer than he remembered.

He couldn't move too fast. Zenja had invited him to come and sleep in the bed, and evidently that was all she planned on doing. In less than five minutes, her breathing fell into a soft, consistent rhythm. He ran a finger across her shoulder blade.

"Are you hot?" Roman whispered. "It's seems a little warm in here."

"Huh?" she mumbled. "No. It feels fine to me." Zenja adjusted her position so that the soles of her feet were against his legs. "Take some of your covers off."

There was no way he was getting out from under these covers. He'd drench the bed in sweat before he did that. He wanted his body to be as close to hers as possible. He wanted their bodies to be one.

"It's probably because I was working downstairs," he said.

"Probably," Zenja said drowsily. "Maybe the power company will have our neighborhood up and running by morning."

Tonight reminded Roman of the late-night pillow talks they used to have, murmuring back and forth until one of them drifted off. But right now, he didn't want to sleep; he only wished Zenja didn't want to, either. It was going to be a long night lying beside his wife and not being able to touch her. He tried to push his thoughts elsewhere.

It was the first opportunity he'd had to reflect on the events of the evening. It had taken all that was in him to keep calm when the tornado touched down. His only focus had been keeping Zenja alive, which had happened by God's grace, not his own efforts. Carlos had wanted to do the same thing for Ava, but no amount of human strength could've changed what happened. "I can't believe she's gone," Carlos had whimpered as Roman helped him into the ambulance. "I want her back. I promise I'll treat her right." Then an EMT pulled the doors closed, and the ambulance had driven away in silence, its beacons casting an eerie red glow in the darkness.

All Roman knew was that he would never again say that Kyle's room looked like it had been hit by a tornado. There was absolutely no comparison.

Roman still had his wife, and he planned on it being that way forever. Tonight she'd said the words he'd desperately needed to hear. Ever so softly, Roman brushed his lips over her back. "I love you, too," he whispered again. "Always."

# 27

Roman was making rounds up and down the street to see if any neighbors needed anything while we were out, and I was about to go outside and help him, when Caprice called. The tornado had lost its steam before reaching her side of town, and she listened in amazement as I told her about our harrowing experience.

Most of the families on our street had awakened before us and ventured outside to gather fallen tree limbs or search for mementos that had been carried away by the wind. I could tell that few had slept; if they had, their slumber hadn't been very peaceful. I, on the other hand, had slept like a newborn baby.

"Tell me what I can do to help," Caprice said. "I'll be over as soon as I get showered and dressed."

"No rush right now," I told her. "We're headed out to get some plywood for the doors and windows until we figure out what we're going to do. We still have to call the insurance adjusters and get quotes from the roofing contractors other than the ones riding through the neighborhood like bloodhounds. They smell money."

"I know you're glad Roman was home with you."

"You could never imagine how glad I am," I said. I'd been thinking the same thing all morning. "I pray I never experience anything like that again. Once in a lifetime is enough."

I searched under the sink for a bottle of bleach and some rubber gloves. In the neighborhood wreckage, Roman had found some toys belonging to Jessica and Chris, and he'd brought them to me to clean. "We can repair our homes and replace our things, but we can never replace Ava. This morning I actually picked up the phone to call her."

"Breaks my heart," Caprice said.

"We were supposed to be sipping tea right now while I moaned and complained about Roman coming home," I said. "She was such an encourager. She grew so much in her walk with God in such a short period of time, I'm convicted about letting my faith waver since Roman left."

"Evidently you had a purpose in her life, and she had a purpose in yours," Caprice remarked gently.

Now that it was daytime, I realized how much dirt and grime I'd missed when I attempted to mop the floor last night. The entire space could use some elbow grease, but it would have to wait.

"I'll never forget Gabe walking down the street carrying Ava," I said. Scenes from the previous night kept popping into my head.

"And he still didn't say anything?" Caprice asked.

"Nothing. He appeared like an angel over the horizon without a scuff mark on him."

"It says in Hebrews that sometimes we entertain angels and don't even know it."

"If Gabe's an angel, I'm glad he roams our neighborhood," I said. "And he can bring the rest of his heavenly legion with him, as far as I'm concerned."

"God and your guardian angels were definitely with you last night."

"Maybe they were the ones that made me tell Roman I loved him. Them and fear."

"Whatever's in the heart comes out of the mouth," Caprice reminded me.

"I've never denied loving Roman," I said. "But love alone can't hold a marriage together."

"And why can't it?" Caprice asked. "God is love."

I desperately needed God to be the center string in our threefold cord if I was going to give Roman another chance. I was still fighting my decision. If a man cheated once, wouldn't he do it again? And that's what I asked Caprice.

"Anything's possible," she replied.

I groaned. "That wasn't what I wanted to hear."

"But that's why you have to trust the God *in* your husband. Don't underestimate the power of God and His ability to influence Roman, and don't underestimate your power in praying for him. It's not over until God says it is. Has God told you that it's over?"

I pulled out one of the kitchen bar stools and swept some dirt off the cushion with my hand. "Let's just say I want to keep my options open."

"Options?" Caprice almost exploded. "What are your other options? Or *who*, I guess I should ask."

*Silence.*

"I know you're not talking about that insignificant high-school reunion you had on the cruise. That's a blast from the past, and that's where it should stay."

"You never know," I said. "People reconnect for a reason."

"True," Caprice agreed. "And the only man you need to reconnect with held you in that storm last night, just like he'll hold you through every other turbulent time in your life. Don't be ridiculous. That Lance guy is a distraction."

"Why would you say that?"

"Don't act blind," Caprice said. "Even if you and Roman were to go your separate ways, you're not the kind of woman who runs into the arms of the first man to pay attention to you—at least, I hope not. Yes, he's good-looking. Yes, he has a nice body. But so what? That's just the packaging."

Caprice rarely showed her frustration with me, but I could tell I'd ruffled her feathers. She wasn't the only one frustrated.

"It's not fair that a man can cheat and a woman's supposed to forgive him so easily, like she's lucky to have a man at all. Maybe that's why men do it in the first place—because they know we'll give them another chance."

Caprice let me rant, and I continued until I was in tears. I ripped a paper towel off the roll and pressed it to my eyes. "Vincent never would've cheated on me. He loved me too deeply, the way I *thought* Roman loved me. He wants to come back home without suffering any consequences for what he's done to me or my children."

"Roman's had his own consequences—trust me," Caprice put in before I could say any more. "You may not know what those consequences are, but I'm pretty sure he's had his share of pain, probably more than you could conceive of. He's not the kind of man who can ignore his conscience or fail to face the realization of what he's done to his family."

"Adultery is just cause to divorce your spouse," I said, as if Caprice didn't know Genesis from Revelation. "That's in the Bible, and *that's* what Roman needs to realize."

"The Bible also says that you should forgive a person's offense against you."

"Fine. I can forgive Roman and move on without him." I dried my last tear and tossed the paper towel in the trash. I was tired of crying over the same thing.

"You could."

That was all she said. I was waiting for further explanation, for Caprice to give me a Scripture to refute my claims. But she didn't. That meant one thing: She wasn't going to argue with me about it. Instead, she would take it to God in prayer.

Still holding my phone, I walked out the front door and around to the deck, carefully testing each step to make sure it was secure. The newly potted ivy and the herb garden I'd planted with Zariya over spring break had been overturned. One of the two chipped planters I'd planned to repair and spray-paint by the end of the summer had cracked in half. I assumed that my carefully chosen patio chairs—the ones that hadn't ended up in our living room—were in someone else's yard, along with the custom-sewn cushions Caprice had helped me design. It had taken me forever to find the perfect yellow and teal patterned fabric.

Roman came around the side of the house carrying one of the frames of my patio chairs.

"Hold on a sec," I told Caprice.

"It's dirty," Roman said, holding it up like he'd discovered a treasure, "but it's nothing a good cleaning can't fix. I found the other missing one, too, but I could only carry one at a time."

"Thanks," I said, tucking the phone between my chin and shoulder. Caprice was still silent on the other end, although I could hear Duane talking in the background.

Roman lifted the frame over the railing, and I propped it against the house. He used a hand towel to wipe his brow, then tossed it across his shoulder and stared at me like I was a woman he'd never seen before.

"What?" I asked.

"Nothing. Just looking at my wife." He smiled. "I'll be ready to leave in ten minutes."

Sleeping in our bed had given Roman an extra boost of confidence. I didn't understand how he seemed to have so much energy when he'd spent half the night kissing my shoulder and caressing my hip. He'd waited for me to respond, but I hadn't moved a muscle. I wasn't about to go down that road.

I'd forgotten Caprice was still on the phone until she spoke up. "Call me when you get back," she said. "I know there's something we can do to help out."

"I will, and I'm sorry," I said. "I didn't mean to get snippy with you."

"You're entitled to. You've been through a lot lately. If anybody can take it, I can. You can't run me off that easily."

"And I wouldn't want to," I said. "Do you want to go to the movies tonight? A comedy. I need some laughter in my life right about now."

"Can't," Caprice said. "We have our Friday Night Love event."

"You never finished telling me about it," I said, going back inside to find my tennis shoes.

"It's better if you come see for yourself," Caprice said.

I sighed. "I'll see what I can do. What time does it start?"

"Seven. But don't come alone. It's a couples thing."

"Oh, yeah," I said. I almost declined, but I figured I could put aside my problems with Roman for one night and support Caprice's new ministry. I knew Roman would jump at the chance to go out together, so getting him to agree would be easy.

"You'll have fun," Caprice said. "I promise."

"Promise me you won't make a big deal out of it if Roman and I show up. The divorce decree is still in motion. One night out together isn't going to change that."

"That's because it hasn't been a Friday Night Love," Caprice teased.

"See? That's why I'm not coming," I threatened. I double-tied my shoelaces and pulled a baseball cap low over my disheveled hair.

"Yes, you are," Caprice insisted. "If you come tonight, I'll never beg you to come again. Deal?"

I gave it a moment's thought. "Deal," I said. I could handle one night out with Roman.

# 28

Forget Friday Night Love, I was Friday night tired. Tonight would've been the perfect evening for a supreme pizza with the works (minus the olives), a piece of double-decker chocolate cake, and a romance novel. After working and cleaning all day, my energy was zapped. But friendship was about sacrifice, and I wanted to keep my promise to Caprice. I felt 100 percent better when I emerged from the hot shower. At least, I did until Roman's cell phone started chirping and vibrating with text messages.

It was buried somewhere in the mountain of covers and sheets on the bed. Any other time, I would've made the bed and arranged all the decorative pillows in place, but I refused to lift a finger to clean up one more thing. Roman had been the last person out of bed this morning, and the bed was still exactly as he'd left it. We'd been at home together again for only a few days, and I wasn't about to go back to being his housekeeper.

With every new text message alert, I wanted to prove to myself that I could trust Roman, but by the time the sixth chirp sounded, I was tossing pillows and digging beneath blankets to find his phone. It could've been an urgent matter involving a student, or it could've been Lovie. She could be relentless when she wanted to talk to her precious son.

"I'm almost done," Roman yelled from behind the closed bathroom door. I nearly jumped out of my skin.

"Okay," I answered. "We still have time."

Roman said something else, but it was muffled by the whir of his electric razor. I was familiar with his meticulous grooming routine, and I knew he'd be behind that closed door at least another ten minutes.

Jazz music from one of Roman's compilation CDs joined the sound of his razor. He was in a good mood. He'd casually transferred his toiletry items from the guest bath to the master bathroom. Later on tonight, I'd casually transfer them back again.

Keeping my back toward the bathroom door, I cradled Roman's cell phone low against my stomach in case he made a surprise appearance. As soon as I tapped the sensitive touch screen on his high-tech phone, the list of notifications popped up. There were seven, one of them a Twitter update about the latest scores from his beloved UNC Tar Heels athletic department. The other six were from a number that wasn't identified. I studied the mysterious number and it didn't take long for me to register that I'd seen it before. I knew I'd always remember the last four digits: 2828. It was *her*.

The messages looked cryptic—a jumble of letters that didn't make sense. Maybe it was an accident. I'd received numerous messages from one of the teachers at school whose toddler had gotten ahold of her phone and called or texted whomever he pleased.

I almost brushed off the cryptic messages until I recognized words hidden amid the gibberish: Missinu. I scrolled to the next message and saw another hidden text: Heartbrokenagain. As I studied the last message, I saw yet another: Plzcall.RUokay?

These messages were no accident.

I charged into the bathroom and found Roman a nose-length's distance from the mirror, studying an ingrown hair on his chin. He didn't bother to look in my direction. I gripped his phone, fighting the urge to throw it at him. There were plenty of loose weapons in the bathroom. I could do some serious damage with that razor right now.

Roman stepped back from the mirror, still admiring himself, then took me in from head to toe. I knew the look. He was imagining what was beneath my red wrap dress. At this rate, whatever he'd imagined would have to suffice. No way was I letting him enjoy the real thing.

"Now I remember why I married you," Roman said. "It was those legs that did it to me."

I rolled my eyes, but Roman didn't notice.

"Can you edge my hairline up in the back?"

"You don't want me holding that razor right now. Trust me," I said through clenched teeth. I threw the phone at him, and he caught it with his free hand. Quick reflexes. I should've hurled it at his head, but I didn't want to destroy the evidence.

"Is it Amir again? He's been blowing up my phone since yesterday." Roman set the phone on a towel he'd draped over the sink basin. "He wants to borrow two hundred dollars. Not happening. He still owes me a hundred seventy-five that I know I'll never get back."

The last thing on my mind was the money we'd loaned to *his* family members over the years but had never recuperated. Neither that money nor anybody else's could pay for my peace of mind.

I picked up Roman's phone and handed it to him again.

"What?" he asked, deep lines of confusion furrowing his forehead. His jaw tightened when he saw what I'd seen. He shook his head, then set the phone down as nonchalantly as if he'd just read the weather report. "Nothing to worry about, sweetheart." He spread some sort of cream around the fading bruise under his left eye.

"Is it who I think it is?"

"Yes."

"Then why are you trying to hide the number from me?"

"I'm not trying to hide the number. I purposely deleted the name from my contacts list months ago because I had no intention of keeping in touch. I can't control what other people do."

I propped my hands on my hips. "You can if you change your number."

"Do you know how long I've had that number? Over ten years. People who need me wouldn't be able to reach me."

"And neither would people who *don't* need to reach you."

"We're forgetting the past, remember?" Roman said.

He was pulling words out of the sky. He couldn't try to pacify me with some impromptu sermon. "No, I don't remember that conversation," I said, "but if you *forget* everything about the past, you might *repeat* it. And I wish some things in the past had never happened." My voice was louder than I'd intended it to be, especially with the acoustics in the bathroom. I took a breath and started again. "It's something I can't easily forget. It will probably always be buried in the back of my mind somewhere, and things like unsolicited text messages will always bring it up again."

"Sooner or later, she'll give up when she realizes I'm not going to respond," Roman said.

"Oh, so this has been an ongoing issue?"

"It's happened before. But it's not an issue."

"Maybe not to you, but it is to me," I said. This conversation was making my heartbeat pulse in my neck. Roman was avoiding eye contact. He was so easy to read.

"What is it?" I demanded. "What else happened?"

"Don't make something out of nothing."

I picked up his phone once more and hit *Call back*. "If you don't want to tell me, I'll find out for myself."

He tried to pull the phone from my hand, but my fury must have increased my strength.

"Don't do it, Zenja," Roman pleaded.

I could tell he was trying to keep his voice calm in an effort to avoid infuriating me further. I ignored him. I'd never been a troublemaker, always a peacemaker. But *she* was pulling something out of me that I didn't like.

"Hello?" her voice rang out.

"Is there a reason you're texting my husband?"

Silence.

"I'm reading your cryptic messages, and frankly, it's pathetic."

Roman tried to take the phone again, but I blocked him with my elbow.

"I think you have the wrong number," she said pleasantly.

"No, I have the right *number*, but you've got the wrong *woman*. I suggest you—"

Roman stripped the phone from my hand and ended the call. "Don't reduce yourself to that, Zenja. You're not that kind of woman."

"Well, what kind of woman was I that you couldn't stay faithful?" I screamed.

"It had nothing to do with you as a woman and everything to do with me as a man." Roman shook his head. "Don't let her put a damper on our night together. Don't give her that power."

"Then why are you keeping notes and cards from her?"

Roman looked genuinely confused. Either that, or he was a better actor that I'd thought.

"Yes, I was a snoop," I confessed. "I found a note in one of your bins."

He turned on the hot water and dropped his washcloth in the sink. "Whatever you're talking about, I didn't keep it on purpose. It must've gotten mixed up with some other papers. I'm sorry you had to see it."

"You owe me the truth, Roman."

"That is the truth, Zenja." He wrung out the washcloth and pressed it against his freshly shaven skin, then picked up his cell phone and powered it off, as if that was going to solve our problems. He finished his routine and dressed in silence.

"So, you're not going to say anything else?" I asked, trying to remain calm.

"You're going to have to trust me, baby."

I wished he'd stop using pet names with me. I wasn't his sweetheart or his baby.

Roman walked out of the closet carrying his rack of bow ties and laid it on the bed. He pulled one from the clip and tucked it under the collar of his shirt. He was so skilled at tying the perfect knot, he didn't have to use a mirror.

"How do I look?" he asked. He stuffed one hand in his pocket, leaned to the side, and winked at me. Then he tried to pull me into an embrace.

"Stop it," I said. "You're always making light of serious situations."

"I'm not making light of anything," he said. "I'm choosing to have a good night out of the house with you. What's wrong with that?"

"There are plenty of things wrong with what's going on in this house," I complained. I was sure he didn't want me to start naming everything that was less than stellar, but if he pushed me, I would.

A sober expression overtook his features. "Everything aside—our emotions, our problems, all that—we are alive. We lost a friend, and three other people in Greensboro didn't make it. There were injuries, but you don't have a single scratch. Can't you focus on the positive things?"

I hated when Roman was right. The things that I had to be grateful for far outweighed my problems. But he wasn't getting off the hook that easy. He still deserved the silent treatment.

I left the bathroom and grabbed my clutch from the bed. "I'll be waiting downstairs."

# 29

Familiar faces greeted us when we walked through the doors of the country club. Couples we'd met at dinner parties hosted by Caprice and Duane commented on how they missed seeing us. The love was so thick, I practically had to wade through it. I pasted on a happy face and tried to forget how our evening had begun.

When Duane noticed us, he worked his way across the expansive room, picking up a few appetizers along the way. He and Roman slapped hands and bumped shoulders the rough way men do. They whispered words I couldn't hear that made them both crack up. It was unmistakable—they'd missed each other. Duane was the closest thing to a brother that Roman had. I'd wanted Duane to be as angry with Roman as I had been, until he'd opened the Bible and shared a Scripture with me from Galatians. "'*Brothers and sisters, if someone is caught in a sin, you who live by the Spirit should restore that person gently. But watch yourselves, or you also may be tempted,*'" he'd read that night. I'd known I couldn't argue with him, because Caprice was that kind of friend to me.

Duane's expression changed when he finished joshing with Roman and turned to me. "You look tense, Z. Shake it off. We're at Friday Night Love."

I cut my eyes at Roman, wanting Duane to catch the hint.

"Before the night is over, you'll forget about whatever it was that teed you off," Duane continued.

I doubted that, but I wasn't going to say anything to put a damper on the evening. Roman needed his friend, and I desperately needed mine.

"Where's Caprice?" I asked.

"In the restroom cleaning something off her dress."

"I'll go help her," I said.

Duane pointed me in the direction of the ladies' lounge, but before I could walk away, Roman grabbed my hand. He kissed my knuckles one at a time while Duane watched in amusement.

"Oh, you got a kick out of that," I said to Duane.

"There's nothing wrong with a brother showing some romance," Duane said. "We *are* at Friday Night Love."

"And I do love my wife," Roman said. "With everything in me. Sunday through Saturday."

Roman spoke as if we were the only two people in the room. He was trying so hard, and I was acting out so bad. He was right—he couldn't control who called him and when, just as I couldn't control when Lance called. And he did, when I was mere footsteps away from Roman.

"Put down the fork and step away from the table," he teased when I answered.

"Whatever." I sat down on the settee outside the women's lounge to give my feet a rest. It was going to be a long night in these shoes. "There's more to my life than eating."

"How's it going?"

"Pretty good," I admitted. "Still recovering mentally and emotionally from that tornado. The stress of it all stole my appetite."

"Man, I saw that on the news. I headed back to Charlotte not too long after our session was over, and all we had were severe thunderstorms. What was it there? F1? F2?"

I was surprised that Lance had known about the tornado and hadn't bothered to call me until now. *Strike one.* "It was supposedly at the low end of the scale, from what they said on the news," I said. "But I'd hate to see the damage of something higher."

"How's your house? Did it get hit pretty bad?"

"We'll have to get some roof work done and repair the damage to some walls and windows on the back side of the house. The insurance will cover most of it, but we can't really focus on property damage and insurance claims with our neighbor's funeral coming up on Monday morning. The tornado leveled her house and sucked her right out of it."

"Man, I can't imagine," Lance said. "I'm sorry to hear that."

"I still can't wrap my head around it," I said. "I don't think I'll be able to until I see her in the casket."

"I'll be in the area on Monday if you want to get away," Lance suggested. "Are your kids still out of town?"

"Yes."

"Well, why don't you come back to Charlotte with me for the day? Or you can pack a bag and spend the night. You'll probably need the company."

"I can't do that," I said.

"Why?"

"I have personal things to take care of at home, and on top of that, I'm preparing for an educators' conference."

"If I were you, I'd take advantage of not having the kids at home. Once they come back, you won't have the freedom you have now."

"You're right," I agreed, "but I'm still not whisking off to the Queen City. How about if I meet you at the gym on Monday afternoon instead?"

"For work or play?" Lance asked.

"Work," I said. I needed to see how I felt when I saw him. I wanted to know if I'd have the same kind of reaction as I did last time if he tried to kiss me. *When* he tried to kiss me. I half listened to Lance's rambling. He'd dropped the topic of the tornado and was on a rant regarding his job and other entrepreneurial pursuits that I didn't feel like hearing about.

"I'm out with my girlfriend now, but I'll see you in a couple of days," I interrupted him when I realized I'd zoned out of his entire conversation. "If anything changes, I'll give you a call."

"Okay. Monday," Lance said, sounding annoyed that I hadn't let him shine.

"See you then." After ending the call, I powered off my cell phone and went to find Caprice. She was standing at the bathroom sink using a damp paper towel to dab at a reddish blotch on the front of her white strapless sun-dress. She'd cinched her waist with a wide brown braided belt that matched the layers of wooden beads draped around her neck. She could accessorize her outfits as fashionably as she could dress a room.

"Cocktail sauce?" I asked. I took the paper towel from her and squirted on a dab of soap.

"How did you know?"

"Don't you remember how much shrimp I ate on the cruise? I think they're still swimming around in my stomach."

"If they were, I'd probably be able to tell in that dress. You look fabulous."

"I was thinking the same about you, but I feel like a stuffed sausage. I have everything nipped and tucked under here."

Caprice took the paper towel out of my hand and dropped it in the trash, then turned me around so she could adjust my tag and fix the hook and eye closure that I'd meant to have Roman do.

"Just say thank you and accept the compliment," Caprice said.

"Thank you." I had definitely transformed myself, considering I'd been wearing T-shirts and jeans for the past two days. Instead of smelling like bleach and cleaning solution, I gave off my signature scent—Viktor & Rolf Flowerbomb perfume.

In the mirror, I fluffed my hair. It was no longer limp and sweaty but freshly washed and styled in a mass of curls. My ego swelled with self-confidence as I turned around, admiring my reflection. The fluorescent lighting didn't do much for my skin tone, but the rest of me was pretty fabulous. I hadn't worn the dress since last summer, but the 20-percent spandex fabric and perfect-fitting undergarments made all the difference. Without them, I wouldn't have been able to wiggle into it. "No wonder Roman couldn't keep his eyes off me."

"Friday Night Love," Caprice said, twisting her lips into a devious smile. "Who knows? You might get lucky tonight."

"You don't want to go there. I haven't even kissed him, much less thought about any bedroom dancing. I told you that I let him sleep with me last night, but I what didn't tell you is that for the first thirty minutes, he couldn't keep his hands off me."

Caprice's eyes lit up. "And what did you do?"

"Nothing. Lay there like a bump on a log and pretended I was asleep."

We giggled like teenagers.

"You don't have to get physical to be intimate," Caprice said when we'd gotten our snickering under control. She tried readjusting her belt to hide the stain on her dress, but it made it look like she was wearing a crumpled bedsheet. "There are other ways to meet your spouse's needs. The ladies here tonight already had that challenge issued last week, so you'll need to play catch-up and do a double assignment."

"We have assignments, too? Can't wait." I'd spoken sarcastically but with a grin.

When we returned to the main room, more than twenty more couples had arrived, by my estimation. Caprice told me that these events usually drew at least seventy couples, engaged and married alike. We stopped at the appetizer table, and I ate two crab cakes and a veggie shish kebab. There was no way Roman could think about kissing me now, since he was allergic to seafood. I willed myself to pass by the dessert table, with its chocolate éclairs and green apple turnovers. I wanted to recreate Caprice's look, and a belt could hide only so much.

"I'm not feeling this whole challenge thing," I confessed to Caprice. "I've had enough of those over the last year."

"Sweetheart, you already accepted a challenge when you didn't throw Roman and his duffel bag out the door the day he came back." Caprice bumped her shoulder against mine. "You'll have fun and get the chance to be creative."

"I'm an elementary school vice principal. I get to do that all the time."

"Not like this," Caprice said. "You won't regret it."

"At this point, I guess I don't have anything to lose," I said, looking across the room at Roman. He met my gaze.

"Actually, there's plenty to lose," Caprice said. "But we'll talk about that later."

# 30

## ROMAN

*She's so beautiful,* Roman thought as he watched Zenja. No other woman mattered. Once upon a time, he'd claimed that he would be a bachelor for life. He couldn't imagine being tied down to one woman. But time and true love had changed things. Zenja had wrecked everything he'd believed, and now he wouldn't—couldn't—see himself with anyone else. Not his high-school love, Rhonda, or even Sandra, his first serious relationship after college. And definitely not Jewel.

Roman trusted God, but winning Zenja's whole heart again would be a process. When he'd kissed her hand earlier that evening, he'd noticed that she still wasn't wearing her wedding ring. That was alright. He'd change that when the time was right.

He'd also seen her eating crab cakes—which meant he wasn't going to get to taste her sweet lips—while he and Duane were talking with their mutual friend Mack. The three of them had made several trips together to Charlotte for a Carolina Panthers football game. They'd had their share of frank discussions about the pressures and responsibilities of being a man. Mack was the only one of them to have been raised and reared by a father who cared. Roman and Duane had been left to figure it out on their own, and at thirty-eight years old, Roman was still trying to make sense of some things. Being a man wasn't easy—being a husband and father was even harder—but somebody had to do it.

Mack took his prayer life seriously, so much so that he'd started a prayer call line for men at five thirty each weekday morning. It had been going strong for nearly three years now, but Roman hadn't dialed in once.

"I'm going to try and call in twice a week, to start off," Roman told Mack when he'd mentioned the prayer line again.

"Hey. Gotta start somewhere," Mack said. "I'd be happy with once a month."

Mack's wife walked up behind him and slid her arms around his waist. "Excuse me, gentlemen," she said, turning her husband around and gazing up at him. "You've been working overtime all week. It's supposed to be my time tonight."

"I'm coming," he said. "Give me a second."

"I have your plate waiting," she said, then turned to go.

Roman averted his eyes. He wasn't about to watch another man's wife walk away, especially when that man was as robust as Mack. He'd played defensive tackle during college and even did a short professional stint. He stood six feet five inches and weighed a solid 300 pounds. Enough said.

"Duty calls," Mack said, reaching out to shake his Roman's hand. "Good to see you back in the fold, my brother. Seriously."

"Appreciate that. It's good to *be* back," Roman said, and meant it.

Roman and Duane were set to find their own wives when Caprice approached the microphone to corral all the women into a side room marked with a sign that read "For Ladies Only." The room emptied as a flow of skirts, dresses, dangly earrings, and designer purses made their way behind the double doors. Roman took his grumbling stomach to the buffet table, where he piled his plate with flank steak strips and garlic mashed potatoes. He forked on a few pieces of steamed asparagus for good measure. All Zenja's mealtime policies for the children had rubbed off on him, including the rule about having something green on the plate.

"Hey there," Zenja said. "You couldn't wait for me, could you?"

"A man's gotta eat," Roman said. "No telling how long Caprice is going to have you locked in there." He cut a piece of flank steak, and Zenja pulled it off the fork with her fingers. She closed her eyes and chewed slowly, savoring the flavor.

"If you could taste heaven, I bet it would taste like that," Zenja said, accepting another piece of meat off the end of his fork. "I hope we won't be long. That steak is bringing my appetite back."

"I can wait to eat after you're finished in there," Roman said, though he hoped she'd turn down the offer.

"Enjoy yourself." She rested her hand on his bicep.

Roman flexed his muscles. He was sure Zenja hadn't thought much about the touch, if at all, but he wanted her to feel a brick. Roman would join her the next time she worked out. Dr. Morrow had suggested that he participate in activities she enjoyed and spend as much time with her as she would allow. Roman planned to do it all—shower her with attention, love, and gifts.

"Pray for me," Zenja said jokingly.

"I do, baby. Every minute of the day." Roman knew Zenja had been playing, but he wanted her to realize that she was always on his mind, as well as on God's.

Roman watched Zenja cross the room. She looked just as good going as she did coming. Mack's wife didn't have anything on her. When she'd nearly reached the door, Zenja turned back, as if she'd felt his intense stare. She let several other women file into the room ahead of her. Even as each woman passed, Roman never lost sight of Zenja's eyes. He prayed she would see his sincerity, his commitment, and his love. He prayed she would look past his mistakes, past every decision that had caused her pain. He prayed that his renewed commitment to God, his marital counseling sessions, and his new promise of getting up at the crack of dawn to pray would cause the change he wanted in himself—the change Zenja needed to see.

# 31

God, tell me I'm ready for this, I prayed. *What if we're better apart than we are together? What if he cheats again? You're the only One I can depend on. And what about Lance? What if he's a sign that I should move on?*

Roman was still watching me when I ducked inside the room and let the door float closed behind me. I found the seat Caprice had reserved for me in the front row and was surprised to see her sister, Carmela, assisting her up front. Bubbly Carmela was all smiles, as usual, and she looked like a walking flower garden in the *Steel Magnolias*-inspired dress she flaunted. I couldn't have pulled it off without looking ridiculous, but it made her as cute as a Southern belle. The only thing missing was her Southern gentleman.

Carmela looked out across the sea of women, and her eyes lit up. She probably had a box of business cards stashed in the pink and purple gift bag she was carrying. There were plenty of potential new customers for her makeup sales, weight-loss shakes, and knockoff hand bags.

Once Caprice was situated, Carmela slid into the chair behind me. She air-kissed my cheeks, which was a good thing, since I didn't want her ruby red lip gloss smudged on my face. It looked like the long-lasting variety.

"Shouldn't you be someplace where the men are single?" I whispered to her.

"Let me tell you a secret." Carmela leaned in closer and cupped her hand over her mouth to say, "Married women always know about single men who are upright and available. Sometime over these next few weeks, someone is going to think I'm the perfect match for her brother, cousin, brother-in-law, coworker, or son. You wait and see."

Carmela was just as obsessed with getting married as she was with starting new businesses.

"I hope your knight finds you," I said.

"Knights are for women who need rescuing." Carmela snapped her fingers quietly. "This queen needs a king."

I snapped my fingers in response. "Well, alright."

Caprice approached the podium and held up her hands to quiet us down. She was in her element—ministry to women—and her glowing face reflected her passion and purpose. Once the women realized it was time to get things started, the buzz behind me hushed.

"I know you ladies are excited, and I want to get you back out there to your honeys, so I'll make this quick. Of course, I called you in here to give you your challenge for the week. But before I do that, does anyone want to share an experience from this past week?"

One brave soul stood up before any of us could cross our legs or tap our heels. We turned in her direction.

The woman clasped her hands under her chin. "As you all know, our first assignment was to respond to our husband's needs."

*Here we go again*. I groaned, even though most of the ladies around me erupted in applause.

"What's wrong?" Carmela asked.

"Don't mind me," I said, then turned my attention back to the woman.

"For the past few months, my husband has been trying to lose weight," she continued, "but he has a hard time staying away from sweets. I drove his car the other day and found a box of honey buns in the trunk." She tsked. "Can you imagine? I hide shopping bags, and he hides honey buns."

The last time I'd looked in Roman's trunk, I'd found those apartment guides. Honey buns were a minor problem.

"It was evident that he needed help making healthy choices, so I went to the grocery store and bought a bunch of fresh fruit, cut it, and divvied it up among sandwich bags, to make it easy for him to grab and go. Now when he gets hungry or gets ready to go to work, it's there for him. He really appreciated it—and I mean *really*," she said with a swish of her full hips.

Caprice started the applause. "As you can see, there's more than one way to respond to your husband's needs, ladies." Her eyes settled on me. "And sometimes it's the *small* things that mean the most, which is why I have a *little* something I'd like to give out as a door prize."

Carmela sashayed back to the podium with the gift bag and a glass bowl of red ticket stubs. Each of us had received a ticket when we checked in at the front registration table. Carmela shook the bowl and held it over her head so that Caprice could reach inside.

"Tonight's gift goes to..." She pulled one out and looked at it. "The ticket ending in seven-one-six."

I didn't bother searching in my clutch for my ticket. I'd never won anything. Not a raffle, not a silent auction, not even a free sandwich from a fast-food restaurant.

"That ticket has got to be in here somewhere," Caprice said, scanning the crowd. "Again, the last three numbers are seven-one-six."

I felt a tap on my shoulder. "I'm seven-one-five," the lady behind me said. "Weren't you right after me in line? What's your number?"

"Oh," I said absentmindedly. I peeked in my clutch and found the ticket under my lipstick and purse-sized perfume sample.

"That's the number!" The woman poked me excitedly, then stood up. "Over here!" she announced, pointing.

"I promise you all that this wasn't a setup," Caprice said, holding up her right hand like she was being sworn in as a witness at a trial. "That's Zenja, my best friend for life, for those who don't know."

Carmela couldn't stop gushing when she presented me with the gift bag. "You'll love it. Roman will love *me* for it. I picked it out myself."

The other women started chanting for me to reveal what was under the glittery pink tissue paper. For a little theatrics, I held the bag up to my ear and gave it a shake. It was so light that there couldn't be much inside at all. I reached in without looking and pulled out a scanty piece of red lingerie. When Caprice had said a *little* something, that's exactly what she'd meant. I know my deep cocoa skin probably didn't reveal my blush, but I felt the heat rise to my cheeks. The women laughed, whistled, and oohed and aahed.

The tag on the lingerie read "One Size Fits Most." *Most of what?* I mused. *Most of my arm?* That thought alone was hilarious. It was going to take more than an occasional training session with Lance to get the job done.

"Remember to tell Roman he has *me* to thank," Carmela said. She patted herself on the back.

Little did she know, but I planned to ditch the gift bag, fold this number into the size of a postage stamp, and stuff it inside my purse. It would be hidden in the bottom drawer of my armoire, and Roman wouldn't know a thing about it.

Caprice quieted everyone again so she could continue. "This week's challenge is to encourage your husband. Simple as that. Be mindful of the areas where he needs to be uplifted, or maybe even pushed. But don't forget—you're still responding to his needs."

"Are the men getting challenges, too?" I asked Carmela.

"I have no idea," Carmela said. "Duane is in charge of them."

After discussing some Scriptures, hearing several encouraging testimonies, and singing a worship song, we were dismissed to find our husbands again. Before heading out, I followed through with concealing the lingerie in my clutch, then ditched the gift bag in a trash can. I found Roman standing in a corner with his phone pressed to his right ear. He covered his left his ear to muffle the music and other sounds in the room. He didn't notice me stampeding toward him on a mission to find out who was putting such a huge smile on his face—until a group of ladies intercepted me.

"That little number you won was the cutest thing," the first lady said.

"If you don't want it, you can give it to me," the second woman chuckled. "Red is my favorite color."

"I couldn't squeeze an ankle in it, but that doesn't mean I wouldn't try," the third joked.

By the time I was at Roman's side, his cell phone had been shoved in his pocket. "I see the secret meeting is over," he said.

"Who were you talking to?" I asked.

"Nobody important." He grabbed my hand and spun me out onto the dance floor before I could detour the night in the wrong direction again.

Roman held me tightly around the waist, and I fell into the rhythm of his sway. "There are slim pickings left on the buffet," he admitted. "While you ladies were talking, the men were eating."

*That's one way to get me into that miniature lingerie set,* I thought. *Starve me to death.*

"Evidently the caterer left some food at Duane and Caprice's," he added, "so Duane invited us to come over after this and eat."

Eating food at Caprice's house was the least of my concerns. Respond to his needs? Encourage him? If Roman had been talking to *her,* the only house he'd been eating food from was the doghouse.

# 32

Immediately after crossing the threshold at Caprice and Duane's, I changed out of my red wrap dress into a yellow polo shirt and a pair of khaki Capri pants. It was one of the three outfits I still had stowed in their guest room closet. I'd begun keeping clothes there after I put Roman out. For months, the Mowrys' house had been a revolving door for me and my tears. Caprice would sit with me in the den and let me cry, scream, and otherwise vent my sorrow and anger. I'd spent so much time on that deep-cushioned couch, my behind had left a permanent indention.

The den was set apart from the main area of the house, and Caprice used half the space as her prayer room. Instrumental hymns were continually playing in the background, with the volume set just high enough to be heard if the room was quiet. "Amazing Grace," "The Old Rugged Cross," "His Eye Is on the Sparrow"...I found comfort there. The residue of whispered prayers and conversations with God gave the room an unexplainable peace, and I wanted to bask in every drip of it.

"Let's eat outside," Caprice said when I walked downstairs. "Believe it or not, there's a slight breeze."

I followed her out to the patio, where she'd lit the citronella torches encircling the table. Despite her attempts to keep the pests away, a couple of mosquitoes found dinner on my shoulders within a few minutes.

"So, what did you think about tonight?" she asked, leaning back in her chair. It was probably the first time she'd been off her feet all night.

I rubbed the itchy bumps on my arms. "Which part? The part where we were late because I almost didn't come? Or the part where I won that skimpy piece of lingerie? Besides those two things, I really enjoyed myself."

"Wait a minute. Rewind." Caprice paused in cutting her piece of flank steak. "What do you mean, you almost didn't come?"

"Roman received a few text messages from 'you know who.' She was sending these cryptic notes, saying things like she missed him and that she was heartbroken. Roman acted like it wasn't a big deal, so I called her back."

"You didn't!" Caprice stared at me in disbelief. Yet that was something she would've pulled as a college sophomore, when she'd gotten her heart broken umpteen times by Kelvin, her on-again, off-again boyfriend. I knew—I'd seen it with my own eyes. Slashed tires. A smashed window. An argument with another girl at a party on campus. Back then, *revenge* had been Caprice's middle name. But God had changed her and given her a husband who loved as hard as she did.

"I did," I affirmed. "And she tried to pretend like I'd called the wrong number."

"And what did Roman say?" Caprice had lost all interest in her meal.

"He hung up before I had the chance to say what I really wanted, which is probably for the best. Then he told me to ignore her and the text messages because she didn't mean anything to him."

"Believe him," Caprice said. She twisted the top off a bottle of steak sauce and shook a few splashes on her plate.

How could she say those two words so matter-of-factly? So easily?

"I feel where you're coming from, but I don't expect you to understand," I told Caprice. "His phone is still an open line of communication, and he refuses to change his number. He claims that nobody would be able to contact him. As far as I'm concerned, that's a good thing."

"I will agree with you on that," Caprice said. "But it's not going to help if you constantly harp on him about it. No matter how you dress it up, most men don't like being told what to do. We're their wives, not their mamas."

"How about I strongly *encourage* him to do the right thing?" I said. "This week's challenge is right on time."

"Your strong encouragement will sound like nagging to him. If you really want to convince him, wear that new nightie. He'll throw his cell phone out the window and run over it with the car."

"I bet he would," I mused.

We ate in silence for a while, serenaded only by the crickets, cicadas, and frogs in the wooded area behind Caprice's home.

"Knowing all that you know," I finally said, "you honestly think I should give Roman another chance? I'm serious. I need straight talk. No holier-than-thou stuff."

"Yes," Caprice said without hesitation.

"I was prepared to move on without him. I'd mentally prepared to be a single mother and a divorcee."

"Well then, prepare for something different," Caprice said. "Prepare to let God use your marriage for His glory."

I sighed. "That sounds so promising when you're not actually living it. Everyone talks about being in the fire and coming out as pure gold, but no one tells you how hot the fire can get. It's easy to shout 'Hallelujah' when it's someone else's testimony and not your own."

"Proverbs three, verses five and six," Caprice said. "Trust in the Lord with all your heart and lean not on your own understanding. In all your ways acknowledge Him, and He will direct your paths." She reached across the table for my hand. "Roman has been rebuilding his faith and relationship with God even before he took a step back into your house. He's been talking to Duane for a few months, and even though my husband has never shared their private conversations with me, I've picked up on things here and there. Let's just that when I'm lying in bed with my eyes closed, I'm not necessarily asleep. I couldn't tell you at the time because I didn't want you to shut down before God had a chance to speak to your heart. The last thing I wanted to do is get in God's way."

"What if we don't work?" I reasoned.

"What if you do?" Caprice retorted. "But that's not to say it's going to be easy. This crumbling of your marriage didn't just start when Roman had an affair."

Every time I heard that word, I had to catch my breath. *Affair.* It was the brutal, honest truth.

Caprice squeezed my hand before letting go. "I believe in God. I believe in marriage. I believe in you."

"I should've agreed to go to marital counseling when he wanted me to." I regretted the times I'd ignored and even scoffed at Roman's suggestion. "Things never would've gotten this bad." There was more. More that I was fighting with inside. "And it's been only seven days since he came back. *Seven days,* Caprice, and I'm about to let this man back into my life. What will people say?"

"What people?" Caprice asked. "First of all, very few people knew that you were separated in the first place. And, second, if they did know, who cares what they think? Do they have to live your life? No. You can't let people push their opinions into God's plan for your life. Whether it's been seven days or seven years, God has the final say."

Caprice looked over her shoulder into the house. We watched through the patio doors as Roman and Duane returned to the kitchen.

"You can't say a word," Caprice made me promise, "but Roman started going to marital counseling on his own. I probably shouldn't be telling you, but I want you to see how committed he is to your marriage. For almost three months now, he's been meeting with Dr. Morrow, one of the pastors at our church."

My heart fluttered looking at Roman. *Forgive. Restore.* The words I'd heard on the veranda the first day of my cruise popped in my mind again. I knew God was speaking to me. Tears brimmed in my eyes and slid slowly down my cheek. Before they could fall off my chin, Caprice continued.

"Your marriage is worth it," she said, turning me toward her. "Don't let *her* win. God can turn even the most hopeless-looking situation around. You know that for a fact."

I definitely did.

Hopelessness had pulled me into its claws after Vincent had died. It began with a glass of wine every night after Kyle and Zariya were finally in bed. After three months, life returned to normal for everyone except us. People no longer called to see how we were doing, to say they were bringing us dinner, or to offer to take the children to the park so I could have some time alone.

The silence at night tortured me. I was a widow. I was alone with my thoughts, living in a home with unwashed baby bottles in the sink, plastic building blocks strewn across the floor, and a closet full of Vincent's clothes.

Vincent had died on the seventeenth, and the seventeenth of every month haunted me. Six months after his death to the day, I was a walking zombie because I'd been operating on little sleep and even less food. One evening, I rushed home to my bottle of red wine. Caprice had picked up

Zariya from school and would take care of her dinner. I didn't need anything to eat. All I wanted was wine and sleep. I parked the car in the garage, went inside my condo, turned on the soap operas I'd recorded, and drank a glass of wine. One glass soon turned into the entire bottle. I was dreaming of my wedding day when the phone woke me up.

"You sound sleepy," Caprice said. "I was going to bring Zariya home, but maybe I should keep her until tomorrow. She has clothes here, so it's no problem."

"P-perfect," I stammered.

"How's Kyle?"

"Hmmmm…?" I was drowsy and drunk, fighting to feel alert, or to at least sound like it.

"Kyle," Caprice repeated. "Is he already down for the night?"

My flailing arms knocked the empty wine bottle and stem glass off the end table. The playpen in the middle of the floor. *Empty*. The swing where he liked to be rocked to sleep. *Empty*.

"Oh, God!" I screamed. I threw open the door to the garage with such force that the knob busted the drywall. Panicked, I ran around to the back passenger door and fumbled to get the harness of Kyle's car seat unbuckled. His face was dripping with sweat, but his shrill screams were music to my ears. At least he was alive. Hungry, scared, and as confused as a five-month-old could be, but alive.

"My baby! I'm so sorry. Mommy's sorry," I said, bouncing Kyle in my arms. I ran my fingers through his head of sweaty curls and kissed him over and over. I didn't realize how tightly I was holding him until he started to whine. "Shhhh…shh…shhhhh…" The sound calmed both of us. I made Kyle a bottle, and he sucked at the nipple ferociously. His brown eyes looked at me like I'd saved him, even though I'd been the one who'd put him in danger.

God had immediately taken the taste and the desire for alcohol out of my mouth that Tuesday evening while I stood in the kitchen. I had promised both Him and Kyle never to drink again.

Yes, I knew what God could do.

Duane slid the patio door open. "We figured y'all would be missing us by now," he said. "Mind if we join you, or is this one of those ladies-only sessions that we need to stay clear of?"

"We'll come in," Caprice said, standing up. "These torches aren't keeping the bugs off us anyway."

"How much do I owe you for this counseling session?" I asked Caprice as I helped her collect our half-eaten meals to carry inside.

"The greatest thing you can do for me is put in the work," Caprice said. "Faith without works is dead."

# 33

## ROMAN

On Friday night, Duane had given Roman and the other men bookmark-sized cards to tuck inside their wallets and two others to keep somewhere they would see them often. Roman taped one to his keyboard and kept the other in his Bible. He'd made it a point to place it on the same page as Ephesians 5, the Scripture passage he'd been studying for the last month or so. He'd read the verses himself and heard them preached from the pulpit by more than one minister, but he couldn't say he'd actually practiced them in his life. That was how Roman knew Friday Night Love was a godsend.

In the kitchen on Sunday morning, Roman set the coffeemaker to brew two cups of hazelnut. Zenja would be up soon. She wasn't a late sleeper. Roman was usually the last person in the house to get up on weekends, but he hadn't been able to sleep much lately. There was too much on his mind to keep him awake, even when his body was tired. House repairs. Insurance adjusters. Car shopping. The call he'd received Friday night about joining a band. Ava's funeral tomorrow morning. Zenja. His marriage. His children. After that first night in the bed together, she'd banished him back to the guest room, and he'd found his deodorant, razor, and toothbrush on the basin in the hall bathroom. Clearly, she wasn't ready. All Roman could do now was wait patiently.

Every morning around four, God spoke to him during his prayer time. He'd been studying and praying the first chapter of James, especially verses 2 through 4: *"My brethren, count it all joy when you fall into various trials, knowing that the testing of your faith produces patience. But let patience have its perfect work, that you may be perfect and complete, lacking nothing."*

Roman wanted his marriage to be whole. His prayer wasn't even that it be returned to the way it was before. He was done with the ordinary, because his God was extraordinary. The more he prayed for Zenja, the more he saw his wife through God's eyes. She was a woman to be protected, loved, and spoiled.

"Morning," Zenja said, her voice low and still groggy from sleep. She shuffled across the kitchen floor in her bare feet and noticed the coffeemaker percolating. "Oh, good. I could use a pick-me-up."

Her feet and ankles were the only parts of her body that Roman could see. She'd wrapped herself in a long silk robe and tied it so tight that there was no chance the belt would slip loose. Too bad for him.

"How did you sleep?" Roman asked.

"So-so," Zenja said, sitting on a bar stool. "Thinking about Ava."

"Me, too." Roman walked over to her and gave her a one-armed embrace. Her head fell against his chest, and he softly pressed his hand against her cheek, wanting her to stay there as long as possible.

"You're going to the funeral, right?" she asked him.

"Yes."

"Good. I know how you dislike funerals."

"Dislike" wasn't a strong enough word. Roman detested everything about them, from the distinct smell shared by every funeral home to the depressing music to the coffin displayed at the front of the church.

Zenja lifted her head and massaged the bridge of her nose. "I'm going to church this morning."

Roman had been thinking the same thing. He wanted to walk inside with her, hand in hand. He hadn't attended their home church in such a long time, but there were some places where a person was always welcome.

"I'll go with you," Roman said, suddenly more energized. He pulled two coffee mugs from the cabinet and filled one for Zenja. "If you want to go ahead and get ready, I'll cook breakfast."

"You? *Cook* breakfast?"

Roman swung open the refrigerator door and started pulling out eggs, onions, green peppers, and cheese. "My famous omelets. When's the last time you had one?"

"It's been forever. I forget why you call them 'famous' in the first place."

"After breakfast, you'll remember," Roman said, dribbling some olive oil into the skillet he'd set on the stovetop. Zenja was watching his every move, but he continued with his morning chef duties like he didn't notice. When he cracked the first egg, she picked up her mug and swept upstairs.

"Oh yes, she's definitely mine again," Roman whispered to himself, whistling as he worked. When he'd cooked her omelet to five-star perfection, he put it on a breakfast tray, along with a glass of cranberry juice, and carried it to their bedroom.

Zenja walked out of the bathroom. "Room service? I could get used to this." She sat on the edge of the bed, accepted the tray from Roman, and forked a piece of fluffy yellow omelet into her mouth. "This is delicious," she moaned.

"I'll make you an omelet every day for the rest of my life if it'll make you happy," he said.

Zenja sipped her juice. "I'll be happy until my cholesterol climbs dangerously high," she said.

"Okay, maybe you're right," Roman chuckled. "Let me think of another promise and get back to you."

"I can only imagine what you'll come up with."

Within an hour, Roman was dressed and in the car, headed for the church he and Zenja had started attending together nearly five years earlier.

"Looks like they've done some renovations," Zenja remarked as they turned into the parking lot. A new high-tech sign featuring church events and worship services had replaced the old billboard of slide-in letters, which had needed to be updated every weekend by one of the assistant pastors.

"So, you haven't been here, either?" Roman asked.

"I couldn't. For one thing, I didn't know if you'd show up, but mostly I didn't want to field any questions from nosy folks. People act concerned, but really they just want to be in your business. Some Sundays, we'd go to Caprice's church, and other Sundays I'd take the kids to the church around the corner from the house. But it's good to be home."

"It seems more crowded, too," Roman observed. "That's a good thing."

"Well, Pastor Hunter did initiate that street evangelism team some time ago. It seems to be working."

The parking attendant held up a hand to stop Roman while he directed another line of waiting cars into the side parking lot. Roman reached over and put his hand on top of Zenja's.

"This feels right, doesn't it?" he said, with all sincerity. "The day I lowered the last of my boxes in the trunk and drove away, I wasn't sure if this could happen. I'm glad God doesn't see things the way I do."

Zenja lowered her head. "Honestly, one day, I feel like we can work it out, and the next day I feel like you don't deserve me." She massaged his palm with her thumb, as if to soften the blow of her words.

Roman still felt like he'd been punched in the gut. "I can respect that."

"All we can do is take it one day at a time," she said, not looking up. With her other hand, she fingered the pages of her Bible.

Roman freed his hand from hers and touched the cover of her Bible. "This is how we're going to make it," he said. "We can get back in the Word and stay in right relationship with God. I don't know about you, but until about five months ago, I didn't want to hear from anybody, not even God. I should've been running to Him instead of away from Him."

"Me, too," Zenja admitted. "I've never hurt like this before."

"But we have two best friends now," Roman said. "Grace and mercy."

"And Lord knows I need them." Sighing, Zenja leaned back against the headrest.

The parking attendant signaled for Roman to proceed, and he found a spot. Once inside the sanctuary, they selected a seat in the middle section of pews about halfway to the front. The praise and worship leaders played a soft medley of songs while everyone waited for service to begin. Roman glanced over the printed program, then handed it to Zenja.

"They've expanded their ministries," Roman said. "Maybe we can find one we can join together." He adjusted his linen suit jacket and slid over as a lady joined them on the pew. He didn't see her face, only her endless legs, which were barely covered up by her miniskirt—and "mini" was a very accurate word.

Roman turned his attention elsewhere, to the cross suspended above the pulpit. He had a feeling he wouldn't be looking to his left for the entire service. Zenja had been pulled into a conversation with the elderly woman seated beside her. Somehow they'd gotten into a discussion on the educational system, and it just so happened that prior to retiring, she'd taught for twenty years at Zenja's alma mater, Bennett College. Roman closed his eyes so he could enjoy the music and block out everything around him.

A soft tap on his shoulder and a murmured "Excuse me" changed that, even though he tried to pretend he hadn't heard or felt anything.

"Excuse me," the woman said again, "but don't I know you?"

Roman glanced in her direction but didn't maintain eye contact. He knew exactly who she was. "People say I have a familiar face," he said, brushing her off. He reached inside the pocket of his jacket for a handkerchief and pretended he had a sudden urge to wipe his eyes.

"No, no," she said, leaning forward to study Roman's face. She had tilted her body so that her knees pointed in his direction. She picked up one lengthy leg and crossed it over the other. A pointy-toed shoe bobbled in front of him.

Roman pulled at the knot of his bow tie. "I teach at UNC–G," he muttered.

"I don't have any reason to go on campus," she said. "Well, besides to satisfy the occasional craving for one of those delicious hot dogs from Yum-Yum."

"Best hot dogs in town, they say." Roman glanced at his watch. He wished they'd hurry up and start the service. It was five minutes after the hour, but the big screens on either side of the pulpit were still displaying a slide show of announcements.

"What's your name?" she asked.

Roman hesitated. He didn't know another living soul with his name. How could he lie in church? He was already pretending that he didn't know this chick. That was about as close to a lie as he could get without opening his mouth.

"Roman," he mumbled.

The woman snapped her fingers. "Roman. Who could forget a name like that? You dated one of my coworkers for a while. Jewel."

The blood drained from Roman's face. Hearing another woman speak his name must've triggered Zenja's antennae. Though she was still talking to the former professor, she shifted slightly in her seat. That could mean only one thing: One of her ears was tuned in to his conversation.

"Remember?" the woman persisted. "I brought her over to your apartment once when she had to leave her car at the dealership. I'm Alena. Nice to see you again." She slipped her slim hand in his direction.

Roman shook it with little enthusiasm. What was he supposed to say? *"I remember that. Nice to see you again, too. How's Jewel doing?"* No. None of the above. His meeting and exchange with Alena had been brief. He never knew why she'd walked Jewel to his apartment door, anyway.

"You two should get back together," Alena continued. "She came to work with a much better attitude when you were dating. It must be fate that I'm here. You should give her a call."

Roman cleared his throat and faced forward, hoping she would get the hint that he wasn't interested in conversing further, but she nudged his arm.

"So, are you going to call or not?"

"No," Roman answered.

"Why? You make the cutest couple."

Roman didn't find the need to lay out his reasons to a stranger. He could name plenty of them, number one being that he was back with his wife. He just wanted this chick to shut her mouth and mind her own business.

Zenja cleared her throat, folded her arms, and crossed her legs. Now he had two pairs of heeled lethal weapons aimed in his direction.

Then Zenja leaned forward, placed her hand on Roman's knee, and whispered to Alena, "Because he's back with his wife, that's why he's not going to call. Ever. So do me a favor and take that message back to your coworker."

It was the second time this weekend that Roman had seen a more aggressive side of Zenja, and all because she'd been claiming him as her husband. She'd stroked his ego without even knowing it.

"Oh. Um, sorry," Alena stuttered. "Maybe I..."

"Maybe you should find another seat," Zenja finished for her. She pointed a finger up front. "You might enjoy the service more if you sat closer to the front. Way up there. Near the altar. By the cross."

"That's a good idea," Alena said, wasting no time squeezing past four other people who'd joined the row.

Roman reached for Zenja's hand, but this time she wasn't as responsive as she'd been in the car. Her palm felt like a cold lump of clay.

"I'm sorry you had to hear her say those things," he said.

"It's not *her* fault," Zenja said, yanking her hand from his grasp.

One of the ministers approached the podium and asked the congregation to join him in prayer. Roman immediately bowed his head. He needed all the prayer he could get.

~

For Roman, church had been like a stream of water, refreshing him in every way. Despite the rocky start to the service, Zenja had looked just as thirsty for the living water Pastor Hunter had offered.

"That was the perfect way to begin the week," Zenja said as they strolled to the car afterward. Her disposition toward him had softened. "I'm glad we came together."

"So am I," Roman said. "Almost like old times."

"Almost," Zenja agreed. "I felt closer to God today than I have in long time."

"Me, too," Roman said.

He noticed a couple standing a few cars over, waving enthusiastically at him and Zenja. "Do you know them?" Roman asked, his teeth clenched in a wide smile.

"Friday Night Love," Zenja whispered. "But I don't remember their names."

"Don't worry," Roman said, shedding his linen jacket. "They probably don't remember ours, either."

The man approached them, grinning wide enough to show most of his nicely capped white teeth. "Don't tell me—Roman, right? Like in the Bible. Duane pointed you out on Friday, but I never had the chance to come meet you."

"Good memory," Roman said, extending his hand.

"I'm Carey," the man said, "and this is my wife, Waverly."

"This is my wife, Zenja," Roman said. He'd been waiting to do that.

"You won the raffle, right?" Waverly asked Zenja. She winked at Roman. "How did that work out for you?"

Roman raised his eyebrows at Zenja, but her expression revealed nothing. She was, however, quick to change the conversation.

"Wasn't it a nice night?"

"It was," said Waverly. "I have absolutely enjoyed myself to the fullest at those events for the past two weekends." She unclasped her gold dangly earrings from her earlobes and dropped them into her purse. "I can't tell you how much we've grown together in such a short time. God is amazing," she gushed at her husband.

"To say the least," Zenja said.

Roman nodded his head in agreement. He was still wondering what raffle prize Zenja had won.

"We better get going," Carey said. "We just wanted to say hello. I saw you from across the church and thought you looked familiar."

"Well, we've looked familiar to quite a few people this morning," Zenja said.

The sun was bright, and Roman pulled his aviator sunglasses out of his suit jacket pocket. "See you guys next time," he said, hustling Zenja toward the car.

Roman was ready to go. He could already feel the sweat pooling under his armpits, and even though breakfast hadn't been all that long ago, he was famished.

Carey and Waverly strolled off hand in hand, and Zenja started for the driver's side of their car. "I'll drive. I know your wrist is feeling better, but you should still give it a break when you can."

The discomfort was only sporadic now and not nearly as painful—nothing an ibuprofen couldn't handle. "It doesn't hurt right now, but it tends to get stiff if I don't use it much. I think it's fine." Roman flexed the muscles along his left side. His cuts across his chest and lower neck were already starting to heal. His bow tie had only irritated it slightly, but he didn't feel right wearing a suit without his signature accessory. It was like leaving home without a watch.

Roman unlocked the door with the keyless entry, and Zenja slid past him into the driver's seat anyway. She took his coat out of his hands and tossed it in the backseat, along with her purse and Bible. "Give yourself a break. Save those hands for when you actually need them."

Roman chuckled to himself. He could think of plenty of useful ways to employ his hands, and they didn't entail driving.

"I already know where your mind is going," Zenja said. "We just left church. Bring it back to Jesus."

"We're married," Roman said. "That *is* Jesus." He climbed in the passenger door and adjusted the seat until he was almost fully reclined.

"Get comfortable, why don't you?" Zenja said.

Roman stretched his mouth wide in a yawn. "What is it about Sunday afternoons that make people want to take naps?"

"I might get back in the bed myself," Zenja said. "Either that or do some work on the back patio. I'd like to replant some herbs, but maybe I'll wait until Zariya gets home. I still have my five hundred dollars to use that Caprice won singing karaoke on the cruise."

Roman's mind was in their bedroom, where his thoughts had wandered when Zenja had mentioned wanting to go back to bed. Candles. Soft music. Strawberries. If Zenja wanted romance, she'd get it. There were things he wanted to say, but he'd keep them to himself. Then Zenja's last words registered.

"Caprice did *what*? You didn't tell me that. I can't believe you let her do it."

"She talked me into it," Zenja said. "Turned out she was the best performer on the ship. And in exchange for my embarrassment, she agreed to split the prize money with me."

"Wait until Zariya hears this," Roman said. That girl constantly kidded her godmother about her lack of singing skills.

"I miss my babies, but I'm in no rush for them to come home," Roman confessed. "We haven't had much time for just the two of us."

"They have to come back sooner or later," Zenja said.

"Just like you have to tell me what you won in that raffle, sooner or later."

Zenja didn't respond but turned on the radio.

Roman reached up and turned it off again. "What did you win? I'm curious."

"Nothing for you to worry about."

"But something for me to enjoy, evidently. I saw that look what's-her-name gave me."

"Waverly," Zenja reminded him. "And whether you'll enjoy it is a matter of opinion *and* my decision. Besides, I don't think I should let you see my prize until you change your cell phone number. That seems like a fair trade-off."

Zenja had thrown a ball from left field. Roman had thought that conversation was over and done with.

"Oh, so you want to play that game?" he asked. "I can be patient."

He closed his eyes as the car accelerated. Yes, he could be patient because he knew that *when* things happened, it would be worth the wait. Duane had seen the lingerie beforehand—a little red number—and had already hipped Roman to the fact that Zenja had been the lucky recipient. She always looked tasty in red.

# 34

The meteorologist on Channel 8 was mistaken about the imminent rains on Monday morning, and I couldn't have been more grateful. Sunshine greeted the waking city instead. A dreary day would've only deepened the sorrow of the Menendez family.

I'd been numb since yesterday afternoon, when we were stopped at a traffic light beside a minivan identical to Ava's. After church, Roman and I had grabbed lunch at a buffet restaurant, and I'd stuffed myself. When we returned home, I'd retreated to the bedroom. Alone. I knew Roman was concerned about how I was feeling, emotionally, but that wasn't the only reason he'd kept peeking his head inside the bedroom door. Every time, I'd shooed him away, telling him to go about his business. It wasn't about to go down like that. Men could have such a one-track mind despite what else was going on in their world.

The past few days, it had felt more like Ava was out of town for the family's annual vacation at Hilton Head. However, I was reminded of the reality every time I pulled out of my driveway and saw the ruins and rubble that remained of the Menendez house. I missed the squeals from Jessica and Chris that had long been as dependable as the sunrise. Every house on our street was under some type of construction. Brick by brick, shutter by shutter, we'd all been picking up the pieces.

As soon as my eyes opened, I thanked God for allowing me to touch Ava's life, even if in the smallest way. But who was I kidding? There was nothing small about introducing a person to a magnificent God. Over the years, we'd exchanged small tokens of our friendship on birthdays, holidays, and just because. I recalled how she'd told me, barely four months ago, that my leading her to salvation had been the greatest gift of all. I brushed away a tear. Today would be rough.

I rolled over to the middle of the bed. Roman's scent had permeated the sheets again. Sometime during the middle of the night, he'd gotten bold and come to my bed. I'd been too tired to object. As soon as he'd climbed in, I'd scooted over to the edge as far as I could without falling out. And then I'd lodged a barrier between us—the body pillow I usually used to support my back. I hadn't heard him rouse this morning, but the pillow was still in place.

I inhaled as deeply as I could before letting the air seep from my lungs like a balloon being deflated. I couldn't postpone the events of the day, so I dragged myself out of bed and went downstairs to cook breakfast for Roman. The funeral wouldn't start until eleven, but Roman still had to teach Music Theory at eight thirty. The least I could do was return the favor for the omelet he'd impressed me with yesterday morning. I didn't want to heat things up in the bedroom, so the kitchen would have to do for now.

Once downstairs, I could clearly hear the knocking, clanging, and banging of the contractors who'd finally begun work throughout the neighborhood. Across the street, a crew of at least eight men was working to repair a roof and rehang shutters.

I found Roman in the garage, looking like he'd endured a sleepless night. I'd never liked that he used his side of the garage for his man cave, but now he'd given it another makeover. I'd assumed his items were going to be taken to the nearest donation center. I guessed I'd assumed wrong. Two brown winged arm chairs flanked a marred coffee table that sat atop a navy rug with bleach splatters.

It looked too much like apartment #3528, as far as I was concerned. I'd been in Roman's apartment twice—once when Kyle had gotten sick and wanted me to pick him up, and again when Zariya had insisted I come over to help save her botched science project. I recalled how the cords from his cable box, amplifier, and computer had run across the floor like pieces of black licorice spilled out of the box. There'd been several framed photos of him and the children—none of me—on one of the end tables. After seeing that, I'd gone home and removed all the photos of Roman from my bedroom. If it hadn't been for the children, every image of his face would've disappeared entirely from the house.

For the short amount of time that I was at his place, I was uncomfortable. I knew on the days my children weren't there that it was highly probable that *she* was. Initially, my suspicion was based solely on women's intuition. I hadn't noticed any physical evidence of another woman's presence. But on my second visit, I saw air freshener plug-ins in the living room and an aloe vera plant on the windowsill—two things Roman would never buy.

That was the reason this revamped garage setup wouldn't last long.

"I couldn't sleep last night," Roman admitted. "I came out here and started messing around. Thought through some things. I wanted to think about it before I told you, but a guy named Bernard I met on the circuit a few years ago called to see if I would stand in for his regular saxophonist next Friday. He's the one who called me on Friday night. There's a possibility his band will need someone permanent because the man's wife just had twins." He paused. "I want to join the band, but only if you agree."

Music was Roman's passion. He loved just about every style—jazz, the blues, classical, gospel, contemporary, Latina, bluegrass, country music, you name it. Denying him would be selfish on my part.

"I don't want it to be a cause of strife in the family," Roman continued. "If it ever went that far again, I'd walk away without a second thought."

We'd been down this road before, with Roman spending weeknights at practice and weekends traveling and playing at events in the city, in the surrounding Triad area, in Charlotte or Raleigh—wherever a gig popped up. Making music was like breathing to him, but it had suffocated our marriage. Why did he want to come home just to be away again?

But God had handed me a test for this week's challenge, and encouraging Roman meant accepting what came with it.

"What about your wrist?" I asked.

"It'll be fine. I bought a brace to wear." Roman was giving me puppy dog eyes.

"I know it's in your heart to do it," I finally said.

"This time, it'll be different," he assured me. "We'll have Kenneth's daughter from down the street babysit the kids so you can come with me as often as possible."

"She's leaving for college in the fall, remember?" I slid out of my right bedroom slipper and studied my foot like there was nothing more important at the time than touching up the chipped polish on my pinkie toe.

"I'll figure it out," Roman said. "You won't have to worry about it."

It sounded good now, but Roman was a procrastinator. I'd seen the reminder he'd posted for himself on the refrigerator to call his chiropractor. I doubted he'd done that yet, either.

Roman picked up a small cloth and began buffing the sides of his shoes.

"Yes," I said. "Do it."

My blunt response caught Roman off guard. I turned and walked back inside, but I could hear him running after me. He grabbed my waist from behind and picked me up.

"Don't hurt yourself," I warned him.

He kissed the side of my cheek. My shoulder. My forearm, all the way to the tips of my fingers.

I twisted out of his grasp and went to the kitchen, where I put the teakettle on the stove and set the water to boil so I could drink a cup of raspberry zinger tea in honor of Ava. Then I got to work preparing a package of frozen hash browns, sausage, and scrambled eggs. Roman thumbed through his lesson plans and organized the backpack he carried instead of a briefcase. He sat down to join me and surprised me by pouring himself a cup of tea. Roman wasn't a tea drinker. He preferred coffee with enough creamer to make it look like a milkshake.

"Ava's favorite, right?" he asked.

"Yep." I nodded and smiled. I couldn't believe he'd remembered.

Over breakfast, Roman and I reminisced about memories we'd made with Ava and Carlos. It was the happiest moment either of us would have that day.

~

Roman's hand was wrapped so tight around mine that my fingers cramped. He took a step forward, but my grasp pulled him back. I wasn't prepared to walk through the doors of the church and see Ava lying in a coffin. When I finally did, it sucked the breath out of me. My other hand clenched Roman's arm as we walked forward together to view her body.

Ava was absolutely gorgeous. She was dressed in a flowing white dress that looked even more pure against the bronze glow that remained on her skin. Though most of the mourners were dressed in black, navy blue, or gray, the Menendez family wore white. Jessica was dressed in her angel costume from last year's Christmas pageant. She even wore the wings rimmed in silver glitter, and her halo tilted slightly as she rested her head on her grandmother's shoulder. I'd worked with Ava to break Jessica of the habit of sucking her thumb, but now it was shoved securely in her mouth. Chris's face was burrowed under his father's arm, as if he was hiding from the casket and the comforting words of the mourners.

I walked over on wobbly legs to offer my condolences to the family. I knelt down and whispered in Jessica's ear, "You look beautiful."

"I'm dressed like Mommy," she said. "She's an angel now."

"Yes, she is." Tears pooled in the corners of my eyes. Then I reached for Carlos, and he took my hands in his. We hadn't seen him since the night of the tornado, and he looked like he'd aged ten years since then. He kissed my hand and mouthed, "*Thank you.*" I didn't know what he was thanking me for, but I smiled through my grief, then followed Roman to the pew two rows from the back. We sat down, and I rested my head on his chest, the thump-thump of his heart reminding me how blessed we were to be alive.

After an hour of friends and family sharing memories of Ava, the service culminated with the releasing of doves. Roman and I followed the funeral procession to the burial site to honor Ava's final resting place. There were few words between us. We reflected in our own silence, as did most of our neighbors in attendance.

"Hold up." Carlos's voice stopped us as we were stepping through the well-manicured grounds of the memorial garden. The shoulders of his off-white suit jacket were stained with the foundation, mascara, and tears of the women who'd sought solace there or offered sympathetic embraces.

"I wanted to thank you both for how you've supported and encouraged my family," he said. "Zenja, you meant more to my wife than she probably ever told you." He paused, appearing to carefully consider his next words. "I know things weren't the best between you two for a while, but you cared enough to push past your own hurt and listen to my wife. I'm sure she shared some things about me that could've made you look at me in a different light, but you've never treated me like it. She talked more and more about God because of you." His Adam's apple bobbed. "And even though I never really understood or shared her faith, I respected it. Her face—you saw it—was so peaceful. And as much as it hurts not to have her here with me, I do know she's in a better place." Carlos pounded his chest with his fist. "With God, we *will* get through it." He pulled a slip of paper from the inside pocket of his jacket and handed it to me. "I found this in her Bible, and I'll keep it with me for the rest of my life. Jessica can already recite it by memory."

> *Trust in the Lord with all your heart, and lean not on your own understanding; in all your ways acknowledge Him, and He shall direct your paths.*

Carlos's words and the Scripture he'd been holding close to his heart brought me an inconceivable peace. It was the same verse Caprice had shared with me, and I knew it wasn't a coincidence. God wasn't coincidental; He was very strategic.

After a final embrace, a white limousine crept toward us, and Carlos joined his family inside. I'd never seen him so humble. We watched the limo drive away until it was only a white speck in the distance. Other mourners lingered, tossing red and white roses on top of Ava's coffin, but I wanted to keep the rose I'd been handed. I had given Ava her flowers when she was alive—a full bouquet of tulips on Valentine's Day. I thought she would have wanted me to keep this one.

"Do you want to go out for lunch?" Roman asked.

"I'm not really hungry," I said. And I couldn't believe Roman had an appetite. He'd devoured everything on his plate at breakfast, while I hadn't been able to stomach more than a few bites. I looked at my watch. It was one o'clock. "I have another session with my trainer at four," I told him, "but I need to make a couple of conference calls at home first. If you have any other errands to take care of, you might want to do that before I head out."

*Why are you going to see Lance?* I questioned myself. Personal trainers were a dime a dozen. But I had to check just once more. He was the only man I'd been even remotely attracted to during my separation, and I needed to assure myself that I wasn't making an irrational decision to get back with Roman. I'd kissed Lance, for goodness' sake. A lot. He'd held me, and it had felt amazing. Roman had been in an auto accident, and we'd survived a tornado together. Those emotional events might be clouding my judgment. I knew I was acting double-minded, and my emotions were erratic. But after this, I'd know for sure. I hoped.

In the parking lot, the gravel crunched beneath our shoes. "I don't have anything to do that can't wait," Roman said. "Maybe I'll join you. It would be good for me to work start working out. My body probably wouldn't feel so stiff all the time."

"You have to schedule your session in advance," I rushed to say. "Plus, you need to be careful with your wrist if you plan on playing on with the band. I wouldn't do anything that might strain it."

"You're probably right." Roman opened the passenger door, and I slid onto the leather seat that had been baking in the June sun.

Roman was too busy looking at the way my skirt crept up my thighs to question my motives in advising him not to join me at the gym. "That trainer has an easy job on his hands," he said.

"Thanks," I said.

"You know I used to help train the football players in college," Roman said, leaning on the open door.

"Are you having another flashback?" I asked. Roman loved retelling stories from his college days. I'd heard so many tales of extracurricular activities, parties, and band performances that I couldn't understand how he'd graduated with a degree in anything other than socializing.

"Can't a brother have his moment? I still think I could work you out. I *really* could. Really." Roman held the door tightly so that I couldn't pull it shut.

I had a feeling we weren't talking about working out in the same kind of way. Roman never gave up. Never.

# 35

Squats. Lunges. Triceps and bicep curls. My body scolded me for not having done a single exercise since my last session with Lance, unless you counted lifting my fork. Once again, I was starting from square one, but I pressed through. My forty-two-year-old body might never again look like my twenty-two-year-old body, but that didn't mean it couldn't come close.

"I see you mean business," Lance said, standing over me.

I was too exhausted to answer, so I just grunted. I'd hit the floor mat for a few sets of push-ups and abdominal exercises, and he was trying to make small talk. When I was finally able to catch my breath, Lance tossed me two hand towels—one to wipe my face, the other to clean the sweaty mat.

"That workout was brutal," I panted. "What were you trying to do to me? I'm going to be in so much pain tomorrow."

"Don't worry about it. Pain is weakness leaving the body," Lance said, repeating his mantra.

"I know, I know," I huffed. "And all this time, I thought I was pretty strong."

Lance lightly thumped my temple with his fist. "Maybe strong-headed."

"Can't argue with you there." I twisted my torso to one side and then the other, to cool down and stretch my muscles. I was wearing one of those dri-weave shirts that were supposed to pull sweat away from the body. I wouldn't waste my money on another one.

Lance joined me on the mat and led me through a series of stretches. It wasn't right that a grown man was more flexible than me. I wrapped my arms around myself and rubbed all the sore spots around my obliques and lower back.

"Here, let me get that for you." Lance crawled behind me and spread his legs on either side of mine. A knot rose in my throat as his fingers kneaded the top of my neck, across the span of my shoulders, then down the length of my spine. His fingers hit my problem spots with such precision and the perfect amount of pressure. I wanted to ask him if he was certified in massage therapy, too, but when I opened my lips, a moan escaped. I covered my mouth in embarrassment.

"I must be doing something right," Lance said, dropping the strict bark of his trainer voice. "There's more where that came from."

Suddenly his fingertips felt like snakes writhing on my back. I attempted to get up, but my legs didn't cooperate as quickly as I needed them to.

"Take it easy," he said. He placed his hands on either side of my waist to help give me a boost.

"I need to get home," I said, suddenly disoriented and dizzy. I still hadn't eaten, and my body wouldn't let me forget it. Lance twisted the top off a nearby bottle of water and handed it to me. I chugged down half the contents in a single swig.

"Would you like company?" Lance asked, lifting his tank top over his head.

There was nothing good about this. Nothing at all. I headed for my bag. "I already have company," I said.

"Kids back already?"

"Actually, my husband," I said. *Yes, my husband.* I felt an uplifting in my spirit when I said it. I had the answer I needed. God had spoken loud and clear.

Lance caught up to me, having quickly changed into a muscle T-shirt featuring the gym's new logo. "Moving the rest of his things? You seemed down today, but I thought it was only because of the funeral. Now I know why. Going through a divorce is like having the flu. You'll feel worse before you feel better."

"No, actually, Roman has moved his things back in, not out."

"Roman?" I could tell he was musing over his name. "So, he's trying to make a comeback?"

I didn't answer.

"And you're letting him? This is one of those times when being headstrong would work in your favor." Lance tossed the two dirty workout towels in a nearby bin, then zipped his bag shut. The gym was starting to buzz with the after-work crowd. All the flyers and postcards I'd noticed around town were working quickly to build the business. It didn't hurt that Lance's business partner, Drew, had decided to offer a free week of personal training and a 50 percent discount on membership costs for the first three months.

I headed to the front of the gym and swung open the huge steel door. It was final. What God had joined together, no man could separate. I'd allowed Lance to reel me in because he'd given me the slightest bit of attention, and I'd wanted to pay Roman back for what he'd done to me. But now I was the one carrying the regret.

Lance followed me out of the building into the blinding brightness of day. "Don't let him come back," he said. "If he did it once, he'll do it again."

I shielded my eyes and looked up at him. "Do what?"

"Cheat. And you didn't have to tell me, because I know. What other reason would you have to put him out?"

I crossed my arms over my chest. "I came for training, and now I'm getting marital advice?"

"You may have wanted training, but you wanted me, too." Lance bit his bottom lip and looked at me with lustful eyes. A group of women in matching pink bandanas walked by, so he lowered his voice. "I'm speaking from experience. I never thought Treva would do it to me once, much less twice."

Roman cheating on me again was one of my biggest fears.

"You're only giving him another chance to hurt you again," Lance said, drilling home his point. "Why would you do that?"

It didn't make sense to me, either, but since when did love always make sense? Love could be crazy sometimes, yet real love was patient and kind; it kept no record of wrongs. Love never failed. When I didn't understand things, I had no choice but to trust in God.

"It's called forgiveness," I said, refusing to be poisoned by Lance's negativity.

"You'll survive without him," Lance said, popping the latch on the rear door of his SUV. He pulled out a mesh bag of red and black boxing gloves. "Think about yourself for a change. Do you *really* want to be with him?" He let the bag dangle by his feet as he stared at me in the middle of the hot, crumbling asphalt of the warehouse parking lot.

Maybe I couldn't trust Roman 100 percent, but, like Caprice had said, I *could* trust the God in him. I did want to be with my husband, and there was nothing Lance or anyone else could do to change that.

"I really do want to be with him," I said confidently. "You have no choice but to accept my decision. Our time on the cruise may have seemed fun and daring, but it was wrong, Lance. Bottom line. We'll take it for what it was and move on."

"Let me know how you feel next week," he said. "It might be another story by then."

He threw the mesh bag of boxing gloves over his shoulder. If I'd had one of those strapped on my hand, I would've delivered a nice uppercut to his bottom lip.

"Do you have your eating plan?" Lance asked nonchalantly. He didn't believe that our meetings were over.

I patted the side pocket of my bag. Tonight's dinner would be a spinach salad with mixed veggies, although I really wanted to cook my mama's recipe for Crock Pot chili, filled with beans, chunks of cheese, and mounds of sour cream. And I couldn't forget the corn bread. I was an emotional eater, and I was overstuffed with emotions right now.

"I'll wait for your call," Lance said, then headed back for the gym.

I got in my car and headed toward The Fresh Market to buy groceries so I could prepare dinner for me and *my husband*. Lance was in for a long wait.

# 36

## ROMAN

A bush-sized bouquet of peach-colored roses hid the courier's face.

"Delivery for Zenja Maxwell," a young male voice said, mispronouncing her first name.

"Close enough. This is the house." Roman signed the paper on the clipboard, then accepted the flowers, his mind clicking through occasions he might have missed. With such a colossal gift for Zenja in front of him, he didn't even have transportation to go on a hunt for anything comparable. Zenja's birthday wasn't for another two months, and their sixth anniversary had been in February. He'd spent that lonely night watching old Westerns. Unless Zenja had gotten a promotion at work and hadn't told him yet, he'd exhausted the possibilities.

Roman pushed the door closed with his foot and carried the weighty glass vase to the kitchen, where he set it on the table. Whoever had sent it hadn't spared any expense. He stuck his hand in the middle of the bush to search for a card. That's what it was—a bush. How many dozen roses were there? Three? Four?

The note on the card was typewritten: *Hope you can lift these with your sore biceps.*

Before Roman had a chance to wonder further who they were from, the doorbell chimed again. This time, it was two blooming vases of fruit bouquets—pineapples, cantaloupe, honeydew melon, grapes, pineapple slices, and watermelon—all shaped like flowers and surrounded by chocolate-covered strawberries. The card read: *Better than biscuits.*

Roman was no fool. It didn't take long to put two and two together, especially since the third delivery was a basket of marketing items—a baseball cap, a T-shirt, a water bottle, and two wristbands—emblazoned with the fluorescent green and black logo of Warehouse Fitness. He'd never heard of a gym or personal trainer laying out this kind of welcome package for a client. Anger seethed through his body.

*No wonder she wanted to go to the gym alone,* he thought.

Roman was half watching Sports Center, half looking over the teaching outline and assignments for his class when he heard the hum of the garage door almost thirty minutes later. Zenja's supposed training session had started at four o'clock, and it was nearly seven thirty now. It was a moment before Zenja walked inside, her arms full of paper bags spilling over with so many groceries, they blocked her view of all the surprises awaiting her. She eased the bags down on the counter.

"Can you give me a hand?" Zenja called out. "Sorry it's late. I didn't mean to take so long. I was choosing vegetables, and then I got sucked into one of those cooking demonstrations and had to go to several stores to find what I wanted."

Roman followed her back to the garage, and she loaded his arms with three bags.

"You know it was a trick, right?" she went on. "Every one of us watching bought the ingredients to try it at home. And no, I've never cooked a beef and plantain casserole in my life. Who has?"

She picked up a gallon jug of green tea with honey and closed the trunk. She'd returned home happy—too happy for a woman who, hours earlier, had sobbed through an entire funeral. She had yet to notice that Roman hadn't said a word.

Zenja trailed him inside, and when she finally noticed the deliveries, her eyes brightened in surprise. "Roman?" she said. "You've got to be kidding me." She tore the plastic from the fruit bouquets, picked up a skewer of pineapple slices, and took a bite. "Super sweet. Just like I like it." She smacked her lips. "I could've saved some money on fruit at the store if I'd known you did this." She stuffed her face in the flowers next. "And roses? Not my usual tulips, but they're beautiful."

Just like Roman had done, she pushed her way to the center of the arrangement and pulled out the card. Her expression dimmed when she read it.

"Do all the trainers at the gym give their clients this kind of treatment?" Roman finally asked.

"Well, he's an old friend from high school, that's all," Zenja said, suddenly fidgety. She waved it off. "Don't worry about it."

"You never mentioned you were being trained by an old friend," Roman said.

"That's because I didn't see it as a big deal," Zenja said as she started unpacking the grocery bags. She set romaine lettuce, mixed greens, and cucumbers on the counter.

*Rabbit food,* Roman thought.

"It looks like this old friend wants to start something new. Or maybe things aren't so new. I haven't been here. I don't know what's been going on."

Zenja stopped digging in the second bag. "And don't forget why you *weren't* here."

Roman had expected her to say something like that.

"Like I said, it's nothing to worry about anymore," Zenja assured him.

"Anymore?" Roman tried to calm himself.

Silence. The sports commentary on ESPN blared in the background, talking about an upcoming boxing match, of all things. Zenja swung open the refrigerator door and tossed the vegetables in the crisper drawer at the bottom. She was avoiding his questions.

"You could've said something about doing training sessions with your ex," Roman pressed. He'd have to make assumptions to get the answers he wanted, since Zenja wanted to be tight-lipped.

"Ex? Who said anything about him being an ex? I ran into Lance on the cruise, and he mentioned that he was partnering with a guy here in Greensboro to open a gym. I was just trying to show him some support."

*Lance.* Now he had a name. "Is that all you showed him?" Roman asked.

"Roman!" Zenja swung around, her voice rising. "Roman, you really don't want to go there with me."

"High-school friend or not, he wouldn't have done all this, unless there's something more you aren't telling me. And how did he get our address?"

Zenja shrugged her shoulders. "Probably from the waiver forms I had to sign at the gym. He hasn't been to the house, if that's what you're asking. He lives in Charlotte."

Zenja set a recipe card on the counter and started lining up her ingredients. Olive oil. Stewed tomatoes. Yellow onions. She was fumbling, hoping he'd move on to something else, but Roman wanted answers, not dinner.

"What happened on the cruise?" Roman had lowered his voice, having seen Zenja's hand on her hip. The minute he made her angry, she would shut down, and they'd lose ground on all the progress they'd made. He was still trying to work his way out of the twin bed in the guest room.

"Don't ask if you don't want to know," Zenja said.

What did she mean by that? "I want to know." Roman swallowed. He could feel his nostrils flare. He'd hoped that he was overreacting. Evidently not.

"It's been weighing on me since I left the gym," Zenja nearly whispered. "I was trying to figure out how I could tell you, because I want us to be honest with each other. But I don't want you to build a wall to block me out. I'm sorry."

*Why is she apologizing before I know the story?* Roman wondered. This wasn't good at all.

Roman trailed Zenja into the living room. He turned off the television, and they sat on the couch, her at one end, him at the other.

Roman's cell phone rang, but he ignored it, leaving it in its case at his hip. Even when it rang a second, third, and fourth time, he wouldn't pull his eyes from Zenja's. She recounted her time on the cruise with the man who'd had the nerve to send *his* wife gifts at *their* home. There had been kisses. Zenja confessed only because he'd asked. Lots of them, she admitted with pain in her eyes. A day at the beach. Some nights together on the ship. Caprice hadn't known, Zenja assured him.

Roman stopped her. If there was more, he couldn't take it. He was already conjuring images in his mind. He would never know completely how his infidelity had affected his wife, but if the way he felt at hearing about her lips on another man's was an inkling, Zenja had had every right to put him out.

# 37

Maybe you should get that," I said after Roman's cell phone rang for the fifth time. He'd been ignoring it for good reason, but now it was irritating me as much as what I'd said had exasperated him. We needed a break from this entire tense conversation. Anger and agony clouded his eyes and tightened his jaw. He was holding it in, but I knew Roman was ready to blow. He'd wanted the truth, so I'd given it to him. We were both hurting, but I was relieved to be free of the guilt.

"It can wait," Roman said.

"What if it's important?"

"It can wait," he repeated, the veins in his temples pulsing.

I stood and went to the kitchen, glaring at the monstrosity of a flower arrangement on the table. Lance really had some nerve. If we hadn't had that conversation today, I would've been flattered, but this act was downright disrespectful. He knew Roman would see them.

I removed the lid from the garbage can, yanked as many roses as I could from the vase, and stuffed them inside as a shower of peachy petals fell to the floor. I picked up another handful and shoved them in until the sides of the trash bag ripped. Roman came and helped me muscle the bag out of the trash can, then pulled the drawstring closed.

"Can we keep the fruit?" I asked with a slight smile. "It would be a shame to let it go to waste." The last time I'd had pineapple, it had been on a pizza, and my mouth watered just looking at the fresh yellow slices.

Roman unwrapped the cellophane from the other blooming fruit arrangement. He pulled out a skewer and fed me one of the chocolate-covered strawberries, followed by a piece of cantaloupe.

"There's no way those are going in the trash," I said, savoring the sweetness.

Roman tried the pineapple. "You're right," he said. "We'll keep the fruit."

Our conversation ended when I looked into his eyes and repeated two simple but powerful words: "I'm sorry."

"I'm sorry, too," he said. He'd spoken those words to me before, but this time, they didn't have to penetrate a cold, hardened heart.

Then Roman said, "Today, we start over." He put his hands on my shoulders, then slid them down my back until they rested comfortably at my waist. Heat rose through my body. "Zenja, will you be my girlfriend?"

"I'll do better than that," I said. "I'll be your wife." I tilted my head up and rested my chin on his chest. He leaned down and kissed my lips. Pineapple. His lips tasted like sweet, tangy pineapple.

When Roman's cell phone rang for the sixth time, I unclipped it from his belt myself. "It's Lovie," I said. "She's not going to stop calling until you answer."

He slid the phone from my grasp. "Hi, Lovie," he said, pulling another chocolate covered-strawberry from the bloom.

As Roman listened to his mother, the cheerful countenance slipped from his face like a mudslide. He leaned on the counter and covered his face with the span of his hand. I couldn't make out Lovie's actual words, but her voice was high-pitched and frantic.

"Where is Queen?" Roman asked. "Put her on the phone."

I pressed a hand gently to his back, but he didn't respond. That quickly, he'd shut out everything around him. Pop had probably fallen sick again. It seemed his body was breaking down one piece at a time, but he always managed to bounce back. He was a stubborn man.

"Hi, Queen," Roman said. *Pause*. "Yes, I'm okay. Just take care of Lovie." *A long pause*. "We'll be there in the morning."

"*We*"? I thought. *We* didn't have to go to South Carolina. Having access to the car was the least of my concerns. I'd manage to do without it; I could always call Caprice if there was anything I needed.

Roman scooted a chair away from the kitchen table and slumped down in it. His arms fell to his sides. I sat on his knee, lifted his arms, and wrapped them around my body, then pulled his head against my chest and held him. His breathing was heavy.

"Pop died," Roman struggled to say. "He's gone."

The weight of Pop's death settled over our house for the rest of the night. Roman retreated to the garage and his music; he played his keyboard and saxophone and tapped on the single snare drum he owned. He pushed away all my attempts at affection and said he didn't feel like talking. Even though I didn't understand, I accepted the way he needed to grieve, and went upstairs to pack our bags.

"He's pulled himself into a shell," I said to Caprice over the phone as I surveyed Roman's suit options. He had moved most of his clothes back into the master bedroom closet; other than a few extra bow ties, I noticed he hadn't added much to his wardrobe. I couldn't help but look for the bow tie he'd been about to purchase on that fateful day I'd found him with Jewel. I flipped through his collection twice, but it was nowhere to be found.

"Let him do what he needs to do," Caprice said. "He'll talk when he's ready. All you have to do is be there. Respond to his needs. *Encourage* him," she reminded me.

I found a tan suit still wrapped in plastic from the dry cleaners and draped it across the bed. "Being there for Roman is the easy part; it's dealing with Lovie that's going to be the real issue. She's not going to want me there, and I'm not sure how long Roman will want to stay. Personally, I've never been able to tolerate her for more than three days."

I hated that my relationship with my mother-in-law was actually not a relationship at all. Vincent's mother and I had been so alike that we could finish each other's sentences. I talked to her as often as I talked to my own mother, and there'd never been a problem between us. When I'd told her of my plans to remarry, she'd treated Roman with utmost respect. Lovie was the exact opposite. On top of that, she barely acknowledged my children. So, unless she changed her ways, there was only so much she would get from me.

"It's not about you," Caprice said, exactly as I'd expected her to. "Despite all the problems you two have had in the past, this is a woman who has lost her husband, and you know how that feels. She was with him longer than you've been alive. If she's nasty toward you, just pray, grin, and bear it for now. You'll have your day to address it."

"You're right," I said. "Her entire life revolved around him. I'll get through it, no matter how long we're there."

After I had packed our bags and showered, Roman emerged from the garage and came upstairs to the bedroom.

"How do you feel?" I asked, folding down the comforter and sheets on his side of the bed. It felt wrong to send him away to another room.

"Better now," he said. "Thanks for letting me have some time alone."

"I can sleep in the guest room if you'd like more room to stretch out," I offered.

Roman yawned. "Absolutely not. I need you beside me."

"I know you prefer showers, but how about I run you a hot bath?" I suggested.

"That would be nice. Then we can leave first thing in the morning."

"That's fine," I said. "I'm sorry all this is happening. Seems like if it's not one thing, it's another. We've had some rough times since I got home from the cruise. Maybe I brought some bad luck back in my bag."

"Or maybe I had some in my duffel bag," Roman said.

"I've always hated that stupid purple thing," I said, chuckling slightly.

"I guess God trusts us with trouble," Roman said, unzipping his overnight bag to see what I'd packed for him. He added two more pairs of socks and underwear, making it enough for an entire week. I moaned inside.

"We should pray. Together." Roman moved our bags off the bed, then knelt at the footboard. I eased to my knees to join him. Getting down would be easier than getting up. It had been a long time since I'd actually knelt to pray, and I'd forgotten how humbling it was to be in a physical position of surrender to God. With our hands locked, we prayed together for the first time in over a year.

"God, we ask that You would give us strength and wisdom during this time in our lives," Roman began. "You know everything that we've had to face in the past weeks. So much in such a short time. No one can get us through it except You, so we place everything in Your hands. Our home repairs, the Menendez family, the insurance companies' dealings with our house and car, Zariya and Kyle, Lovie."

Roman paused, and I turned my head ever so slightly and peeked out of one eye. Tears were flowing down his face.

"Bless my wife," he said next, sniffling. "Give her everything that her heart desires, and show me how to be the husband You want me to be for her. Let my love speak her language and no one else's. Thank You for giving us another chance. Thank You for giving *me* another chance."

Roman was overcome with emotion, and he covered his face with both hands. He'd been holding in so much, and now it had spilled out. My lips trembled. I thought about what Caprice had said—that he'd been going to marital counseling alone. Roman had laid it all on the line. And he'd done it for me.

My own tears came as I began to pray. "Father, bless my husband. Continue to let him see that You're the Father he always wanted. We thank You for being his friend, confidant, counselor, and protector. And I thank You for molding him into an upstanding man of God. We want to know You more, not just in the bad times but also when things are going good. Show me how to love and respect Roman and how to see him through Your eyes. Forgive and cover our sins between and against each other so we can move forward, in Jesus' name. Amen."

We didn't rush from our places. Once Roman stood, he helped me up and pulled me into his arms so tight that I had to catch my breath.

"I think I'll take that bath now," Roman said when he finally let me go.

I added lavender oil to the bathwater. There was nothing I could do to soothe his inner pain right now, but I could help him relax. I lit the candles that were positioned around the circumference of the tub and turned off all the overhead lights.

Roman shed his clothes, then stepped into the water and eased down until it covered his shoulders. Lights and shadows flickered around the silhouette of his body. I dropped his dirty clothes into the hamper and eased the door closed. My desire for my husband was increasing, and I knew in due time we'd join together again as one. I could feel it in my soul. As I'd knelt beside the bed after our prayer, God had promised me that our marriage would be completely and wholly restored. And God had always kept His promises.

I was in a light slumber when Roman slipped into bed. Even though my back was turned toward him, I could tell he'd been crying again by his sniffles and the way his shortened breaths blew on my shoulders. That night, as the moonlight slipped through our window blinds and an owl hooted outside, I responded to my husband and gave him exactly what he needed—my shoulder to cry on.

# 38

Lovie watched from the front porch while we unloaded our bags. I could tell she was surprised to see me because her face wore a look that asked, "*What is* she *doing here?*" Half shock, half disgust.

Roman dropped his overnight bag at the bottom of the porch steps, and Lovie wilted into his arms. "I can't believe he's gone," she cried. "I just can't believe it."

"Neither can I, Lovie," he said into her hair.

I waited at the rear of the car. It was their moment, and Roman was the only man Lovie had in her life now. Despite all the tears he'd shed last night, Roman had awakened this morning like his faucet had run dry. He'd cooked breakfast, loaded the car, and jumped into the driver's seat before I could object. During the three-hour ride, we'd discussed everything except Pop's death and the arrangements for the memorial service, which Lovie had put in Roman's hands. It was almost like it hadn't happened.

Lovie gripped both sides of Roman's head and kissed him on the temple. She held his hand out and examined his wrist, then ran her thumb across the scars on his temple and neck. "Come inside. Queen is cooking breakfast. I can't eat, though," she said, placing one hand on her midsection. "My stomach is in knots."

I remembered the feeling. If my mother hadn't spoon-fed me the second day after Vincent's death, I wouldn't have eaten at all. Even then, I couldn't keep much down and had subsisted on clear liquids, mashed potatoes, and applesauce until my body would accept solid foods.

"You have to eat, Lovie," Roman said. "At least a little. Zenja and I are fine. I made breakfast for us this morning."

Lovie furrowed her brow. "What were you doing cooking? You're grieving."

"I wanted to," Roman said. "I needed to keep myself busy. I couldn't sleep."

"Me, either," Lovie said. "It doesn't feel right in the house anymore. If Queen hadn't stayed the night, I wouldn't have been able to close my eyes at all." She clutched the top of her robe.

"Let's go inside," Roman said. He turned toward me. "Baby, are you alright with your bag?"

"I've got it," I said. Truth be told, I wasn't in a hurry to get inside, anyway, so I headed toward the house like I was walking the plank. *It's not about me*, I reminded myself over and over. As if she'd sensed the challenge I was about to face, Caprice sent me a text message.

You can do all things through Christ who gives you strength.

She sent a second text ten seconds later.

You'll probably miss this week's Friday Night Love. The next challenge: Show your love for your husband in a creative way. Might be good to try it while you're in SC.

I couldn't fathom how Caprice thought I was supposed to get creative at a time like this. Yes, I'd prayed to God for strength and grace, but that didn't mean my flesh didn't want to rush home and tell Roman I would come back for him after it was all over. And then there was Lovie. I couldn't do anything creative with her constantly looking down her nose at me.

I texted Caprice a message that would cover it all: Pray for me.

Roman, Lovie, and Queen huddled near the stove in the cramped kitchen. There was barely room to turn around with the three of them there, let alone with my adding another body to the space. Southern food was my weakness, and I'd choose it any day over the yogurt, steel-cut oats, and grapefruit on my eating plan. At seven o'clock that morning, we'd stuffed our stomachs with a healthy breakfast, but when I saw the sausage, grits, and cinnamon apples Queen had prepared, I found an empty pocket in my stomach. Evidently Roman had, too. He didn't even bother to sit down at the table but plucked a piece of sausage from the black frying pan and shoved it into his mouth.

Queen buzzed around the small space with a white cloth that smelled like it had been soaked in soap and bleach. I'd never seen Lovie's kitchen so light and airy. The windows were open, and the curtain rods had been stripped bare of the usual fabric panels with the coffee cup print. They were probably being washed, because the air was also thick with the scent of mountain breeze detergent and fabric softener. Queen was on a mission. I knew the tactic well, because my mother had called in a cleaning service two days before Vincent's funeral. Queen was trying to wash the stench of death away.

Unlike Lovie, who still had yet to acknowledge me, her best friend greeted me joyfully.

"Long time, no see," Queen said. "You look great. How long has it been?"

"Long enough for me to put on some extra pounds. I've been trying to lose a little, but I think I found it again," I jested. Last night, I'd purposefully chosen a shirt with vertical stripes to help hide my thickness while under Lovie's scrutiny.

"Well, the weight looks good on you. You look blessed," Queen said. "Doesn't she, Lovie?"

Lovie glanced at me out of the corner of her eye. I guess she had to search hard for her version of a compliment, since Queen stared at her like she needed to say something.

"It *is* a nice shirt," Lovie said. "I used to have some curtains just like it when the boys were young."

I cleared my throat as a warning to Roman that he'd better do some serious praying if he wanted me and Lovie to cohabit in the same house for the next few days. On the ride down, I'd called two hotels to check their nightly rates, but Roman had shot down the idea. Maybe now he would reconsider.

"I definitely feel blessed," I said, ignoring Lovie's dig. "Things have been turning around for me. For *us*," I said, to rub at Lovie's nerves. I hoped Caprice was praying.

Queen rubbed incessantly at a spot on the counter, and Roman did what he always did when it came to Lovie's smart-aleck remarks: Nothing. He never defended me in Lovie's presence, which only made it easier for her to be rude.

"I'm going to put my bags down," I said, escaping the kitchen.

Roman wasn't far behind me. He closed the door to his old bedroom, and I sat down on the full-sized bed with him. The mattress was firm around the edges but soft and lumpy in the middle. According to Roman, it was the same bed and mattress he'd used all through school. That fact didn't sit well with me. With all the television Lovie and Pop had always watched, hadn't they seen any of those prime-time specials about bedbugs?

"I'm sorry Lovie is acting this way," Roman apologized.

"Don't act surprised," I scoffed. "She is who she is."

"She's hurting," he said defensively.

"Whether she's hurting or not, she's always been rude to me," I said. "Your father may not have been the kindest person on earth, but he didn't try to personally demean me. At least, not to my face."

Speechless. Roman was speechless. I had to give it to him for his level of respect for Lovie. He never spoke badly of her, but he still had a responsibility to his wife. I wouldn't press it now, but it was one of the issues we would have to address in our efforts to give "us" another chance. In the meantime, I swallowed my pride.

"I'll be okay," I assured him. "You and Lovie do what you need to do for your father's funeral arrangements."

It turned out that Pop had made his wishes known. He wanted to be cremated following a short family viewing at the funeral home. In his own words, he didn't want "folks he barely knew gawking over" him. He also didn't want his memorial service to last more than an hour. Lovie and I kept our distance from each other while she and Roman wrote the obituary and the order of the service. Around eleven, she asked Roman to drive her to the mall to find a pink dress because seeing her in that color always made Pop happy. That was news to me. Pop had always acted like nothing bought him joy. I graciously bowed out of their shopping excursion and opted to stay at the house with Queen.

Lovie was right—the house felt empty without Pop. His size and his presence had taken up so much space. The cane and walker he'd used to scoot around were propped against his worn brown recliner. The fabric was tattered on the bottom cushion and on the armrests from supporting his heavy, doughlike arms. The back of the chair was dirty with sweat and years of not being cleaned.

I walked over to the wall to look at photographs from happier days in the life of the Maxwell family.

"Times sure have changed, haven't they?" Queen said, walking into the living room. She'd put on an apron and a pair of yellow rubber gloves that covered her arms up to the elbows.

"This is the family I wish I knew," I said, flicking the dust off my fingers.

I pointed to a photograph of Pop, Roman, and Joshua sitting on the hood of a blue Ford Mustang. Lovie leaned against the car, striking a pose worthy of a magazine ad. Most of her face was covered with large Jackie Onassis-style sunglasses and an oversized sun hat with a swooping brim. The joy in her smile was undeniable.

Queen took the frame from the wall and wiped it with the cloth she was holding. "This family died with Joshua. Thomas and Lovie took their last breath together with their baby boy. Roman's the only one who moved on with his life. I think Thomas always envied that. In fact, I think he hated Roman for it." Queen started taking the rest of the picture frames off the wall. "Dealing with that tears Lovie to pieces."

Lovie had barely acknowledged my existence and had said my shirt looked like her old curtains, yet my heart ached for her.

"I'll be back," I told Queen, then went to the back bedroom and changed into a pair of jeans and a T-shirt. When I returned dressed for work, Queen handed me a cloth. Together, we carefully stacked each picture on Pop's faded chair and proceeded to wipe grime from the walls. Once we were finished, we polished the frames and put them back on the wall in as close a configuration to the original as we could.

We worked silently yet in unison. I followed Queen's lead as we wiped the other walls, dusted, vacuumed, emptied the trash, recycled old papers and magazines, washed the remaining window treatments and rugs, and put spring-blossom-scented air fresheners in every room. There was life in the house again, and Queen and I both knew it.

"Do you want to keep going?" Queen asked me after we'd taken a short break. We were sitting at the kitchen table nibbling on leftover sausage and drinking Lovie's super sweet tea that I'd diluted with water.

"Absolutely," I said. Caprice would be proud. By honoring Lovie, respecting her home, and helping to create a sanctuary of peace, not only could I creatively show God's love to her but to Roman, too. "Let's see if they're on their way back," I suggested.

Roman's voice was no louder than a whisper when he finally answered his cell phone.

"Are you okay?" I asked him.

"Waiting for Lovie to finish up in the dressing room. She's tried on every outfit in the store and stared at herself for at least ten minutes in each one. I've never seen this much pink in a single place."

"Be patient with her," I said. "It's probably been a while since she's been able to shop for herself. Granted, these aren't the best circumstances, but you know she rarely left the house."

"She can stay out all day if she needs to. I'll take her wherever she wants," Roman said. "As long as you're okay with it," he quickly added.

"I'm fine. She needs you. Stay out as long as you need. Take her somewhere nice to eat, too," I prodded him. The longer they were out of the house, the better. Queen still wanted to tackle both bathrooms and spruce up the front porch.

We worked to clean and sanitize the hall bathroom, moving around each other like partners in a choreographed dance. She scoured the sink and fixtures while I scrubbed the baseboards and mopped the floor. We wiped off Pop's toiletries and placed them back in place on the side of the sink basin. The only thing we took the liberty of trashing were his numerous medications. Lovie didn't need the lingering reminder of his sickness.

Around five o'clock, Roman and Lovie arrived home at a house that was drastically different from the one they'd left that morning. They opened the door and entered slowly, as if they couldn't believe they were at the same address. Queen and I were sitting at the kitchen table playing Scrabble. After three more hours of exhausting work, we'd had enough time to shower, shop for groceries, and come back to cook a dinner of cubed steak, mashed potatoes, cabbage, and corn bread. Roman and Lovie had already eaten out, but Queen and I had been ravenous for a home-cooked meal. I was completely off my eating plan, and I couldn't have cared less.

Lovie walked around the room, running her hand along the kitchen counters. "You didn't have to do this, Queen," she said.

Queen rearranged the Scrabble tiles on her wooden stand. "And Zenja, too. I wouldn't have been able to do most of this without her."

Roman followed behind Lovie. They stopped to admire things they probably hadn't noticed in years. Lovie was most impressed with the sparkling picture frames and photographs no longer camouflaged by dust.

"Thank you," Roman said to both of us. "I know this took a lot of work."

Lovie said not a single word to me, but I didn't cringe as I normally did. Actually, it made me pray. I fiddled with my two remaining tiles and asked God to heal all Lovie's wounds—whether they were from me, Roman, Pop, or self-inflicted.

Queen lined up her last four letters on the board. L-O-V-E.

"That about says it all," I said, tallying up the final score. Queen had won by forty-three points.

"Not *about*. Love *does* say it all," Queen said, standing up to clear off the board. "Love has the final say." She swept the tiles into the box with her palm. "You're in good hands, Lovie. I'll be back in the morning. Is there anything else you need?"

"You've done more than enough," Lovie said, pouring herself a full glass of tea. She frowned at the first sip. "Who messed up my tea? It tastes like water."

Neither Queen nor I answered. I didn't need another strike against me.

Queen's eyes cut my way. "That stuff was way too sweet," she said.

"You've never had a problem with it before." Lovie dumped her tea in the kitchen sink. "But I'll forgive you since you have my home shining like the White House."

*Talk about exaggeration,* I thought.

"I don't know how I can repay you for the kind of friend you've been to me all these years," Lovie squeaked, sounding on the verge of tears.

Queen took her best friend's hands in hers. They were the same height, and their apple-shaped figures had similar contours. They'd been friends for so many years, they looked alike. "You can repay me by living," Queen answered. She pumped Lovie's arms up and down. "Because we're all one breath away from the end."

# 39

# ROMAN

The morning of the day he died, Pop had complained of heartburn, which was nothing out of the ordinary. He suffered from acid reflux and a long list of other compounded illnesses attached to his excessive weight. Before Lovie had stepped into the bathtub, she said, he'd asked for a drink of water. She'd given him a full glass topped with ice, then retreated to the bathroom to soak in water with Epsom salt to relieve the pain in her aching knee. After her bath, she'd found his head slumped forward and the cup of water nestled between his knees. She assumed he was asleep, so she seized the opportunity to seek quiet refuge in her room and work on crossword puzzles. After an hour, she'd gone to wake him for his evening medicine regimen. That's when she'd realized that his sleep would never end.

That had been three days ago. Now it was time for Roman and Lovie to say their final good-byes.

The memorial service for Thomas Maxwell was just what he wanted, with very few people in attendance. Roman knew it was more because of how Pop had treated people and less because Lovie was honoring his last wishes. The people sitting in the pews behind him were there to support him and Lovie.

Roman thought his mother looked more youthful than she had in years. Queen had curled and pinned her hair away from her face, then convinced her to let Zenja apply some makeup. After thirty minutes of refusing, she'd finally agreed. Zenja had accentuated her high cheekbones and made her eyes look bigger and brighter. Roman noticed the slightest hint of a smile when Lovie checked her appearance in the mirror.

"I knew there was a pretty woman somewhere in there," she'd remarked, patting her hair into place.

"A gorgeous woman," Roman had said. But there'd been no thank-you for Zenja. Roman couldn't let his mother's behavior continue. He would eventually have to address the elephant in the room, but right now, his thoughts were on putting his father's ashes to rest. They'd chosen an immaculate gray urn for Pop's ashes and set it on a table up front. Roman had purchased it—the first thing he'd bought for his father in years that wouldn't be rejected.

When the presiding minister asked if anyone would like to share any words about the deceased, it was so quiet, Roman could hear the happy shouts of children at the playground a block away. Neither of Roman's uncles budged. Pop had become estranged from most of his family, and even in his death, they didn't have a good word to say about him.

Lovie squeezed his arm hard, urging him to move. She'd told him to say a few words to honor his father, but Roman hadn't been able to put his words together the night before. He adjusted his bow tie and went to stand up front beside the framed photograph of Pop. In the picture, he was 250 pounds lighter and wearing a navy blue bow tie with yellow polka dots. Thick black hair. Eyes and skin bright and not yet yellowed by the toxins of alcohol.

Roman scanned the faces of his family members. Zenja slid closer to Lovie and offered her a hand of comfort, which Lovie refused.

The microphone squealed as he tried to adjust it. He turned it off. He didn't need it, with fewer than thirty people in the room. He tugged at his bow tie again. It was choking his throat. Zenja smiled and gave him a reassuring nod. She placed her hand over her heart. *Speak from your heart,* she was saying. And Roman did.

"It's no secret that Pop and I didn't have the best relationship...truthfully, not much of relationship at all." He cleared his throat. It was so quiet, he could hear his own breathing. "But he's still my father. Man to man, we weren't able to work out our differences, but Pop instilled some things in me as a boy that I'll never forget. He was committed to his wife." Roman noticed several people nodding. "The rite of passage for both me and Joshua when we were in kindergarten was to learn to tie a bow tie. Lovie taught us reading and math, but Pop wanted us to look good. I'll be forever indebted to him for that, because that's how I snagged my wife. She was impressed with my skills. So, if nothing else, that was enough."

Everyone chuckled except Lovie.

Roman looked at Pop's picture. "Love you, Dad," he said before retaking his seat between the two women in his life. They both laid their heads on his shoulders. He hadn't had the chance to right the wrongs between him and his father, and now it was too late. Roman didn't want to live his life with another regret.

# 40

"Can I get something off my chest?"

I spun around, startled by Lovie's voice. How had she approached the kitchen without my hearing her? I'd either been caught up in my own thoughts or was delirious from lack of sleep after tossing and turning in the mattress pit. For most of the night, I'd stared at Roman's faded poster of Michael Jordan defying gravity on the basketball court or the water stain on the ceiling.

With Lovie's face scrubbed free of makeup, I could clearly see the lines at the corners of her eyes. Then again, it was probably because of the way she was eyeing me. Sneering.

"Sure," I said. "Would you like some coffee?" I could tell she was taken aback by my kindness. Her arms, which had been locked across her chest, dropped at her sides.

"No, I wouldn't like any coffee," she said. "But what I would like is for you to let my son be. Let him get on with his life, and you and your children get on with yours. Nothing good has happened to him since he moved back in with you. He was nearly killed in a car accident, there was the tornado, and then his father died. Aren't those signs? Don't you know God has a way of talking to us?"

*No she did not.* She'd never mentioned God before, and now, all of a sudden, she'd found Him and was receiving messages from heaven? *Please.*

"And you blame that on me?" I asked, incredulous. "Do you really think a tornado ripped the roofs off the houses of our neighbors and even killed one of our close friends because of me? It was Roman's decision to come back to his family. I wasn't expecting it. In fact, I'd already filed for divorce. He still has the papers, and he's free to walk away at any time if he wants to."

"But I won't," Roman interjected.

We both turned.

"I've known life without Zenja, and I never want to do that again." Roman appeared in the doorway as quietly as Lovie had. Sleep still rimmed his eyes, and it looked like his slumber had been as restless as mine. I didn't know how that could be, though, since he'd snored the entire night.

"She filed for divorce, Roman. Doesn't that say enough?" Lovie threw back at him.

"And I had an affair," Roman admitted. "What does that say about me?"

Lovie huffed. "It says that she wasn't living up to your expectations as a wife, so you had to go elsewhere to have your needs met."

Lovie's insult hit me to the core. God's grace and my love for Roman helped me refrain from saying what was on my mind. The retaliation wouldn't be worth it. Once the words were spoken, I'd never be able to take them back.

Roman rubbed small, slow circles into my lower back. "No, it shows that I'm a flawed man who did a stupid thing. When things weren't ideal in my life, I was crazy enough to get caught up in adultery. But despite all that, Zenja's choosing to see me how God sees me. That doesn't make her *less* of a woman, it makes her *more* of a woman. You should be happy I have a wife who loves me as much as you do, if not more."

Those were the first words I'd heard Roman say to Lovie in my defense.

"She could never love you more than me," Lovie insisted.

Roman flung his arms in the air. "It's not a competition. Zenja has endured your criticism for years. She's endured your treating her like she's invisible for the past three days. No, make that the past six years. Since she's been here, she's ironed your clothes, washed your walls, and scrubbed your bathtub. If you can't do anything else, you can at least give her the respect she deserves."

Roman guided me by my shoulders until I was face-to-face with my mother-in-law. I stood my ground, she hers.

"Look at her," Roman told Lovie. "She's not invisible. *This* is the woman your son chose. *This* is the woman my soul loves. You are my mother, but Zenja is my wife. She. Comes. First."

We were both crying—Lovie and I—but I doubt it was for the same reason.

Outside the window, the world began to awaken. A garbage truck rumbled and screeched down the road, setting off the neighbor's irritating hound dog, whose barks had also contributed to my sleepless nights in South Carolina.

"There's nothing I wouldn't do for you, Lovie," Roman continued. "But Zenja has given me another chance, and I intend to show her that I can be the kind of man you raised me to be. I love her, and there's nothing you can do about it."

"Well," Lovie said, fiddling with the ties on her housecoat, "I didn't know that was the way things had happened, and I certainly didn't know that was how you felt. Most of the time you talk about Zenja, you complain about this or that."

*Busted.* Whether it was right or wrong, most people had a sounding board when they wanted to vent about their spouse. Mine was Caprice. I just hated that Roman's had to be his mother, of all people. No wonder she was inclined to dislike me. That explained a lot.

Roman turned to me. "I'm sorry," he said. "I shouldn't have done that. From this point on, you don't have to worry about me taking our business to Lovie." He gently prodded his mother with a hand on her shoulder.

"I'm sorry," she mumbled halfheartedly.

"Apology accepted," I said.

I would take an apology any way it came. Roman had defended me, and that was all that mattered right now.

"Lovie, we're headed out in a few hours," Roman said. "We've got to get back to things at home, but you're more than welcome to come with us for a few days if you want to."

I nearly fainted. Roman hadn't discussed this with me. Lovie and I may have taken a first step that morning, but we had miles to go. We hadn't reached that crossroads yet, and both she and I knew it.

"No, I'll be fine right here," Lovie rushed to say. "If I need anything, Queen is a phone call away."

"And we are, too," I said. "Maybe we can get you up to Greensboro for Labor Day. That's when my parents usually come down, and you'd have a chance to spend some time with Zariya and Kyle."

"We'll see how the wind blows in September," Lovie said.

"Good," Roman said, kissing her on the cheek. "Can't wait."

When he moved to do the same to me, I turned my face toward his and pursed my lips to let him know he was welcome to a taste of my mouth. He pecked once, but my lips held his for a softer, longer touch the second time.

"Sorry, Lovie," he added, embarrassed at our display of affection in front of his mother. "But that was better than breakfast."

"Then that settles it," Lovie said. "I don't have to cook this morning."

"I never said that." Roman started opening cabinets.

"I think it's time I show you how to make Roman's favorite drop biscuits," Lovie said to me.

"I'd love to learn," I said, giving Roman a wink.

Lovie pulled a large mixing bowl and a cookie sheet from the drawer under the oven, then reached for the canisters of flour and sugar on the countertop. "Look in the pantry for baking powder, and get me some butter," she instructed me.

Roman stepped out of the way, seemingly amazed that we were working together without flinging sharp utensils at each other.

"I'll tell you this much: If you make these biscuits for him at least once a week, he'll never tip out on you again."

"Lovie," Roman warned.

"That didn't sound right, did it?" she said as she set the oven temperature to 450 degrees.

I set the baking powder and butter on the counter with the other ingredients. "Well, if the biscuits will work, let's get to it," I said.

Lovie gave me a nudge, which was the closest thing to a hug that I'd ever gotten from her. I'd take it. God is good.

# 41

## ROMAN

Zenja had been asleep since they'd crossed the North Carolina state line. Roman was anxious to get back to his normal routine and was equally ready to start working with the band. They'd practiced twice without him already this week, which meant he would get only two chances to play with them—tonight and once more later this week—before next Friday night's gig. But Roman wasn't worried. He knew all the songs except one, and that wouldn't take long for him to pick up.

Roman pulled into the garage and turned off the ignition. When he opened his door, the car lights came on, and Zenja's eyelids fluttered open.

"We're home," he said.

"You've got to be kidding me." She pressed the button to bring her seat back to an upright position. "I slept better in the car than I did on that raggedy mattress at Lovie's house."

"Don't talk about my mama," he joked.

"We're on better terms now," Zenja said. "I definitely wouldn't want to mess that up."

Roman popped the trunk and took the bags inside while Zenja went to check the mail. Roman inspected the new patio door, which had been installed under Duane's supervision during their absence, for which he was thankful. Duane had also offered to have his and Caprice's regular housekeeping service come by while he was there to give the house a deep cleaning. Roman was glad he'd agreed. The place gleamed like a model home, and there wasn't a speck of dust, a hint of dirt, or a fingerprint smudge to be found. He planned to call the company tomorrow and contract them for a bimonthly cleaning. Once Zariya and Kyle returned and they were pushed back into their normal routine of school and outside activities, Zenja didn't need the hassle of staying on top of the housework. Roman didn't like cleaning. Never had. So, if he wasn't going to lend a hand, the least he could do was pay money to make sure it happened.

"Am I in the same house?" Zenja said when she came inside carrying a colossal stack of mail. "I feel like Lovie."

"I had Caprice's housekeeping service come by," Roman said, puffing out his chest.

Zenja smiled. "I could get used to this."

"Done," Roman said. "All you have to do is ask, and if it's in my means, it's yours."

"How long is this generosity going to last?" Zenja put down the stack of mail and walked over to admire their new door. She looked out through the frosted glass at her patio oasis.

"That's next," Roman said, reading her mind. "Do you still have your money from that karaoke embarrassment?

"Every dime of it," Zenja said. She walked back to the kitchen, flipped through the mail, and handed Roman an envelope she'd opened outside. "It's the insurance check for the car. I'd rather shop for cars than patio pillows."

Roman hadn't expected the money to come so soon. He'd also thought he'd have to fight through some red tape. "Nice welcome-home present," he said.

"Too bad you have practice tonight," Zenja said. "We could've walked through some car lots and then headed out for Friday Night Love. I hate to miss it again. We've only gone once, and we've bailed out already."

"Not bailed out, just had a change of plans," Roman said. "I can drop you off. Nobody will care if you're there alone."

Zenja shook her head. "I'll care."

"Then come with me," Roman said.

"I'll be bored."

"But we'll be together, and that's all I care about," Roman said. "For our sake, I want you near me as much as possible."

"Fine," Zenja conceded. "Since I agreed to your playing with the band, I might as well come with you while I can. We'll look for a car later. Maybe we can find something pre-owned and pocket the rest of the money or use it for school shopping for Zariya and Kyle."

"Or for a getaway for a late anniversary celebration. I'm taking you back to the Bahamas, to the Atlantis, so the only memories you'll have from there will be of us together," Roman said.

"You don't have to do that," Zenja protested.

"But I am. I'm going to make you forget you ever knew a man named Lance."

Roman noticed how Zenja's expression changed. She looked at him like she used to. With desire. With passion. He would let her make the first move, but she'd gone back to sorting through the mail.

Holding the check from the wreck made him think about his lie of omission. The phone calls and text messages from Jewel. The crash just seconds later. He hadn't mentioned them to Zenja at all. He'd pressed her for the truth about her and Lance but hadn't been honest about himself.

The longer Roman waited, the worse the damage—Zenja's reaction—would be. She'd find out sooner or later. It might be years later, but lies were nearly impossible to conceal forever.

Zenja was engrossed in an article in one of her educators' journals, but she suddenly stopped reading and stared at him. "You're quiet *and* you're pacing," she said. "What is it?"

Roman hadn't realized he'd been walking the floor. "There's a story behind this check that you don't know about," he began.

"And that is?" Zenja closed the magazine and set her gaze on him instead.

"I haven't been totally honest with you."

"I don't like the sound of this conversation," Zenja said. "And I'm not sure I want to know the truth."

Roman didn't give her the option. "The young man who ran the red light was definitely the cause of the accident, but right before that, Jewel had been calling and texting me—"

"Hold it right there." Zenja interrupted him with a hand in the air. "Never, ever say that woman's name in my house."

Roman scratched the side of his face. "*She* had been texting and calling me repeatedly that evening," he continued. "I went out for a ride to give you some space and to pick up dinner. I only answered the phone to tell her to back off. It's possible that I would've seen the driver if I hadn't been distracted with her. We'll never know. But I wanted to tell you."

Zenja exhaled, her face flushed with relief. "Not what I wanted to hear, but what's done is done. Like you said, the driver might have hit you either way." Zenja shook her head. "And you still don't think you should change your phone number?"

*Forget the cell phone number.* Roman dropped the final bomb. "She came to the hospital to see me. You'd gone downstairs to get something to eat."

Zenja stood for a long time, her eyes fixed on the floor in front of her. Roman didn't know if he should approach her or stay clear in case of a sudden attack.

"And I lied," Roman continued. "She and I did things we shouldn't have, but it meant nothing. And I mean nothing. *She* meant nothing."

"Do you honestly think I believed you when you said nothing happened?" Zenja asked. She put her head down for a moment, then looked back up at him. "Do you know what I think about that?" Her voice was barely above a whisper.

"What?" Roman asked.

"Come closer," she said, beckoning him with her pointer finger. "I really want you to hear this."

Roman took his chances. If her palm left an imprint on his cheek, he deserved it. But it wasn't her hands at all that landed on his face. It was her lips. Soft, gentle lips.

Their mouths locked lightly at first, and then with the passion of a couple whose spark had been reignited. Roman swept Zenja up in his arms. Desire ran through his body, pushing him up the stairway and toward their bedroom. It was finally time.

He nearly stumbled, his nerves getting the better of him, but the misstep didn't override the passion brewing inside him. Still cradling Zenja, he kicked the door open, then felt her hands drop from his neck. She flattened her palms against his chest and pushed herself away from him.

"I can't," she said, panting. "Not yet. I don't feel right."

"You said yourself that we can't always go off our feelings," Roman said, breathing just as heavily as she. "It *is* right." He tried to kiss her again, but this time, her lips were lifeless. He covered her mouth with his, but still no response. "You said you'd be my wife again. Please, Zenja." Roman wasn't above begging. It had been too long. Too much longer and he'd explode.

"You have to be patient," Zenja said, adjusting her clothes. "Isn't patience a fruit of the Spirit?"

"I'm not thinking about a Scripture right now," Roman said, reaching for her again. "I want my fruit right now."

"Roman!"

"Zenja!"

"I need time," Zenja said, smoothing her hair down.

"Thirty minutes? An hour?" *This is torture.* Roman flexed his hands into fists and then opened them again. He paced.

"I can't say how long," Zenja said. "Maybe tomorrow, next week, next month." She couldn't even look at him. She went into the master bathroom and closed the door. The lock clicked.

*Oh, it's like that?*

Roman admitted defeat. What choice did he have? He tapped on the door. "I'm going to the garage to practice, if you need me. If you really, really need me." He heard her turn on the water in the sink. She was probably trying to cool herself down. It was going to take more than some cold water to douse that fire.

"I think I'll call Caprice and see if she needs help getting anything together for tonight," Zenja said. "What time do I need to be back?"

"Six is fine," Roman said. "We'll make it a date." He pressed his ear to the door. What was she doing in there?

"Not my idea of a date."

Roman heard her open and close the door of the linen closet. He stalled to see if she'd reemerge from the bathroom with a changed mind. He picked up his pajamas and some other random items they'd left lying around the room on the morning they'd left for South Carolina. The master suite was the only part of the house he'd asked the cleaning service not to touch.

"It's all in what you make it," Roman finally called out, already making plans for a night out that Zenja would appreciate, because he wanted an evening that they wouldn't forget.

# 42

I had to talk so somebody other than Roman about my frustrations and insecurities. The details of our intimacy had never left the confines of our bedroom, but this was a special circumstance that required some serious prayer, and if nobody else prayed for me, I knew Caprice would.

Caprice and I were stuffing small candy boxes with heart-shaped mints and affixing them with tags that said, "We were MINT to be." It didn't surprise me that this was Carmela's idea, but instead of helping us with the real work, she'd dropped off the supplies at Caprice's so she could attend yet another networking lunch.

"You can't keep that lingerie hidden in the drawer forever," Caprice told me after I'd bared my soul to her. "Sooner or later, it'll be time to give Roman a personal fashion show."

"Believe me, I want to," I said. "But I can't keep my mind from playing certain images. My husband was with another woman. How can I get past that?"

"Your mind is like a battlefield, and your ammunition is the Word of God. You need to meditate on some Scriptures that will push out those other thoughts."

I sighed in frustration. That was easier said than done.

"It'll take some time," Caprice said truthfully, "but God's Word can do anything." She picked at a paper cut on her middle finger. "It's different for men. They don't have to love a woman or be emotionally attached to have sex with her. I'm not saying it's right, or that they can use that to justify their actions, but it's true. Men are visually stimulated, and sometimes, when they see it, their flesh wants to conquer it, especially if they haven't stayed grounded in the Word of God. At the time of Roman's affair, he wasn't seeking and chasing after God like he is now. All the enemy needs is a door to be cracked open, and he'll kick that sucker down."

I passed Caprice another tag. "Well, I don't want to be looked at like something Roman wants to conquer. I'm his *wife*."

"Which is exactly why he wants to be with you. He doesn't see you in the same way that he saw her. You can be sure about that."

"But can you believe she came to the hospital? And Roman didn't say a word about it, even after all my confessions about me and Lance."

I'd had to put everything on the table with Caprice about what had happened with Lance on the cruise. She was clearly disappointed, but she seemed more relieved that I'd closed that door.

"You chose your battles wisely," she told me. "That wasn't worth fighting over. You're fighting for your marriage, remember? Not the trivial distractions, Lance and *her* included."

At this point, I'd become a broken record, but my feelings were better out than in. "I can't help but wonder where we'd be if I'd gone to counseling when Roman had asked me to. I didn't help the situation by refusing. I just didn't think I was the one with the problem, so I left him to figure things out on his own because I was too stubborn and prideful."

"You can't fix what's behind you, only what's in front of you," Caprice said.

"I've prayed for God to show me more about me, and I tell you, He hasn't held anything back," I said, tying a tag on the last candy box.

Caprice slid me a ring of fabric swatches so that we could proceed with the next order of business—choosing material for a bench she wanted to reupholster.

"Wouldn't you rather God tell you than somebody else?"

"Definitely," I said. I held up a swatch of a chevron pattern of teal, navy blue, and yellow. "I don't know about your bench, but I love this pattern for my patio cushions and pillows. We found only two of mine after the tornado, and they weren't even worth salvaging."

Caprice marked my swatch with a black dot on the back, then tossed the ring in the basket full of fabric at her feet. "I don't feel like looking at those anymore. I'm on overload. Everything is starting to look the same. I'll let Duane pick out what he likes."

"You're brave," I said. "I'd never let Roman do that. The only things I trust him to choose are bow ties."

I followed Caprice into her den, where she also must have had the itch to do something different. She'd hung Roman shades on her floor-to-ceiling windows and accented one of the walls with red textured wallpaper. Two framed black-and-white prints leaned against the wall, waiting to be hung by Duane's steady hand.

"Friday Night Love is at the new art gallery tonight, right?" I asked, admiring her new wall art.

"No, that's in two weeks. Tonight we're going to the bowling alley." Caprice frowned. "It was the men's choice."

"Going to practice with Roman isn't such a bad idea, then," I decided. "But I do like connecting with other women and married couples. It makes a difference knowing there are other couples who are committed to building godly marriages. We need Friday Night Love. We really do."

"Come to the Friday Night Love events when you can, but right now, take this opportunity to focus on you and Roman," Caprice advised. "In the meantime, make your own love on Mondays, Tuesdays, Wednesdays, and Thursdays. And I mean that literally and figuratively."

Caprice was Caprice, and that's why I love her.

Caprice picked up an envelope from her coffee table—a refurbished trunk she'd found at a consignment shop. She pulled out a stack of cards and handed them to me. "Here are all the assignments," she said. "It's not as much about making it a seven-week challenge and coming to every meeting as it is about being aware of ways we can honor and respect our husbands. When both husband and wife are focused on pleasing their spouse, everyone's needs are met."

I thumbed through the challenge cards: *Respond to his needs. Encourage him. Show your love for him in creative ways. Put him first. Expect the best. Cherish your time with him. Talk highly of him to other people.*

"The challenges aren't really that bad," I admitted. "They're things we should be doing anyway."

Caprice flipped open her laptop and pecked away furiously on the keys. "I'm e-mailing them to you right now," she said. "We might not see too much of you guys over the next few weeks."

"Why do you say that?"

"Because you're climbing your own mountain, and God's plan may be for you two to journey to the top together."

"I kind of feel the same way," I said. "But I wish Roman would say something about his going to marriage counseling. If I bring it up, he'll know that you spilled the beans."

"He'll tell you."

I swiped at my bangs, which kept falling in my eyes. It was definitely time for a trim. "When he does, I'll suggest we start going together."

Caprice turned her laptop so I could see the screen. She's listed the challenges. "Look at the first letter of the first word in each challenge. What does it spell?"

"R-E-S-P-E-C-T," I said. "Respect?"

Caprice nodded. "Ephesians five thirty-three: '*However, each one of you also must love his wife as he loves himself, and the wife must respect her husband.*' Duane has been talking to the men about the Scriptures in Ephesians, too."

"Clever." I smiled. "What a cute way to walk out the Scriptures. It'll be something I'll never forget."

"That was the point," Caprice said. The alarm on her phone beeped. We had the tendency to lose track of time when we were talking, so we always set it when we got together. "That's our warning," she said. "Time for me to get dressed and for you to pick up your man."

"Have fun bowling," I told her. "I always end up with five broken, chipped fingernails."

"I plan to sit this one out and cheer Duane on." Caprice stood and shook her hips. "Already packed my pom-poms."

"You're everybody's cheerleader," I said, suddenly feeling sappy. "You've cheered and encouraged me over every rough place in my life. You talk about me and Roman climbing this mountain..." I paused. My nose was starting to run. Caprice handed me a facial tissue. "You talk about me and Roman climbing this mountain," I said again, "and I know, if no one else is waiting at the top for us, you and Duane will be there. I can't thank you enough for believing in my marriage when I didn't. Instead of bashing Roman, you let God deal with me and my heart. You, my sister, are a friend from heaven."

Despite Caprice's best attempts to hold herself together, she'd started to cry, too. We were a babbling mess of hormones until Caprice started to laugh.

"You know you look terrible when you cry," she said. "You should really look in the mirror and practice crying with a prettier face."

"Oh, shut up," I said, sniffing. "Evidently you haven't seen what you look like, either."

Caprice plucked more tissues from a nearby box. "That's alright. Our husbands love us, ugly faces and all. People should add that to their marriage vows. For pretty or for ugly."

Caprice walked me to the front door, then gave me that sisterly embrace that told me everything was going to be alright. And it would. Not only had God given Roman another chance, He'd given me one, too.

# 43

Roman ushered me into the event hall where the band would be performing the next week. In the midst of the room filled with bare circular tables, one was skirted in a white linen tablecloth with an arrangement of mirrors and candles in the center. He led me to it, pulled out one of the chairs, and sat me down face-to-face with a silver-framed photo of us on a weekend getaway to the Blue Ridge Mountains. A lot had happened in the last three years from the time we'd bundled in our sweatshirts and jeans and taken the spontaneous trip to find a cabin. We'd lit more than the fireplace that night.

"A date is what and *where* you make it," Roman said.

"How did you pull this off?" I asked, noticing three gift bags off to the side. He hadn't had the time or the transportation to coordinate such a surprise.

"Your appetizers will be out in a minute," Roman said, not bothering to entertain my question. He leaned down and kissed my cheek. I turned so that our foreheads touched, and I felt it. The shift. A change. Our breathing fell into a synchronized pattern.

The blast of music was the only thing that pulled us out of our private world. The four other band members had taken their place on the risers without my notice.

Bernard, the keyboardist, tapped his microphone. "Should we play a love ballad?" He ran his fingers across the keys and tickled out the song we'd selected for our first dance at our wedding reception.

"Oh, so that was planned, too?" I asked Roman.

Roman shook his head. "Actually, it wasn't. Complete coincidence." He picked up his saxophone case. "Enjoy your appetizers and dinner. Don't forget to open your gifts."

Once Roman had taken his position with the band, a server dressed in a black tuxedo appeared and presented me with an appetizer tray. I ate a little of each but restrained my appetite so I'd be able to enjoy my entrée, which the server informed me would be Cajun chicken Alfredo with penne pasta and broccoli.

"Glass of wine, ma'am?" the server asked me.

"No, thanks," I said, holding up my hand in protest. "Water's fine."

Shortly after the band started its first set, my cell phone rang. I quickly silenced it and checked the caller. It was Lance. He'd called three times while we were in South Carolina and left three messages. I decided not to dignify his attention with a response. Lance had wasted his time and his money. Eventually he would get the point and go away.

I texted Caprice: Bowling or candlelight dinner and music? Loving my nite.

She texted me back immediately: One broken nail. Over it. Back to the sidelines I go.

The band took a break halfway through their rehearsal, and Roman joined me at the table. "Why didn't you open your gifts?" he asked, stuffing his mouth with the steaming pasta the server had set in front of him.

"I wanted to wait for you," I said. I pulled the tissue paper from the first bag, and a gift card to one of my favorite shoe stores fell out. "This is starting off good," I said.

"Shoes to thank you for letting me walk back into your life, and for not walking out on me." Roman smiled broadly, like it had taken a while for him to come up with something so clever.

"I see you've put some thought into this," I said, using my napkin to wipe some Alfredo sauce off his chin.

"You know me," he boasted. "Plus, I know shoes are a girl's best friend."

"Actually, it's diamonds," I said. I shook the bag in hopes that I'd missed something shiny.

"Maybe next time." He handed me the next bag, which was slightly bigger than the first.

Inside was a daily devotional for couples and a washcloth. "I get the devotional. But the washcloth?"

"The more time we spend together in God's Word, the closer we will grow together. I want us to read and pray together every morning to set the tone for our entire day." He took the washcloth from my hand and spread it across his open palm. "And the washcloth is for my promise to wash you with the Word, like it says in Ephesians five twenty-five and twenty-six." Roman pretended to wash my arm with slow, gentle, purposeful strokes, as he recited the verse: "'*Husbands, love your wives, just as Christ also loved the church and gave Himself for her, that He might sanctify and cleanse her with the washing of water by the word.*'"

Fire ran up my arm with every touch. "I'm impressed," I said. "You might make me cry tonight."

Roman refolded the washcloth and put it back in the bag. "You have something to wipe your face with if you do," he said. "I think that's the only Scripture I know by heart besides 'Jesus wept' and the Twenty-third Psalm."

"What you need to know is buried in your heart." I picked up the third gift bag and pulled out a jar of honey. "I'm really stumped on this one," I said. "And don't say anything kinky because you'll totally mess up the mood."

"There should be a note," Roman said, sticking his hand inside the bag. He produced a note card and handed it to me.

*How sweet are your words to my taste, sweeter than honey to my mouth!*
—Psalm 119:103

*Your lips drop sweetness as the honeycomb, my bride; milk and honey are under your tongue.* —Song of Solomon 4:11

"I had to think of a way to describe that kiss you gave me at Lovie's. Sweetest thing I ever tasted," Roman said. "And not only is honey supposed to have healing properties, but it's the only food that never spoils. That means your kisses will never grow old to me."

"Your kisses are the only ones I'll ever want," I said coyly. "Now, whether or not they taste like honey, I'll have to determine that next time."

Roman spun the jar around on the table. "Limitless possibilities," he said, before Bernard called everyone back to the stage. "You can use it in the kitchen, the medicine cabinet, the bedroom."

"Don't start," I warned him. "Get back to your saxophone before you start some trouble over here."

"That's exactly what I'm trying to do," Roman said. He brushed my cheek with the back of his hand.

I held onto his wrist. "How's it feeling?"

"Not bad," he said, letting me massage the length of his forearm. "It's sweaty from the brace more than anything. If you weren't here, I wouldn't be wearing the thing."

"Wifey knows best," I said.

"Always has," Roman said, shoveling another bite of pasta into his mouth.

Bernard tapped on the microphone again. "Let's go, guys. I've got a wife and a two-year-old at home and both of them want their daddy. Let's get out of here at a decent time."

Roman resumed his place on the stage. He was meant to be there. It was part of his DNA to play and create music for others to enjoy. I was glad I'd said yes to his participation, and in my mind, I was already rearranging my schedule and clicking through my list of babysitters so that when his band had a gig, my face would be in the crowd. This week's challenge was a joy for me: *Put him first*. I'd have to make sure Caprice added a caveat: *Put him first (after God)!*

I tucked the jar of honey back in its nest of tissue paper along with the note card. If it was honey Roman wanted, it was honey Roman would get.

# 44

The following Friday night, Roman and I arrived a little more than an hour before the doors would open, since the band needed to do a sound check and warm up. Jazz Fridays were always popular at the T.C. Lounge, and the owner had told them to expect a packed house.

Roman had spent the week teaching classes in the morning and practicing most afternoons while I attended an all-day training conference for educators. On Wednesday evening, we'd finally found a car to Roman's liking. It was similar to his wrecked blue Volvo, except this one was newer with more bells and whistles. When Roman had said he wanted us to spend as much time together as possible, he hadn't been kidding. At his insistence, he'd been chauffeuring me everywhere I wanted to go, including to the shoe store to put his gift card to good use. We'd already used every one of my gifts from last Friday night, even the honey. Not in the way Roman had hoped, though. Not yet. Regardless, it had been the perfect sweetener for my nightcap of green tea.

At first, people trickled into the room at the T.C. Lounge, but twenty minutes till showtime, there seemed to be a sudden rush of music lovers. The host and wait staff scooted among the tables to serve food and drinks before the lights dimmed.

The spinach dip had been so delicious last Friday that I ordered it again, along with a ginger ale to sip on while I watched Roman. Had I not been married to the man, he still would've caught my attention. How was it that he'd become more handsome over the last week? God had given me a new attraction to him. I was seeing everything about our marriage in a new light.

But right now, I hoped my eyes were deceiving me.

*She* walked in like she owned the place. It wasn't her first time here, because as she swept by me, I heard two of the hostesses greet her by name.

I had my back toward the entrance, so I assumed she hadn't noticed me. I was seated at the same table where Roman had promised to wash me with the Word, but tonight's feeling was far from the euphoria of that evening. I took a long gulp of ginger ale to wash down my angst. I wondered what Roman's reaction would be when he saw her. And he would see her, even though he was engrossed in conversation with the drummer right now. She went directly to a table near the stage that was marked with a "Reserved" sign, like mine. When we'd arrived, I'd had the choice between my table and one closer to the action. I kicked myself for choosing the wrong one. My gaze followed her svelte figure. I couldn't keep myself from watching her... and wondering.

*Why, Lord? Why does she have to be in front of my face?*

The house lights went down, so I couldn't see beyond the few tables in my immediate vicinity. I checked the back of the room for Caprice and Duane, who'd agreed to join us after Friday Night Love. I didn't know why *she* was here, but God couldn't have planned it any better for my best friend to be by my side. I needed her support.

*Where are you, Caprice?* I kept looking over my shoulder. I called and texted her but got no response. People trying to find a seat in the dark room kept eyeing the three empty seats at my table.

"Yes, those are taken," I had to say three times before the music started.

I turned my attention to my husband. *My husband.* We were probably both watching him, but that was all she would ever do to him. Roman may have been her dream, but he was my reality.

A narrow shaft of illumination from a penlight bounced across my table. "Here you go," the hostess said, seating Caprice and Duane.

"This place is packed," Caprice whispered. "I tried to call you back."

I looked at my phone and saw her two missed attempts. I'd forgotten that I'd silenced my phone when I'd first walked in. "They're just getting started," I said. "I didn't think about ordering you guys something to eat. Sorry about that." I slid the spinach dip and chips toward Duane.

"We ate at Friday Night Love, so I'm not hungry," Caprice said, taking in the surroundings. "This is nice. Could you have imagined a better night?"

"I couldn't have imagined the night would be like this at all," I said. "And I don't mean that in a good way."

"Why?" Caprice scooted her chair close to mine.

"Roman's little snake in the grass is here," I said. My eyes had adjusted enough to see Caprice's eyes widen in surprise.

"Unbelievable," she said. "How do you feel?"

"Mad. Shaken up. Curious. Thank God Roman and I have been spending so much time together and starting our mornings with prayer, or else I'd have some not-so-pleasant words to say."

"How about these words, then? Victorious. Renewed. Confident. Married." With each word, Caprice tapped the table. Then she handed me my glass, and I took another long sip of flat ginger ale, which helped to soothe my dry mouth.

"I have those feelings somewhere in here, too," I said.

"Dig deep, girlfriend," Caprice said. "Find a Scripture. You've got enough in you that you can draw one out when you need it."

I closed my eyes to zero in on the whine of Roman's saxophone and to let God speak to my heart from the devotion and Scripture we'd read that morning. *"'For I know the plans I have for you,' declares the* L*ORD*, *'plans to prosper you and not to harm you, plans to give you hope and a future.'"*

I pulled my strength from God's Word, knowing that He alone had ordered my steps. Without a shadow of a doubt, I knew that before the night ended, I would stand face-to-face with *her* again, and this time, it wasn't a bow tie that had led me to her.

# 45

## ROMAN

Roman could barely make out the features on the faces of the people in the crowd. The lights above the stage skewed his view so that everyone except for the people in the front looked like swaying shadows. At least they were enjoying the music. His music. The way Roman made his saxophone sing even sent shivers up his own spine.

He knew the area where Zenja should've been sitting, but he couldn't see her face. Each band member had a solo part in this song, so once Bernard began to thrill the crowd with his incomparable skills on the keyboard, Roman focused on finding his wife in the mass of people. The owner hadn't exaggerated. Roman doubted there was an empty seat in the house.

An elderly gentleman seated near the front kept the tempo with the cane perched between his knees. He bobbed his head like he could feel the music down to his toes. *A musician, no doubt.* Two tables down from him on the left was a circle of ladies who appeared to be on a girls' night out. One of them was wearing a crown and a pink boa. Birthday girl or bachelorette, Roman figured. He drummed his thigh, waiting now for Joey, the trumpet player, to have his time in the limelight.

Roman scanned the crowd to his right. He went numb. His throat went dry. Jewel fanned her fingers below her chin; a quiet hello meant for him. Roman didn't flinch or show any sign of emotion toward her. He felt no attraction or desire for the woman he'd nearly allowed to sever the bonds of his marriage. Just like Song of Solomon said, he'd let a woman lure him with drips of sweet honey from her lips. Never again. He turned his attention to the middle of the room. There was only one woman who would consume his mind tonight, whose lips alone had the sweet honey he wanted.

Joey was winding down, which meant Roman was next to perform. He closed his eyes, steadied the mouthpiece at his lips, and made it sing.

"Play that sax," somebody called out.

There were little bursts of applause here and there, and when he finished, the claps were like thunder. The rest of the band joined him for the final eight bars, and then Bernard pulled the microphone close to his lips. "We're going to take a brief intermission, but we'll be back in about twenty minutes. Enjoy yourselves. The Soulful Connections have a lot more to give."

As Bernard went on to tell people how to book the band for events, Roman slipped off the stage and disappeared into the thick arrangement of tables. The house lights brightened just enough for him to make his way without stumbling through the obstacle course. Zenja wasn't at the reserved table, but Duane was. Roman signaled for Duane to follow him outside, then headed toward the main entrance. He was forced to stop briefly for the patrons who wanted to give him a pat on the back, tell him about their failed musical aspirations, or compliment him on his skills.

"You're a bad brother."

"I haven't picked up a saxophone since my college marching band days. You make me want to see what I've got left in me."

One woman, who'd stood to block his exit, said, "Too bad you're wearing a wedding ring. Does it mean anything to you?" She was wearing a dress that hugged her body like snake skin, her hair was pulled into a high chignon on the top of her head, and her oversized earrings brushed the tops of her shoulders. Her red lips spread in a smile—a beautiful smile, at that—but those came one in every two women. Zenja was one in a million.

Roman paused and looked at the woman. "This ring—and my wife—mean everything to me." He brushed past her and didn't stop again until he reached the front foyer. He looked around. No Zenja. No Caprice.

Zenja was observant. She must have seen Jewel. Hopefully she hadn't disappeared somewhere to cry with Caprice. Regardless, Roman wanted *his* wife in *his* arms right now. He would leave right now if he had to. He'd pack up his saxophone and head home without a care of what anybody else thought.

"Roman."

He wished the voice had been Zenja's. He didn't turn around. He knew Jewel was approaching him, and he wasn't going to acknowledge that he'd heard her. The tip-tap of her heels closed in behind him, and within seconds, her hand touched his shoulder. He shrugged it off.

"I'm glad to see you're okay," Jewel said. "You look great." She stepped around in front of him.

"My wife's taking good care of me," Roman said. He took a step back from her, reclaiming his personal space.

"Oh, is that so?" Jewel said with a smirk on her face.

"Absolutely." It was Zenja who'd answered. From behind him, Zenja clutched his shirt. "I'm his wife. That's what I'm supposed to do."

"That hasn't always been the case," Jewel said.

"But it's the case now," Zenja said, stepping up beside Roman. "Let's lay some things on the table so I won't have to worry about you calling or sending text messages in a couple of weeks when you think I'm not around. Or so you'll know I don't care if you pull one of these little pop-up appearances when my man happens to be alone. *You* were a mistake. A lapse in judgment. *You* were temporary, but I will be with Roman permanently. Together forever."

Jewel looked too shocked for words.

Roman glanced around, wondering if a small crowd had gathered to watch their confrontation, but Zenja was speaking with so much reserve that the people who passed them did so without a second glance. The only ones paying particular attention to them were Caprice and Duane. Caprice looked ready to pounce if Zenja gave her the slightest signal, but Duane seemed collected as usual.

Jewel leaned all her weight on one hip. "So, you let him back home? Quite a wife you are. Most women wouldn't have done that."

"Well, I'm not most women," Zenja said.

"You're right. Because most women wouldn't have let him go from the beginning." Jewel had gotten over her shock and was ready to throw darts. "You wouldn't even support him in his dreams because you were too caught up in doing everything for and with your kids. You basically dangled him out for someone else to snatch."

Jewel turned to Roman. "Did you know that I'm the reason you're here tonight? I knew Bernard was looking for a saxophonist, and I recommended you."

"I've known Bernard for years," Roman said.

"But you weren't on his mind, and he didn't have your number. I did you a favor."

Zenja stepped in with a solemn look on her face. "Then we really must extend our gratitude," she said. "Isn't that like God? He'll use anybody He wants to bless us. Even the devil herself."

*Boom!* Roman thought. *That's my wife!*

He couldn't have said it better himself. Roman slid his arm around Zenja's waist and pulled her away from Jewel. They walked back into the room to enjoy the night, leaving Roman's past behind.

# 46

## ROMAN

Roman turned off the house alarm but didn't go through the normal ritual of flipping on the lights downstairs. The only lights they needed were always on—the night-lights leading from the upstairs hallway into their bedroom.

He and Zenja hadn't been able to keep their hands off each other on the ride home. They'd locked their lips in passionate kisses at every stoplight. Roman thanked God for the tinted windows on his new car and for timing the lights so that they were caught at every traffic signal.

Zenja didn't have to tell him that the time was right, because he could feel their spirits drawing toward each other. She didn't speak much but communicated instead with her eyes, lips, and hands.

"How do you feel?" Roman asked his wife.

"Fine," she whispered, easing down onto the bed.

"I don't want to do anything unless you do," he said. He didn't mean it. He wanted to do anything and everything, but he still had to consider Zenja's feelings and her level of comfort.

"I want to be with my husband," Zenja said.

"I love you," Roman said. The single tear he shed fell on her cheek as he joined her under the sheets.

# ZENJA

My tears joined with the one that dropped from Roman's eye. I hadn't known what to expect when this time came. I'd thought I'd have to fight the images in my mind. I'd thought I'd be overtaken with bitterness and hatred, but all I felt now was love and desire for my husband.

God had cleared my mind so that I couldn't conjure up any images even if I'd wanted to. "*Whatever things are true, whatever things are noble, whatever things are just, whatever things are pure, whatever things are lovely, whatever things are of good report, if there is any virtue and if there is anything praiseworthy—meditate on these things.*"

I couldn't stop my tears from falling. They slid out of the corners of my eyes and back toward the pillows.

"I love you, Roman," I said through trembling lips. "You don't know how much I love you."

Roman silenced my ramblings with his mouth. He tried to kiss every one of my tears. I massaged his back, pulling him so close to me that our bodies melted into each other. Then I pushed slightly on his chest so that he'd lift his body off mine. "We're forgetting something," I said.

"What?" Roman asked.

"The honey," I crooned.

Roman catapulted off the bed so fast that I was sure he'd reinjured his wrist or another part of his body. "I'll be right back." His feet pounded down the steps, and I could hear him opening and closing the kitchen cabinets.

I slid from under the covers, ran to my armoire, and opened the bottom drawer, where I'd buried the lingerie I'd won at Friday Night Love. I pulled it over my head and wiggled my body until I was able to maneuver it over my hips. Minus another ten pounds, it would've fit perfectly, but I wasn't trying to evoke perfection, only passion. I had a feeling that either Roman wouldn't notice, or I wouldn't be wearing it long enough for it to matter.

Roman ran back into the bedroom and stopped in his tracks. I massaged my hands along my thighs and smiled.

"You wanted to know what I won, right?"

Roman tossed the jar of honey on the bed. "I don't know who the real winner is, you or me."

Then he picked me up and carried me to our bed. Undefiled. We worshipped together in a way that only a husband and wife can. That night, I made him forget that he'd ever met *her*. I made him forget her name. That night, I treated my husband to some Friday Night Love.

# 47

Our Friday Night Love rolled into Saturday, Sunday, Monday, and Tuesday night love, until we were met with Wednesday, Thursday, and, finally, another Friday. Our bedroom became our nesting place and the spot where we reconnected, physically, spiritually, and emotionally. If Roman hadn't needed to go to campus, if I hadn't had to attend another educators' workshop, and we hadn't had contractors coming daily to patch up the back of our roof, we probably wouldn't have stepped outside the door. We'd closed off the outside world and created our own.

It was the best six days we'd ever shared as husband and wife. And finally, on the seventh day…we rested.

While Roman went to his chiropractic appointment, I lounged around the house with little to do besides work on a 500-piece jigsaw puzzle. The outside frame of the picture was finally coming into shape when my cell phone rang, disrupting my concentration. "Hello, Zariya," I said. "What's up?"

"I'm ready to come home." I could tell she was pouting. "Kyle is getting on my nerves, and Gemma and Grandpa won't let me do anything. They wouldn't even let me go to the movies with Brandy."

*Here we go again.* "Isn't Brandy sixteen?" I asked.

"Yes, but you said yourself that she's responsible."

"But she's also older than you."

"Only by three years."

"Three years is a huge gap at your age, so unless you're going to have adult supervision, you can hang it up. Why can't you two go with Gemma to the movies?" Even as I made the suggestion, I laughed to myself. Zariya would never agree to that.

"Everyone is trying to ruin my life," Zariya whined, not amused.

I offered my usual explanation. "We're not ruining your life, we're protecting it."

"At least at home I can go see *my* friends. I'm in prison here. Please come and get us," she pleaded.

My daughter sounded so pitiful that I almost caved in. I could empathize with her. My mother would make me go to my aunt Pat's for two weeks every summer, and it always felt like I was serving a sentence, too. She had cats, tons of them, that tiptoed around the house and jumped over me or at me when I least expected it. Aunt Pat said they were being playful, but I slept with the bedroom doors closed at night so they wouldn't try to claw my eyes out when I was asleep. Zariya and Kyle had begged to stay a month, so I was going to make them stay the entire time. They'd survive. I was still walking out my Friday Night Love challenges. *Put him first.*

"Well, you're going to have to stay for a little longer while Dad and I work some things out," I told her. And I did mean work them out.

"So it's true? Dad's back home?"

"Yes, he is," I said, admitting it outright to her for the first time.

"Kyle, come here quick," Zariya yelled. "Use the legs God gave you and move faster."

I shook my head. Zariya was supposed to be one of my summer projects. Besides working on my patio, I was supposed to be working on her smart mouth. She put her cell phone on speaker so I could hear both of them.

"Ma?"

"Hey, baby boy," I said. "How's it going?"

"Good," Kyle said.

"How's your arm feeling?"

"Good," he said, again. Typical male. One-word answers.

"He's playing a video game," Zariya tattled. "That's why he's not listening."

"Put down the game for a minute, Kyle," I said. "I have something important to tell you."

"I hope it's not bad news," Kyle said. "I don't want to hear about anybody else dying. I can't sleep sometimes at night when I think about Mrs. Ava."

"I know, baby boy. I can't, either," I said. "But I promise this is good news. Dad's back home, and we're going to work on our marriage and our family."

"I know," Kyle said nonchalantly. "Dad already told us."

"Duh," Zariya butted in. "I know he did, but it really doesn't make a difference until the woman says it."

"That's not true," I said, noting yet another thing that I'd have to work on. "Your dad and I are going to do a better job of making decisions together. We have some things we need to work on as a family, and we're going to do it with God."

"That's a good idea," Kyle said. "I read something like that in my devotional before I went to bed last night. It talked about trusting in the Lord instead of always thinking that you know what's best. If we trust in the Lord, then He'll clear the path that we have to walk. Something like that."

I was impressed. I'd made both of them take their Bibles and age-appropriate devotionals to their grandparents' so they could read them nightly before going to bed. It was my way of making sure they dumped whatever mess they had in their head from the day so they could end it with God in their minds. Zariya, especially. Her earbuds were always pumping music into her head, and I know my parents didn't monitor her computer and television activity as much as I would have preferred.

"Thank you for taking your time with God seriously," I said to Kyle. Unlike usual, Zariya hadn't added her two cents, which meant she probably hadn't cracked open her Bible and devotional. I could imagine my mom had appeased her and bought every teenybopper magazine she begged for when they went to the grocery store.

"You're welcome," Kyle said.

"Alright, guys. I need to get dressed before Dad gets back. We'll call you later."

"I can't believe you don't have clothes on yet," Zariya said. "That's like a sin at our house to walk around with pajamas on after ten o'clock. You must've been up late last night."

"I had some things to take care of," I said, rushing to get off the phone before Zariya's mind went to other places. She was at that age where she knew she hadn't been delivered by a stork. "And now I need to get up and get lunch made for your Dad."

"Let me guess what you're making. Lasagna?"

"No," I said, sliding my feet into my bedroom slippers and heading downstairs. "Your dad's favorite. Drop biscuits."

# 48

## ROMAN

"We're out of honey, and I like to use that on my drop biscuits," Roman said slyly. He'd been pinching off pieces of biscuit all day, and by dinner, he'd eaten almost the entire pan. He felt heavy and bloated, but it was worth every bite. He'd never admit to Lovie that Zenja had mastered her recipe in such a short time. Or maybe they tasted exceptionally good because he was still on a cloud of euphoria.

"I wonder what happened to all that honey," Zenja said. She was about to head upstairs to change her clothes for the Friday Night Love event at the art gallery.

"Don't worry," said Roman. "There's more where that came from." He handed her the Bible he'd brought downstairs from the bedroom earlier that day. "I borrowed your Bible this morning when I called in on Mack's prayer conference call this morning. What are those little cards all about?"

Zenja opened up the front cover where she'd tucked the cards. "You're about as nosy as your children," she said. "They're the Friday Night Love challenges that Caprice gives to the ladies each week. She gave them all to me ahead of time."

Roman covered the pan so he wouldn't be tempted to eat the last two biscuits. "Let me see those cards again." He slid them out of her hands and flipped through them. "I would say you've almost passed with flying colors."

"Almost?"

*"Respond to his needs.* Check. *Encourage him.* Check. *Show your love for him in creative ways.* Check and double check. You did that one on Wednesday night. Twice."

Zenja rolled her eyes. "No. That happened when I cleaned Lovie's house."

"You have your opinion; I have mine," Roman said, climbing the stairs. It was imperative that they arrive on time tonight. If they were running late, it wasn't going to be his fault. Zenja had no idea that the two of them—not the local artists—were going to be the main feature.

*"Put him first,"* Roman continued. "Check. And thanks again for making the kids stay in New Jersey."

"No problem," Zenja said, "but time is running out. I need my babies with me soon."

"Two weeks," Roman said. "Then we'll drive up and get them."

Zenja sat down on her settee and fumbled with a few pieces of her puzzle that was nearly finished. "We should make a pit stop in D.C. on the way back," she suggested. "With Kyle's growing interest in politics, I want to make sure we nurture that. I can make his social studies lessons come alive."

"Yes, Vice Principal Maxwell, ma'am," Roman teased. He knew the drill. It would start off as a lesson for Kyle but end up being a learning experience for the entire family. He could already see Zariya pouting while Zenja dragged them around to the Lincoln Memorial, the Washington Monument, and the Capitol Building. Roman would suffer through most of it as long as he had a chance to walk through the White House and visit the long-awaited Martin Luther King Jr. National Memorial.

"What else am I supposed to be doing?" Zenja asked while he continued to look at her cards.

*"Expect the best of him,"* Roman read. "I can't answer that one for you."

"I could say I passed that challenge. On Tuesday night, I expected—and you delivered—the best." Zenja winked. "So double-check that one, too."

"I have the feeling that we're not supposed to just meet these challenges in the bedroom," Roman said.

"To each his own," Zenja said. "We have the rest of our lives to work on that stuff. But personally, I like the way things are working out."

Roman's ego swelled as he set up the ironing board to steam the wrinkles out of his white linen pants. Zenja should call him the mailman because he was ready to deliver, no matter the weather. "*Cherish your time with him,*" he continued.

"Every minute," Zenja said. She walked into the closet and came back out with a black sleeveless sundress. "I'd forgotten how nice it feels to spend time with you as friends."

"Friends with benefits," Roman said with a sneaky smile. He eyed her choice for the night. If he remembered correctly, it was the long one that puddled around her feet. *That's not going to work,* he thought. He had to think quickly. "Caprice said everybody's supposed to wear white tonight."

Zenja looked puzzled. "Since when? I talked to Caprice less than thirty minutes ago, and she didn't say anything about a dress code."

"She told me yesterday when I stopped by the house," Roman said. "She probably assumed I told you. My fault."

"Are you sure? Let me call her," Zenja said, looking around for her cell phone.

Roman stopped her. "Zenja, trust your husband." He flipped through her cards again. "That one should be somewhere in here."

"The last one, for T, is *Talk highly of him to other people,*" she said, then disappeared inside the closet again. She came back out with a dress that Roman had bought for her two days ago, when they were supposed to be shopping for shirts for him. He had spotted the dress on their way past the women's department and steered her in that direction so that the night he'd envisioned would be perfect.

"I need to talk to Caprice about that last one," Zenja said. "It should really be 'Speak highly.'"

"The teacher in you can't help but whip out that red pen," Roman said. He watched Zenja as she abandoned her puzzle and shimmied out of her sundress. She looked up at him and blushed like a schoolgirl.

"Don't start none, won't be none," she said.

"Is that sentence grammatically correct?" Roman teased.

"We could stay here, you know?" she purred, running her hands down the silhouette of her body. "Caprice would understand."

Roman was tempted to grant his wife her wish, but since he'd enlisted the help of other people for this special evening, he had to turn down her request. He averted his eyes. That was the only way he could keep himself contained. There was no seduction like what a man received from his own wife. He'd make it up to Zenja tonight. And next Friday. And the Friday after that. And the Friday after that. And the next…

"Baby, we can't miss tonight," Roman said, even though he wasn't sure he sounded that convincing. "I told Duane we'd be there."

"Well, call him back and tell him we won't."

"I gave him my word," Roman said. He couldn't drive the point too hard, or Zenja would begin to suspect something. Roman continued to dress, to send the message that he wasn't changing his mind. "The man took off work and sat here for hours waiting for the contractors to come while we were in South Carolina. His wife needs our support."

"Fine," Zenja said. "But I can't promise I'll be in the mood afterward."

Roman wasn't worried about her mild threat. She would definitely be in the mood.

"I was going to take this one back," Zenja said, assessing the new dress's fit to her body. "It was too expensive."

"It was my gift to you," Roman said. "I won't let you take it back." He walked over to help Zenja with the zipper in back. She looked like a chocolate cookie dipped in milk. And he wanted to…

"You don't think it's too dressy?" Zenja asked.

"I don't," Roman said, slipping into his linen pants. "You always tell me it's better to be overdressed than underdressed."

"True," Zenja said. "If I know Caprice, she's probably set up a photographer do a group photo of all of us dressed alike."

"I wouldn't doubt it," Roman said, relieved that she'd bought into his story. "Do you think I should trim my beard?"

"Maybe a little, but not too much. It makes you look distinguished and mysterious all at the same time," Zenja decided. "Give me five more minutes to get beautiful, and I'll be ready. Since we're going, we don't want to be late."

When Zenja went into the master bathroom, Roman quietly opened the top drawer of his bureau, slipped out the box he'd been hiding there, and slid it into the pocket of his suit jacket. Zenja was right. Tonight wasn't the night to be late.

Roman and Zenja were late anyway, and Roman had been forced to take the blame. Caprice had called and asked him to stall for another twenty minutes so that the stragglers would have time to arrive at the art gallery ahead of them. One of the couples had informed Caprice that an accident on I-40 had caused a major backup.

"Do you have to stop for gas right now?" Zenja complained. "You're going to walk in smelling like gas fumes. It never fails. The time you're trying to be the most careful is the time the tank will overflow and gasoline will get all over your clothes."

"You're overreacting," Roman said. He'd entertained the same concern, but he couldn't think of an alternate tactic. He couldn't pretend to be lost, since the art gallery was directly across the street from the spa that Zenja frequented. So, instead of paying at the pump, Roman went inside to pay, then talked to the attendant behind the bullet-proof glass for another five minutes. After that, the attendant seemed annoyed that Roman wanted to dialogue about the declining state of the education system in North Carolina and everywhere else in the country.

When another patron entered the store, his conversation with the attendant waned, so Roman camped out in the restroom. He sent Zenja a text. Too many biscuits. Be out in a minute.

After another five minutes, Roman returned to the car with a twenty-ounce soda and a bag of chips.

"What in the world were you doing in there?" Zenja demanded. She twisted the top off the soda and had a choking fit from the strong carbonation.

"See? God don't like ugly. He choked your words down before you could get them out," Roman joked.

Zenja punched his arm. "Oh, shut up and drive."

So Roman did, staying five miles per hour below the speed limit. "They've been doing a lot of work on the roads in this area," he explained. "I don't want to stir up all that asphalt dust. It might chip the paint on my new car."

"Whatever you say, Roman," Zenja said, staring out the window.

When they finally arrived at the gallery, Zenja unbuckled her seat belt, grabbed her purse, and reached for her door.

Roman stopped her before she could jump out. "Hold up, baby. Let me get the door for you. It would be nice if we walked in together." He slowly slid his arms into his jacket sleeves. "Since we're already late, thirty more seconds won't matter."

"I guess you're right," Zenja said, then waited for him to help her out of the car.

Roman squeezed her hand tightly as they approached the hallway. The floor-to-ceiling windows framed the inside of the art gallery, which Caprice had decorated with her golden touch.

"Roman, I thought you said we were supposed to wear white," Zenja said, noticing the people before she noticed the elegance of the atmosphere.

"We were," Roman said calmly. If Zenja was shocked now, he couldn't wait to see her reaction once they were inside and she realized that this night was about them.

"Then why is everyone else wearing some shade of blue?" Irritation was apparent in her voice.

Roman grabbed her hand. "I'm sorry, babe. Caprice must've said to wear blue this week and white next week."

Zenja shrugged. "We can't go back home and change. We might as well make the best of it."

*Is this my wife?* There had been a time when Zenja would've cut him to half his height for making a mistake like that. Of course, it hadn't been a mistake at all; but as far as she knew, it was. Roman wasn't the only one whom God was perfecting.

At his first counseling session, Dr. Morrow had insisted that Roman focus on shaping himself into a man who was pleasing in God's sight. He said it was about the man in the mirror, whether Zenja changed or not. Yet Roman's growth, as a godly man covering his family, had caused a change in her, as well.

Roman opened the door to the art gallery and saw Waverly and Carey begin to applaud. Slowly, the other couples turned their way and joined in, until the sound of their clapping was the only thing Roman could hear. Yes, this was a standing ovation—and God deserved it all.

"What's going on?" Zenja asked. "What in the world is...?"

The crowd parted, and Caprice and Duane—the only other couple dressed in white—emerged from the back of the room. They walked to meet their best friends, and the remaining couples circled around them.

Zenja half laughed and half cried. "Are we the only ones who got the all-white memo?" she asked as she accepted the bouquet of satin-tied tulips from Caprice. Then she closed her eyes so her friend could dab away the specks of mascara that had stained her lids.

Roman had been the cause of Zenja's tears before—more often than he cared to admit—but these tears of joys moved him. Looking at his wife, he realized he couldn't promise that he would never make her angry, disappointed, or tempted to throw in the towel. Roman couldn't promise her a perfect life, but he could put their marriage in the hands of a perfect God.

Roman took Zenja's hands in his. "Do you forgive me for making you late?" he whispered in her ear.

"This time. But don't let it happen again," Zenja said, patting his backside, which provoked a wave of laughter.

"Don't ruin *my* moment," Roman teased.

Then he stopped. Inhaled. He looked around and made himself take it all in. He had asked certain people to stand at the front of the circle as witnesses and testaments to his growth, and the men hadn't disappointed him. Duane was by his side, and just steps away stood the strong and faithful brothers who'd been instrumental in his life—Dr. Morrow and Mack. One person he hadn't expected to see—and the one who literally took his breath away—was Lovie. Two days ago, he'd mentioned his intentions of surprising Zenja, and he'd never thought Lovie would even consider sharing in this time. Queen stood beside her, the two with their arms hooked together.

Roman lost his composure. All his plans to be the knight in shining armor, gone. The room fell silent as everyone waited for him to say his first words. He bit his bottom lip to steady himself, hoping his voice wouldn't tremble. He didn't want to forget what he'd intended to say.

He turned to Zenja, cupped her face in his hands, and wiped away her tears with his thumbs. "Today I vow again to honor the covenant I made before God. You've stood beside me, knelt beside me, and prayed beside me. You deserve the best, and I want to do everything in my power as an honorable man to give it to you."

Roman swallowed a lump in his throat but never let his eyes leave his wife's. He could hear the sniffling around him as people cried softly. "There's no one in the world I'd rather be with. I knew life without you for a short time, and there were too many sleepless nights and unfulfilling days. It was then that I knew that if I couldn't be with *you*, I'd live this life alone. Just me and my music. Because no one—except God—puts a song in my heart like you do."

# 49

I finally understood the end of my dream. The night I dreamed we were standing together, there was pool of blue water around us. I now realized that it was actually a crowd of witnesses dressed in varying shades of that color.

Roman reached into his suit jacket pocket and pulled out my diamond setting. I hadn't worn my wedding band on my finger for so long that I'd gotten used to it not being there. He slid it on my finger slowly enough for me to realize that he'd upgraded the round solitaire in the middle. It was at least another carat larger.

"Oh, Roman," I said. I tilted my hand so the overhead lights hit the stone in just the right spot to catch the brilliance.

"I tried to convince you that shoes were a girl's best friend, but you set the record straight quick when you said it was diamonds. I hope you two get along," he said, bringing my hand to his face as if he was seeing the diamond for the first time.

"I'm sure we'll get along just fine," I said. "And I hope we can spend a lifetime together."

"Don't blind us with that thing," somebody yelled out.

The laughter and love in the room was even more prominent than the art that decorated the walls. I pulled Roman to me and kissed him with no reserve. The other couples whistled, clapped, and cheered so loudly that it vibrated in my ears. I felt someone slide my tulip bouquet from my hands so I could hold Roman even closer. He was my man...my best friend...my husband. I knew we still had a long way to go, but we weren't where we'd been twenty-eight days ago.

The celebration fell to a hush again once I pulled my lips away from Roman's. Now I was embarrassed that all eyes were on us. I looked around the circle for the first time, seeing all the couples who had vowed to make their marriages stronger through Friday Night Love. Waverly and Carey. Caprice and Duane. Mack and his pint-sized wife. Carmela was there with her ever-present smile, even if she didn't have a man by her side. She'd be my next matchmaking assignment. Then there were Lovie and Queen.

*Lovie?*

I looked up at Roman.

"I know," he whispered in my ear. "It's a miracle."

"If I'd known all I had to do was clean Lovie's house, I would've done that eight years ago," I said through joyful tears. Queen put her arm around her best friend and gave me a thumbs-up. I wasn't much for speaking in front of crowds of adults, but as I looked at the faces of those around us, I knew the words God was pouring into my heart were for them.

"I don't know most of you all on a personal level," I started, "but I do know the God that you serve. You wouldn't be participating in Friday Night Love if you didn't have the desire to keep your marriage strong or pick up some of the broken pieces. That's what we had to do—what we're *still* doing—and sometimes I look down and swear I saw a million of those pieces."

I noticed that it was mostly the women nodding their heads in agreement.

"We all have a story to our lives," I went on, "with plot twists and turns that we never would have expected. You might look at your life and think there could never be a happy ending to all this mess. But, God." I paused and let the words linger. "But God is the author and finisher of our faith, and His Word says that His plans are to prosper us. Why should a person's opinion about our situation carry more weight than God's absolute truth? If you can't believe in your husband or your wife, believe in God. God is love." I looked at Queen. "And a wise woman once told me that love has the final say."

"Amen, sister," Waverly said, stepping forward so that others could hear her. "With your few words, you've said more than you know. Thank you for letting God use *you* and use your *marriage* for His glory."

"Amen and amen," Caprice said. "And it's time to celebrate with Roman and Zenja and with each other." She cupped a hand around her mouth like a megaphone. "So, where are you, Soulful Connections? Let's get the music started." She grinned at Roman. "Surprise."

Bernard, Joey, and the two other band members stepped out from behind a partition that was painted with a mural of downtown Greensboro. Couples began to scatter in different directions to enjoy the appetizers, dance in the corded-off area, or stroll through the art exhibits.

Caprice and Duane enveloped me and Roman in a group hug. "Thank you for not letting us quit," I said to them.

Duane slapped Roman on the back. "My sanity was on the line. If you two got divorced, Caprice never would have let me get a good night's sleep again."

"Our getting divorced would've definitely changed your life," Roman chimed in.

"How so?" Caprice asked.

"Because I would've moved into the cabana in your backyard like a cat you'd fed that wouldn't go away."

"It's a good thing you're staying together, because we don't take in strays," Caprice said.

"I don't know if I believe that," I said, holding out my left hand so she could admire my ring. "For a while, I was like a stray myself who came along with two little kittens. And, come to think of it, you did feed me quite often."

"Well, I've never seen a cat with a diamond like this," Caprice said.

I beamed. "Didn't he do an excellent job?"

"I wanted to either upgrade your diamond or redo your patio," Roman told me. "But since you hadn't bothered to put your wedding ring back on, I figured I'd better give you a good reason to."

Then he motioned to a man standing off to the side. He was the only one in a full suit, but, like everyone else, he was wearing shades of blue in his shirt and pocket square.

"This," Roman said as the man approached, "is Dr. Morrow, my marital counselor."

"Your marital counselor?" I asked, raising my eyebrows. I hoped I was overdoing acting shocked.

Dr. Morrow extended his hand to me, but I reached out and hugged him instead. "You deserve more than a handshake," I said. "Roman's a better man, and these past few weeks, he's gone above and beyond to make sure I'm happy and that we're growing together in God. For everything you've done, thank you."

"Roman put in all the work," Dr. Morrow said. "I'm just the facilitator."

"Dr. Morrow has served on staff at our church for the last eight years or so," Caprice said. "He's truly a godsend."

"And he's sharp, too," Roman said, lifting the hem of one of Dr. Morrow's pant legs to show his blue checkerboard patterned socks.

"A man that knows his fashion and the Word of God sounds like a workable combination. I'd like to join your marriage counseling sessions, unless this is a husband thing," I said, waving my finger between the two of them.

"Absolutely not," Roman jumped in to say. "I couldn't be a husband if I didn't have a wife."

Caprice had been correct when she'd said I would have something to lose by joining Friday Night Love. I'd lost the things that I didn't need: pride, selfishness, self-doubt, and my independence. I had no desire to be an independent woman. I wanted to be a God-dependent woman.

"I have to head out now for another obligation, but I couldn't let the night pass without showing my face," Dr. Morrow said. "I'm glad we finally met, Zenja. I've heard a lot about you."

"The good, bad, and the ugly, I'm sure."

"More good about you than anything," Dr. Morrow admitted. "Everything that was ugly was Roman's fault."

"It's time for you to go before you start some trouble," Roman told him. "As a matter of fact, I'll walk you to the door."

Dr. Morrow shook the static cling from his pant leg. "My socks and I will see ourselves out," he said. "And I'll be calling you about a couple's session."

"I'll be there," I said, grateful that God was giving me another chance to attend the counseling sessions I'd previously turned down. Despite Dr. Morrow's protest, we walked him to the door before setting out to find Lovie.

"If I know Lovie, she's somewhere near the food," Roman said. He steered me through the crowd until we found her loading chicken kabobs on her plate. "You disappeared on us," he said to his mother. Lovie looked refreshed—happier and younger than I'd ever known her to be. I hated to think that Pop had drained the life out of her, but it was evident that her joy had been restored.

"I knew we'd have plenty of time to talk later, since Queen and I are staying at your house tonight," Lovie informed us. She took a long drink of tea and frowned. "Not enough sugar. Who makes sweet tea like this?"

"Everybody but you," Queen said.

I couldn't have cared less about how much sugar was in the tea. I was still shocked that Lovie was staying at our house—the same house that she hadn't stepped in since it had become my permanent address. At such short notice, I'd normally be frazzled about whether my home was in acceptable condition. Furniture dusted? Vacuumed? Bathrooms sparkling? But thanks to Roman hiring a housekeeping service for me, my home's tidiness was the least of my worries.

"Zenja, is there something wrong?" Lovie asked me, snapping me out of my thoughts. "This is probably the biggest shock of your life, isn't it?

"It rates right up there at the top," I said. "And we'll have you anytime you want to stay."

"Good. Cause me and Queen will be burning up the highway."

Changes were hitting the Maxwell household faster than I could comprehend. Zariya and Kyle were going to have to make adjustments in their lives, too. They'd have to readjust to having Roman back home. They'd gotten used to my word being the only say and the final say as it pertained to their daily lives. It might mean Zariya would have to give up her lip gloss and Kyle would lose some of his video game time, but for them, having their father home would be worth it. I could imagine the amazement on their faces when we told them Lovie had spent the night at the house.

"We're going to look at the art," Lovie said, using her fork to move her food around so nothing would fall off her plate. "This is so fancy."

Left alone, Roman and I found a quiet corner. "So, since I've put a ring on your finger and vowed my love to you again forever, does this mean tonight is our honeymoon?"

"We have guests staying over," I reminded him.

"They're staying in our house, not in our bedroom." Roman ran his finger around the middle of my collarbone.

"You can forget it, lover boy," I said. "Absolutely nothing is happening when your mother and her best friend are here."

"Don't worry about them," Roman said. He kissed my right cheek, then my left. "I'm sending them to a hotel."

# 50

## ROMAN

Roman went out onto the patio with a book of matches and two envelopes. He was exhausted from the night's activities, but there was one last thing he wanted to do before the day was over. He'd almost forgotten to do the most important thing that would symbolize the renewal of his and Zenja's marriage.

"What in the world are you doing?" Zenja asked, following him outside. "It's way too hot out here to sit by a fire."

"This one won't burn for long," Roman assured her. He handed her one of the envelopes, then pulled an empty planter closer to them.

"The divorce petition," Zenja said. "You never did get around to signing this, you know? I'll go get a pen." She turned to head inside, but Roman playfully grabbed her arm and held her so she couldn't move.

"Okay, okay, I'm kidding," Zenja said, laughing, as Roman swept her off her feet. He pretended to stumble and almost drop her. "Oh, please. That extra piece of cake didn't make that much of a difference, did it?"

"I plead the fifth," Roman said, setting her down on her feet. He struck a single match and lit the corner of the envelope he was holding. "You gave me two copies of these divorce papers, as if one punch in the gut wasn't enough," he reminded her, then held the flame to Zenja's envelope so hers would light, as well. "Should we say something?" Roman asked, watching the black ash work its way toward his fingers.

"Whatever it is, make it quick," Zenja said. She moved her fingers to the edge of the envelope. "What about 'To forever'?"

"To forever," Roman repeated, dropping his envelope in the planter along with Zenja's. "To forever, and to omelets and drop biscuits." Gray ashes circled to the top of the planter, then lifted in the air.

Roman stepped out of his shoes and took out the folded paper that Nurse Lowe had slipped inside his sole.

"What in the world is that?" Zenja asked.

"The nurse gave it to me at the hospital," he said, opening the paper. It was smudged and damp from having it in his shoe for so long, but it was still legible. "God will perfect the things which concern us," he said, summarizing the Scripture.

"A year ago, could you have imagined that this is where we'd be?" Zenja said. "No, make that twenty-eight *days* ago?"

"If I hadn't imagined it, I wouldn't have come back," Roman said.

"You and that stupid purple duffel bag," Zenja said with a smile.

"Me and that stupid bag," Roman said. "And faith the size of a mustard seed."

Roman and Zenja shared the single patio chair that Roman had cleaned and covered with one of the older pillow sets they'd had stored in the garage. He lifted the hem of her dress high enough to kiss her ankle, then pushed it up as his lips traveled up to her calf and then to her knee.

"I love everything about you," Roman said. He slid his body up so that Zenja could lay her head on his chest.

"I love you, too," she said.

Roman blew away some of the ashes that had floated toward his face. "This reminds me of the Scripture we read in our devotional yesterday morning about God giving us a crown of beauty instead of ashes, and a garment of praise for the spirit of heaviness. With God as our center, our marriage is going to be a beautiful thing."

"Beautiful," Zenja said, her voice growing drowsy.

"Everyone comes into a marriage with certain expectations. I want to keep my promises to you," Roman said. Zenja lifted her face to him, and he kissed her partially closed eyelids. "I want to make your dreams come true."

"You already have," Zenja whispered.

"We've been through the fire," Roman said, as the last remnants of ash floated out into the darkness.

Zenja snuggled closer against him, and he wrapped his arm around her. "But you know what?" she said. "We're coming out as pure gold."

Roman saw the light go out in one of the guest bedrooms. Zenja hadn't let him send Lovie and Queen to a hotel, so he figured his honeymoon session was out of the question. But she had been with him long enough to know that he never stopped trying. Besides, he had almost a year to make up for.

"Do you think we'll ever make it to another Friday Night Love event?" Roman asked.

"Probably not," Zenja said. She stood up unexpectedly and gazed down at him. Roman knew that look. "And I heard tonight there was supposed to be fireworks. I guess things didn't work out."

"It's never too late," he said, scooping her up in his arms. "If you thought Friday Night Love was so mind-blowing, wait until Saturday night."

# About the Author

Tia McCollors used to dream of being a television news anchor, but her destiny led her behind the pages instead of in front of the cameras. After earning a degree in journalism and mass communications from UNC–Chapel Hill, she went on to build a successful career in the public relations industry. In 1999, a job layoff prompted her to explore writing and pursue a career as an author. Following the birth of her son in 2006, she left the corporate arena to focus on her family and her expanding writing and speaking business.

Tia's first novel, *A Heart of Devotion,* was an *Essence* magazine best seller. She followed her popular debut with four other inspirational novels: *Zora's Cry, The Truth about Love, The Last Woman Standing,* and *Steppin' Into the Good Life.* In 2012, she released her first devotional book, *If These Shoes Could Talk: Devotional Messages for a Woman's Daily Walk.* Tia's sixth novel, *Friday Night Love,* kicks off Days of Grace, her first series with Whitaker House.

In addition to being an author, Tia is an inspirational speaker, as well as an instructor for writing workshops. She particularly enjoys coaching women of faith, female entrepreneurs, and stay-at-home mothers. Her speaking engagements and literary works have been spotlighted in a growing number of publications, including *Black Enterprise* magazine, *Who's Who in Black Atlanta, The Good Life* magazine, and the *Atlanta Journal-Constitution.*

Tia currently resides in the Atlanta, Georgia, area with her husband and their three children. Readers can learn more about Tia at www.tiamccollors.com or connect with her on social media at www.facebook.com/fansoftia or @tiamccollors.